Cinderella
and the GHOST

Books by Marina Myles

Beauty and the Wolf

Snow White and the Vampire

A Warlock's Dance
(novella)

Sleeping Beauty and the Demon

Christmas at Thorncliff Towers
(novella)

Cinderella and the Ghost

Cinderella and the GHOST

MARINA MYLES

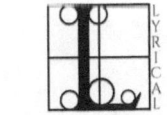

LYRICAL PRESS
Kensington Publishing Corp.
www.kensingtonbooks.com

LYRICAL PRESS BOOKS are published by

Kensington Publishing Corp.
119 West 40th Street
New York, NY 10018

All Kensington titles, imprints, and distributed lines are available at special quantity discounts for bulk purchases for sales promotion, premiums, fund-raising, educational, or institutional use.

Special book excerpts or customized printings can also be created to fit specific needs. For details, write or phone the office of the Kensington Special Sales Manager: Kensington Publishing Corp., 119 West 40th Street, New York, NY 10018. Attn. Special Sales Department. Phone:1-800-221-2647.

Lyrical and the L logo are trademarks of Kensington Publishing Corp.

First Electronic Edition: February 2015
eISBN-13: 978-1-60183-283-2
eISBN-10: 1-60183-283-4

First Print Edition: February 2015
ISBN-13: 978-1-60183-284-9
ISBN-10: 1-60183-284-2

Printed in the United States of America

For my sister, Lisa.
We played Barbies when we were children, giggled
about boys when we were teenagers, and
raised our own kids as adults.
Thanks for being my best friend through it all!

ACKNOWLEDGMENTS

Even though this is the fourth book in the Cursed Princes series, I'm just as excited about it as the first three!

Its journey involves so many people to whom I'm forever grateful: **Peter Senftleben**, my editor and sage who has such amazing ideas and who points out necessary changes so gently. My agent, **Louise Fury**, without whom I'd be adrift on a sea of misdirection. (It may sound dramatic, but it's true!) The skillful crew at **Kensington** that molds my work into something larger than life. To my Arizona writing *amigas*, **Cathy McDavid**, **Terri Molina**, **Pamela Tracy**, **Connie Flynn**, **Libby Banks**, and **Helen King**: You ladies make me a much better writer!

I'd never be able to sit down and type out these stories without the infinite patience and support of **my husband and kids**. I love you!

Finally, I want to thank my English teacher at Cocopah Middle School, **Mrs. Kwitowski**. After reading the summary of this particular story, you smiled and said, "I bet your name will be on the front of a book someday!"

That was all the encouragement I needed.

He who sees without love is only straining his eyes in the darkness.
—Maurice Maeterlinck
Mystic and dramatist
(1862-1949)

When stars align at the hand of the Underworld God, a chosen
few are but puppets on strings.
—Ancient Egyptian Proverb

CHAPTER 1

Present day

Among the inky midnight shadows, Jean-Daniel Girard, formerly *le vicomte de Maincy*, stirred inside his portrait. It was stifling behind the two-dimensional canvas, but it wasn't the stuffiness that made him want to escape it. Instead, the profound sense of change Jean-Daniel felt inside his beloved home was prompting him to emerge tonight.

Peering through the darkness, he materialized from the life-sized painting as easily as water flows from a faucet.

Even though I'm dead, I sometimes come alive *at night.*

He would have laughed aloud at the joke—if he weren't a ghost. That was the kind of man he'd been over three hundred years ago. Blithe sense of humor. Carefree demeanor. Lover of life and all it had to offer.

Now, of course, Girard was nothing more than a spirit doomed to haunt his former residence. Since 1703, he'd been floating around the sprawling grounds and vast rooms of Château de Maincy. Trapped inside the perimeter of the dilapidated estate, he was the specter of a man who'd suffered a tragic death. And as a phantom, Jean-Daniel could hardly believe he had been dead so long.

At least I've had plenty of time to play my favorite game: hide-n-shriek.

He laughed inwardly at that one. Who says you can't take your sense of humor with you?

Mouth quirking, he turned and looked back at his painted image. The so-called "masterpiece" showed him posed in front of Château de Maincy, garbed in early eighteenth-century attire. God, he hated the solemn expression plastered across his face.

In his defense, *nobody* smiled in portraits centuries ago.

As a strange ripple of energy filtered through the drawing room, he touched his wig. *Damn ugly thing.* It had itched immensely when he sat for the portrait. *That painter had been an irritating fellow. Had to get every detail right.*

Now Jean-Daniel was stuck with the unsightly head piece forever.

Fastening his hands on his hips, he let his eyes rove over the "masterpiece" again. Temperamental artist Michél LeBeau had certainly captured the sun-bathed landscape of Maincy with precision. And the contrast between the gray hues of the palace and the colorful, arching trees was spot-on. The artist had even portrayed the essence of Jean-Daniel's impeccable upbringing.

Yet he'd failed to depict Jean-Daniel's soul.

Since then, Jean-Daniel had winced at the comments people muttered when they passed Michél's painting. "My goodness! What a dire-looking fellow that vicomte was!" Or, "His portrait makes me so sad."

Truth be told, Jean-Daniel had been anything but solemn and morose during his time as one of France's distant heirs to the throne. Instead, he'd been the epitome of a lighthearted bachelor, sweeping women off their feet, disappearing from the château for weeks at a time to indulge in wine, dancing, and pleasure.

Those were the days.

Grinning, his stare landed on the brown and white hound dog that sat at his feet in the portrait. Jean-Daniel gave a loud whistle. Rémy stirred, stretched, and then emerged in ghostly form outside the painting.

"Good boy!" He gave the dog an enthusiastic pat before he crouched and scratched the animal behind both ears. "Thank God I have you to keep me company."

Rémy lifted a paw as if to say, "It's just you and me, Master."

Jean-Daniel frowned. "You seem anxious tonight, boy."

Rémy whimpered.

"I know," Jean-Daniel said as he glanced around. "I feel it, too. The lady from the management company set off a strange energy when she came here yesterday. She hasn't been around in a while and I think she's readying the house for a new owner. I sense it in my bones. If I had bones, that is."

Rémy let his tongue hang out in an amused pant.

Jean-Daniel stood. "Do you think the new owner is *her*?"

The dog let out a firm "yap."

"If it is, my heart will finally mend." He exhaled. "And maybe we'll be released from this purgatory."

Rémy barked louder.

Before Jean-Daniel died a tragic death, he hadn't known much about ghosts. Now, unfortunately, he knew too much. Whenever someone died under heartrending circumstances, they manifested as a spirit at the scene of their passing. People asserted Jean-Daniel's untimely death had been a result of murder or possibly suicide. Of course, *he* knew the truth about how he died. Well, *she* knew, too—the woman he'd loved beyond all reason.

With lapis-blue eyes, a stunning face, and gleaming ivory hair, Ella had come to Château de Maincy weeks before his death.

Now, if she resurfaced here in present day (in reincarnated form or whatever one calls it), Jean-Daniel would have to get her to enter his painting and travel back in time. Once she succeeded in returning to 1703, Jean-Daniel wanted her to alter the course of what happened to him.

A fate etched in blood.

He shuddered. Would he recognize Ella when they met for the first time in the eighteenth century? He feared he wouldn't. Yet he held out hope that they'd gradually fall in love—as he remembered them doing all those years ago.

Only then could they rewrite the scene of their tragic parting.

It was all very complicated, but there it was.

Optimism—as tangible and sweet as a cloud of perfume—circled Jean-Daniel while he stood in the drawing room. Pushing his shoulders back, he floated forward. The time for Ella's visit was nearing. That's what his instincts were telling him, anyway. And he was ready.

Gliding out of the room, he drifted along the corridor with Rémy at his heels. He stopped at a bay window and glanced over the château's extensive gardens.

"The only thing that may spoil my plans is that management agent. She mustn't rearrange too many things." He looked down at Rémy, who was listening intently. "You saw her remove the knight-in-armor, didn't you, boy?"

Rémy cocked his head sadly.

"I know the estate is in pathetic disarray, but I've grown used to it." Jean-Daniel paused. "Do you think the agent will store my portrait?"

At that, Rémy sunk to the floor and hung his head over his paws.

CHAPTER 2

Ten hours later in California...

Ella Benoit raced along the corridor of the Santa Barbara mansion she shared with her stepmother. She'd heard the call button beep in the middle of the night. It meant Adelaide needed her.

Gathering her robe around her waist, Ella sped around the corner. *Please be alive.*

Lungs burning, she streamed barefoot into Adelaide's bedroom. Ella's heart pounded as she stared at the buzzing machines and the masses of tubes running to the bed. Her stepmother lay clasping the call button—and to Ella's horror, Adelaide was pale, still, and barely breathing.

"Where's the nurse?" Ella muttered under her breath. Her gut clenched. Why had her stepmother insisted on living out her final days at home? Then again, if *she'd* been given only a few months to live, she might have done the same thing.

"Darlene?" Ella cried. "I need help!"

Nothing.

"Nurse Darlene!" she screamed louder.

A steady line of hospice caretakers had woven their way in and out of the house in the past month. Adelaide was dying of pancreatic cancer. Nasty disease. Fast-moving and relentless—especially when it was diagnosed in stage four.

Darlene finally appeared from the en suite bathroom. Clutching her stomach, she rushed to the bed. "I'm sorry, Miss Benoit. I think I ate something bad last night."

"My stepmother rang the call button. Thank God it's connected to my room."

Darlene took hold of Adelaide's wrist, which hung limply in her hand. "Gracious! Her pulse has really slowed."

While Darlene attended to Adelaide, Ella shot a fretful glance at a photograph of her father sitting on Adelaide's nightstand. Ella had promised him she would take good care of his second wife until the end.

Her father's memory swept over her and tears sprang to her eyes. When Darlene stepped away from the bed, her shoulders rolled forward.

"Has the time come?" Ella whispered.

"I'm afraid so," the nurse replied softly. "Unfortunately, there's nothing more I can do except refresh her morphine drip to make her comfortable."

Ella nodded numbly.

After the middle-aged nurse replenished the plastic medicine bag, she studied the concern in Ella's face. "I'll leave you two alone."

The bedroom fell into silence. Forcing a dry lump down her throat, Ella leaned over and said, "I know I'm not the one you want to be with in these final hours, Adelaide, but I'm here for you." She took her stepmother's hand in hers.

Minutes passed. Ella watched the green line on the monitor rise and fall at slower and longer intervals. She squeezed Adelaide's hand but Adelaide didn't squeeze it back. Just before the monitor flatlined, the old woman turned her head away defiantly.

The day of the funeral arrived quickly. Right up until the moment Adelaide was buried, an emptiness filled Ella. She was having a hard time coming to terms with her stepmother's death. Not because she felt an overwhelming sadness, of course. Adelaide Benoit had been a coldhearted, critical woman—and her poorly-attended memorial service proved just that.

The reason Ella was grappling with Adelaide's death had to do with a consuming guilt. Heavy and repressive, it hung over her like a dark cloud. Had she taken care of her stepmother well enough? Had she failed her father?

Considering that he would be disappointed in her, Ella had gotten ready in slow motion for the funeral that morning. She barely noticed how much the beautiful Santa Barbara weather contrasted with the solemnity of the ceremony. The skies overhead gleamed clear and blue and a slew of birds chirped merrily in the trees above the city's largest cemetery. As she watched her stepmother's silver casket descend into the grave, Ella threw a rose on top of it. There was no denying it now. The woman who'd ruled her life for so long was actually gone.

Don't let it show. Then no one will know. The motto Ella lived by, but had never spoken aloud, ran through her mind. Inside, she felt relief that Adelaide was dead, but she'd become a master at disguising her emotions, hiding the effects of the verbal abuse she had suffered. Being continually beaten down by Adelaide over the years had prompted her to shut the abuse out completely.

Ella looked at her hands. Calloused. Nicked. Hardened from around the clock cleaning, gardening, and cooking she'd done under her stepmother's thumb. Luckily, Ella refused to let her heart harden as well.

"Ashes to ashes. Dust to dust," the priest said. The words signaled the funeral's guests to start dropping handfuls of dirt on top of Adelaide's casket.

Ella took a turn. *There is nothing more final than this.*

Eventually, the priest hung his head and the guests dispersed. Hiding behind a wave of shoulder-length blond hair, Ella stole a look at her stepsisters who stood across the gravesite from her. Now she was alone with the joy brigade.

Hope and Charity. Never had two people been given more ironic names. Squalor and Misery were more like it. Or Tweedle Dee and Tweedle Dum—because one was never present without the other.

Thus, both of them had left Ella behind to care for their sick mother.

She hadn't seen the girls since they traipsed off to New York City to pursue careers in fashion design. Hope and Charity had always been preoccupied with their appearance, so the fashion industry suited them perfectly. Meanwhile, Ella had been stuck in Santa Barbara waiting on Adelaide hand and foot because of the promise she'd made to her father.

The not-so-attractive girls waved to Ella. Selfishness washed over their faces—as it always did. Ella had waited on Adelaide dutifully even when Hope and Charity lived at the house. Although the girls had been perfectly capable of pitching in, they'd refused to lift a finger.

She sighed. *Sometimes I hate my sense of integrity.*

After Hope bid her mother a final goodbye, she met Ella's stare again. Charity copied the action. Teetering comically on too-high heels, the girls moved in Ella's direction, but neither showed signs of crying.

"I understand you stayed with Mother till the end," Hope said as her bright-red hair blew askew in the warm summer breeze.

"Yes," Ella replied crisply. *Who else did you think would be there for her?* She studied her stepsisters at close range. Neither was remotely pretty. Hope's slack chin and beady eyes gave her the look of a possum while shorter and plumper Charity possessed bad skin and over-processed hair that resembled steel wool.

"We got your message that Mother was in hospice." Charity headed for her car. "But we didn't think she'd go *that* fast."

Gritting her teeth, Ella stuffed her hands into the pockets of her baggy slacks. Although she had a figure, she always wore clothes that were one size too big. The reason? Adelaide had damaged her confidence long ago. As a result, she didn't have the nerve to show off her curves.

Confidence gone astray is a terrible thing.

"I suppose you're all alone now." Hope feigned sympathy.

"Didn't I tell you?" Ella bit out quietly. "My Prince Charming is waiting for me right over that knoll."

"What was that?" her stepsister asked sharply.

Ella was too reserved to spew the sarcastic remark in a voice loud enough to be heard. Regardless, she wished it were true. She'd never wanted a man to "save" her from her repressive life, but she hoped to find a special someone with whom she could share her hopes and dreams.

Maybe this special man could show her how to actually live, instead of watching life from the outside looking in.

Charity jammed her tacky sunglasses on her face. "What do you plan to do now, Ella?"

"I really don't know."

"What do you think, Hope?" Charity panted. "When Mum's will is read, do you think we'll find that she left Ella something spectacular?"

The sisters huddled together, twittering obnoxiously.

For once, Ella couldn't argue with her stepsisters' mockery. What money Adelaide had, she'd squandered away. It appeared as if Ella lived the high life inside the Benoits' stunning Santa Barbara mansion—but nothing could be further from the truth. Few people knew about Adelaide's dire finances, including Hope and Charity.

Twenty minutes later, Ella and her stepsisters found themselves gathered around the massive dining table inside the family mansion. Walter Brimhall, Adelaide and Laurent Benoit's attorney for decades, sat at its head. Thin and efficient, Walter sported a neatly-trimmed mustache and salt and pepper hair. From over his bifocals, he scrutinized the small assemblage. His compassionate wife, Mimi, sat next to him.

Mimi was Ella's favorite person in the world. When Ella's real mother died nineteen years ago, Ella's father married Adelaide. Then he adopted Hope and Charity. That was when Mimi stepped into the picture, offering support the way a mother should.

The selfish stepsisters played on their smartphones while Walter gathered his papers. Anger heated Ella's cheeks and she shot Mimi an incredulous look. Mimi mouthed the words, "Everything will be all right," before she turned her attention to her husband.

"Ladies," Walter began, "I dare say we all knew Adelaide as a strong, ambitious woman who enjoyed spoiling her daughters." He paused. "At least her biological daughters."

Hope and Charity exchanged greedy grins.

"Adelaide did much in her sixty-five years," he went on. "She was born in Paris where she met and married her second husband, Laurent Benoit. They settled here in California. After the unfortunate passing of Laurent, Adelaide bought and sold numerous properties. Unfortunately, most of those real estate dealings were not successful."

Hope's and Charity's grins vanished.

"Adding to Adelaide's financial misfortune was the way she spoiled you girls." Walter shot the sisters a critical look.

Tweedle Dee and Tweedle Dum began to squirm in their seats.

"In the end," Walter said grimly, "Adelaide squandered all of her personal assets—as well as the enormous fortune Laurent left her."

Ella's heart thudded. She was aware of these things, but it still hurt to hear them. Her father would have been sorely disappointed that there was nothing left.

"What are you saying, Walter?" Hope screeched.

He cast her a serious look. "I chose to lead up to the reading of the will in this manner for a reason."

The stepsisters tucked their phones away while Walter adjusted his bifocals and unfolded the will. "Let's begin. To my daughters Hope Agnes and Charity Bernice, I regret that I cannot bequeath you anything except my precious poodles, Creampuff and Cupcake."

Hope and Charity went white.

"What in God's name?" Charity yelped. "I thought we'd get the house!"

Walter met the girls' gapes with a scowl. "As shocking as this may be, this mansion is going into foreclosure. Your mother hasn't paid the mortgage for six months and the bank is taking it back."

Hope suppressed tears. "There must be some mistake."

"I'm afraid it's true, Hope. I'm sorry, but if you and your sister had spent more time with your mother, you'd have known her circumstances."

Hope gasped. She leaned toward Charity. "We got the dogs. That's it?"

Shoulders tensed, Walter proceeded to read from the will again. "To my stepdaughter, Ella."

A tingling sensation formed in Ella's stomach. She knew there wasn't any money left, but perhaps Adelaide had left her something sentimental . . . anything to show her appreciation.

"At the request of my late husband, Laurent Albert Benoit—and I stress that this is at his request only—my stepdaughter Ella shall inherit Château de Maincy, an estate in France purchased by Laurent in 1996."

Hope and Charity gasped simultaneously. Ella's entire body prickled with surprise. *What?* She barely heard Walter as he continued reading.

"Upon my death, the title of this estate—which has been held in a trust thus far—shall be passed to Ella. The trust also holds two hundred and fifty thousand U.S. dollars. This amount has been designated exclusively for the care and renovation of Château de Maincy."

Walter set the will down. "Ella, I'm pausing to inform you that Laurent appointed a financial planner to manage the trust fund. This savvy planner has grown its total to four hundred and fifty thousand dollars by investing in the stock market."

Ella's heart threatened to leave her chest. She wasn't excited because she'd inherited an exotic estate in France and a good deal of money. She was excited to have the freedom and purpose that came with the gifts.

"We got a pair of slobbering pooches and Ella gets a French estate?" barked Hope.

"I'm not taking those damn dogs." Charity crossed her arms defiantly.

"Why should Ella get a boatload of money and a château?" shouted Hope. "She's just the stepdaughter!"

The sisters stood and pounded on the table in a rage.

"Girls!" Walter said sharply. "You aren't at a bar demanding a drink! This is the reading of your mother's will. Have some dignity."

Eyeing Ella with contempt, Hope and Charity slid back into their seats.

"The estate in France was left to Ella by her *biological* father," Walter went on. "And it was done so legally."

"Ella," Hope said with forced sweetness, "we've been stepsisters since we were six. You must give us some of that money. My credit card bill is due. And I just bought some new furniture . . ."

"And I just got a new car!" Charity wailed. "We were depending on Mum to help us."

Walter thrust them a stern look. "Ella is not at liberty to draw from her trust unless she needs funds for the château. You may not ask her again."

"I'm sorry." Ella offered the girls a sobering look. Long ago, she'd held out hope that she could form a genuine sisterhood with Hope and Charity. But gradually, that hope evaporated.

Walter folded the will, placed it inside his briefcase, and laced his hands together. "That concludes the reading of Adelaide's last will and testament."

"Speaking of drinks, I need one!" Hope bolted out of her chair. "You can find me at Harry's Bar."

"Me too!" Charity scurried behind her sister.

Ella remained immobile. Mimi jumped when she heard the front door slam shut. Then she rose and put her hands on Ella's shoulders. An attractive, silver-haired woman in her fifties, she always smelled of sweet perfume—a scent Ella found comforting.

"Those horrible girls!" Mimi said. "How did you stand them growing up?"

"I had no choice." Ella shuddered. The girls' torturous ways had started right after her father died. From spiders in her bed, lye in her shampoo bottle, and horrible language that could make guests on The Jerry Springer Show blush, Ella's life had been sabotaged by Hope and Charity. They'd thought nothing of treating her like a servant in her own home. What's more, the vicious girls had managed to ruin any relationship she tried to make outside the Benoit family.

"Hope and Charity were jealous of you from the start," Mimi insisted. "You were beautiful where they weren't. And you were kind, caring, and forgiving where they were spiteful, selfish, and blameful."

Ella found it hard to believe Hope and Charity had been jealous. She'd been pushed down so much she didn't know what there was to be envious of.

Trying to throw thoughts of Hope and Charity out of her mind, she stood. A silver lining hovered within her grasp and she wanted to concentrate on her bright future.

Walter stood, too. As he stuffed his bifocals into his jacket pocket, he said, "Now that we're alone, I want to tell you how happy I am for you, Ella. I know that sounds strange on the day of your stepmother's funeral, but I am."

"God forgive us for speaking ill of the dead." Mimi smiled. "But I'm relieved you got something out of your time with Adelaide."

Ella was relieved, too.

Mimi lowered her voice although there was no one around to hear her. "Adelaide wasn't the most generous person. When Walter and I needed help—"

"It's water under the bridge, my dear," Walter said gently.

Mimi pulled on the edge of her blazer. "You're right."

Each clasped an arm as they led Ella into the foyer. At the base of the curved staircase, Walter spoke again. "As stated in the will, your father's money and the deed to the estate are sitting in a trust. You must travel to Paris to get the keys to the house. At the bank, you must also sign papers verifying that you are the new owner and the appointed trustee."

Mimi chimed in, "We've taken the liberty of purchasing your plane ticket to France. *That's* how happy we are for you."

"You bought my plane ticket?" Ella said excitedly. "You didn't have to do that!"

"It was nothing." Walter showed a rare smile.

Mimi patted her hand. "We're just glad you already have a passport . . . from your trip to France with Adelaide."

That trip was a nightmare. Adelaide had just been diagnosed with cancer—and because her money was running out, she insisted on selling some jewelry so that she could inform her Parisian relatives about her illness in person.

None of them had attended the funeral.

"You leave tomorrow," Walter said.

"Tomorrow?" Ella cried. "But there's so much to do here!"

"We'll take care of everything," the attorney assured her. "Your stepmother named me executor of the estate, so go. Mimi and I intend to auction the furniture to pay for Adelaide's medical bills. So, jet off to a new life."

"You're free, Ella," Mimi said softly. "Free to be who you *truly* are."

Joy washed over Ella. She embraced the Brimhalls.

A moment later, Walter left to attend to further business. Mimi led Ella up the stairs. "I have another surprise for you."

"I don't know that I can take much more excitement!"

As her faded cornflower eyes crinkled at the corners, Mimi tugged her down the hall. "It's waiting in your bedroom."

Ella rushed into her room, as anxious as a little girl on Christmas. Three gorgeous outfits lay spread across the bed. Picking up a navy pencil skirt and matching knit sweater, she twirled with the ensemble to the mirror. She hadn't purchased new clothes in ages—and no one had given her a present since her father died. "It's beautiful," Ella exclaimed. Holding the outfit in front of her, she studied her reflection. The clothes set off her blue eyes and complimented her fair hair, but they were very form-fitting. Could she push aside her insecurities and don a more daring style? A style that might draw attention to her?

Full of doubt, she turned to Mimi. "The clothes are lovely, but I don't know if I can wear them."

Mimi sighed. She removed the sweater and skirt from Ella's hands and then spun her around so they could look in the mirror together. "What do you see?"

"An awkward, unremarkable person. That's what I've always seen."

"No." Mimi argued. "I remember you as a shining little girl who captivated everyone around her."

"Maybe when I was four, but I don't remember."

"Don't let Adelaide control you from the grave, Ella. Like Walter said, leave this place and enjoy a new life in France."

A tiny smile pulled at her lips. "A fresh start does sound wonderful."

"So . . . to make that fresh start even better, here's a little something." Mimi handed her a prepaid American Express card. "It has a five thousand dollar limit. That's all we could afford because we're putting our boys through college, but we want you to have it."

"I couldn't!" Ella's eyes flung wide.

"Nonsense. Adelaide never allowed Walter and me to give you anything while she was alive. Let us help you now."

Ella hesitated. She looked away. "I don't know—"

Mimi smiled broadly. "Indulge us. We never had a daughter."

Not wanting to disappoint the Brimhalls, Ella accepted the credit card. Still, guilt and unworthiness continued to plow over her like a giant tractor. Although she longed for a new beginning in a place where no one knew her, a place where she'd have the chance to do something right for a change, she would only get there by taking baby steps.

CHAPTER 3

Jean-Daniel Girard emerged from his portrait at the stroke of midnight. Trying to gather his energy, he floated to the ballroom with Rémy at his heels. Of all the rooms in his former palace, the ballroom held the most vivid memories. Here, he had enjoyed numerous balls and fêtes—before crushing drama set in.

Jean-Daniel waltzed a few steps as Rémy watched him. Once he stopped, the glow of a full moon streamed in through a wall of broken windows. Unfortunately, the light exaggerated the room's dilapidated condition. Cobwebs draped the corners, floorboards lay cracked and peeling, and a dust-layered mirror hung askance on the north wall.

"You and I know how beautiful this room was. Don't we, boy?"

The dog turned in excited circles, imitating dance steps.

Jean-Daniel had only to close his eyes to envision the opulence of the ballroom in its prime. Shining parquet floors, crisp new draperies, and polished fixtures had lent this place a stunning aura. It'd been the pride of Château de Maincy.

"I can almost hear the musicians playing their instruments and see the guests dancing," he murmured.

Jean-Daniel tried not to dwell on the past, but that was rather like asking the sun to stop shining. Or Mozart to stop composing. It's what he did as a ghost. Hell, what *else* was there to do besides reflect on the chain of events that had brought him to this state of limbo?

"Come along, Rémy." With grace and poise, Jean-Daniel moved

back to the drawing room and glided through one of its walls. The action brought him to a secret part of the château—a place where he stored items he'd collected over the years. *Stolen* was more like it.

There were toothbrushes, newspapers, cuff links, keys, make-up, and various pieces of clothing. The modern items nearly persuaded him that he was connected to the outside world—and not a lonely, pathetic ghost.

"I never liked being on the outside of things, did I, boy?"

Rémy's ears drooped.

Jean-Daniel's favorite objects in this secret room were the watches he'd confiscated from past renters. To say he'd become obsessed with time was an understatement. The fixation went against the carefree demeanor he'd possessed while alive. When Jean-Daniel was a vicomte, he couldn't have cared less what day it was—or how many months loomed ahead to an important event.

Now the anniversary of his death was all he could think about.

Summoning all his strength, Jean-Daniel willed a Timex watch into his hand. The sixty seconds it took for the timepiece's hand to sweep the face of the watch felt like an hour. He hated the way time slowed and nearly stopped inside this secluded house. It made his wait for Ella all the more excruciating.

Thankfully—as he'd said to Rémy a few days ago—things were changing. The anniversary of his death was drawing near and he wished desperately for Ella to appear. If she didn't return to the past to change his fate, he may never be released from this unsated state of limbo.

"Maybe that's why Ella and I fell in love so quickly in 1703," he said as Rémy cocked his head to the side. "Time was of the essence and I didn't even know it."

American Airlines Flight 63 sailed toward Paris with a loftiness that matched Ella's elation.

She'd dragged all her belongings with her—the sum of which fit into a single suitcase and a carry-on. Settled in row seven, she slid the carry-on beneath the seat in front of her. While she busied herself with the task, she tried to ignore the man seated across the aisle. He was blatantly staring. Why, she couldn't guess. Ella hadn't worn the new clothes Mimi bought for her because she didn't have the nerve. Instead, she was wearing her customary baggy slacks and loose-fitting sweater.

She *had* bothered to curl her hair this morning, but the gentleman couldn't possibly be admiring her beauty.

Do I have something stuck in my hair? A piece of food lodged in my teeth?

She hadn't thought to bring a mirror with her.

Her hands shook nervously, but she willed them to stop. *Don't let it show. Then no one will know.*

Blowing out a breath to calm herself, she pulled a faded edition of *Wuthering Heights* from the carry-on. The book brought a smile to her face. She had loved going through her mother's things and had found the book in a memento box when she was twelve. Apparently, Ella's father had given it to her mother when they first fell in love.

"Read it when you turn fourteen," he'd instructed Ella as they sat on the veranda one brilliant Santa Barbara day. "You'll be old enough then since you'll be interested in boys." She remembered squishing up her face in protest.

Her father had laughed. "I want you to learn one thing from this book. Never settle for a love that's less than what Heathcliff and Catherine had." He had paused. "Here. Read the inscription."

Ella had. "*To Colette. May our love grow powerful enough to extend beyond the grave ~ Laurent.*"

Her father had misted up after he read the sentiment along with her.

If I'm a hopeless romantic, Ella thought as she ran her fingertips over the novel's cover, *Dad is to blame.*

An attractive flight attendant passed by. The woman looked down at *Wuthering Heights* and stopped. "Ah, a true classic, Mademoiselle."

"Yes. It's my favorite," Ella replied in perfect French.

The flight attendant perked up then laughed. "You picked up on my accent, eh?"

Ella blushed.

The flight attendant, whose nametag read "Danielle," rattled on solely in French after that. She asked Ella how she knew the language and questioned the reason for her visit to Paris. Ella replied that her father had taught her French and that she'd kept the language up by conversing with her stepmother and stepsisters. Ella went on to tell the flight attendant about the estate her father had bequeathed her.

"Château de Maincy?" the woman gasped. "I grew up two kilometers away!"

"No kidding!" Ella's eyes widened. "Can you tell me about it?"

The man who'd been staring at Ella got up to use the bathroom. In response, Danielle sat on the arm of his seat and leaned over the aisle.

"Château de Maincy is very beautiful. It was built in 1683 for Jean-Daniel Girard, a handsome vicomte who was a distant heir to the French throne. History has it that this vicomte was quite a lady's man—and that he had a dark-hearted twin brother."

Jean-Daniel Girard. The more Danielle said the name, the more it filled Ella with excitement. Why did it sound familiar? Had she read it somewhere? Had her father said the name in the past?

"Supposedly," Danielle went on, "the grand estate was styled to match the vicomte's large personality. It's surrounded by lush gardens and bountiful vineyards." She paused. "At least when I was a girl it was."

"The place sounds amazing," Ella said dreamily.

Danielle raised an eyebrow. "It is. However, there is something you should know about Château de Maincy."

Ella's heart beat wildly. "What's that?"

"It possesses phantoms."

"It's *haunted*?"

Danielle nodded. "I thought the rumors might be kid talk, you know, chatter among children who *want* to be scared. But when I went there one night with my friends, we saw an apparition floating from window to window. A *ghost*."

Ella dropped her smile. "A ghost? You can't be serious."

"Yes." Danielle crossed her heart. "I swear it upon my mother's grave. It was the specter of a man wearing a curled wig and lavish eighteenth-century clothes. I'm telling you it was the vicomte de Maincy, Jean-Daniel Girard, who died a horrible death when he was twenty-five years old."

Ella's skin prickled. "How did this vicomte die?"

Danielle shrugged. "No one knows whether his demise was due to foul play, an accident, or suicide. But what is believed is that Jean-Daniel's ghostly entrapment in Château de Maincy is his curse."

"His *curse?*"

"His doom. It is said that the vicomte must suffer in limbo for all eternity because he's unable to fully cross over from the realm of the living to the realm of the dead. That's why his spirit haunts the house."

"What a terrible sto—"

The return of the man in seat 7C interrupted Ella's conversation with Danielle.

"Good luck to you, Mademoiselle." Danielle grinned as she stood. "I hope you get to see Jean-Daniel Girard for yourself. From what I remember, he's very dashing."

Ella braided her fingers together tensely. She didn't believe in the supernatural. Perhaps her disbelief stemmed from never allowing herself to imagine an existence beyond her hard, cruelty-ridden life.

Would living at Château de Maincy change her mind?

Maybe having a ghost around the house to keep her company would be fun.

And didn't she deserve some fun? When Ella's mother and father passed away, the losses had ripped pieces of her soul away. She'd retreated into an introverted shell. And under Adelaide's thumb, she had been forced to be grateful for what little she had.

There hadn't been any time, money, or energy left over for fun.

Ella glanced out the window. On second thought, having a ghost around as entertainment might not be a positive thing. From a practical standpoint, the château being haunted could definitely raise problems. She'd inherited the estate sight unseen. She possessed little knowledge and information about it—except what she'd gotten off Google. What kind of shape was it in? Had it fallen into tremendous disrepair since her father bought it in the nineties? Perhaps its columns were crumbling by the minute. Maybe its exterior walls were choked with vines and its windows shattered.

It would certainly be difficult to get workers to perform construction work on a haunted house.

Rolling her eyes, Ella set *Wuthering Heights* aside and reached for a fashion magazine left behind by a former passenger. She flipped through the pages absentmindedly but stopped when she saw an ad for Benoit Footwear. It displayed a single, high-heeled shoe in fire engine red. Impeccably made and intricately patterned, the shoe had become the symbol of the company her father started. The empire had supplied him with all his wealth—until he got sick and was forced to sell the line to Macy's. The department store chain was respectable, of course, but it was a far cry from the elite runways of Paris and from customers who preferred haute couture.

Ella snapped the magazine shut. She hated the fashion industry because of how unhappy her father became after the buyout. He didn't make nearly as much money as he'd wanted from the deal. That was when disillusionment hit him and his health took a fatal turn.

She closed her eyes in an attempt to avoid making conversation with the woman seated next to her. One movie and two measly snack boxes later, Flight 63 descended into Charles de Gaulle Airport. Ella craned her neck so that she could see the Arc de Triomphe, the Eiffel Tower, and the Champs Élysées from the window. She'd been sheltered, it was true. But at least she was coming to a country she was familiar with. One whose language she spoke.

Excited, she gripped the armrest. The airplane landed smoothly. Once Ella said goodbye to Danielle, she retrieved her suitcase from the baggage claim and rented a car using the green Am Ex card.

Smiling, she climbed into the front seat of the stylish Audi. *This is getting very real.* Being extremely detailed (a trait she got from her father), she confirmed that she was supposed to go to the Banque Transatlantique to sign some papers, get the estate's keys, and pick up a checkbook from her trust account. Walter had also instructed her to retrieve some things her father had left her inside one of the bank's safety deposit boxes.

Ella took a long time to program the GPS system—her lack of technical aptitude was another thing her stepsisters teased her about. Finally, she found herself cruising around the glittering streets of Paris.

Heart in her throat, she parked the rental car across the street from the bank. When she entered the building, she introduced herself to a handsome manager and asked for aid in her endeavor. The manager offered her a gracious smile.

"Miss Benoit. I'd be happy to help you." He spoke in French in response to her use of the language. "I was not here at the time, but I understand your father was a very valued client."

"Thank you."

He gave her the once-over. "You sound French, but you look American."

Ella blushed. Maybe it was her sloppy, ill-fitting clothes that gave her away. From what she could see, all Parisian women dressed to the nines. From the scarves they tied effortlessly around their necks to the dashes of red lipstick they flaunted, the chic women had an impressive way about them when it came to fashion.

"I *am* American," Ella admitted.

"Ah, I thought so." The good-looking manager asked for her identification and then escorted her to the rear of the bank. He instructed another employee to pull Laurent Benoit's safety deposit box from a large wall. Ella produced the tiny key Walter had given her and once the manager left her alone in a private room, she unlocked the box. Her pulse stuttered. Trying to quell her anxiousness, Ella withdrew a large key made of iron. Heavy and old-fashioned, its scrolling design lent it a charming look.

Now that's a key.

No doubt it belonged to the original owner of the estate, Jean-Daniel Girard. How could she ever forget his name?

If he is a territorial ghost, what will he think of my moving into his estate? She smiled to herself. This was going to be quite an adventure.

She extracted a folded letter from the deposit box.

> *My darling Ella,*
>
> *I've never written a letter that predicates anyone's death, but I just learned I have cancer. Thus, I'm here in Paris to settle the circumstances of you inheriting Château de Maincy following my and Adelaide's passing. You wouldn't be reading this correspondence if they hadn't taken place.*
>
> *Please don't be sorrowful.*
>
> *In retrospect, I know it was hard for you to have a new stepmother and stepsisters. I don't expect you to fully understand the reason I married Adelaide. Suffice it to say, I didn't want you growing up without a mother. In addition, I needed someone strong... someone to inspire me to pull myself together and go on with my life after your mother died.*

Tears welled in Ella's eyes at the mention of her mother. Kind, gentle, and beautiful, that was how people described Colette Benoit.

Unfortunately, Ella hardly remembered her. What saddened her, she supposed, was the *idea* of her mother dying.

> *My lung cancer is terminal. That means I only have a short time left. You are my sweet, unselfish daughter, and because of your admirable qualities, I wanted to leave you something that is yours and yours alone. Château de Maincy is an incredible part of French history, but there are some daunting things you must know about it. The up-keep of the château has been last on my list through the changes in Benoit Footwear. Because the estate was headed toward decay when I bought it, you'll no doubt find it in considerable disrepair today.*
>
> *That's why I have supplied you with a quarter of a million dollars, that I hope will grow over time. Use these funds to restore the house to its former glory. This money comes from an account I kept separate from Adelaide, Hope, and Charity, so feel no pressure to share it with anyone.*
>
> *Take your time renovating the estate. Once it is fixed up, I have a feeling you will enjoy living there. I've found much joy in visiting Château de Maincy. It is an out-of-the-way place which helped me forget the stresses of everyday life. I took you there when you were quite small, but surely you don't remember.*

Ella's lungs hitched. Her father was right. She didn't recall the visit—and disappointment seeped through her. She had very few memories of her childhood.

> *That leads me to another important point concerning the château. I want you to reach in and remove the last item from the deposit box.*

When she did, she extracted what appeared to be a bonnet of some kind. Dingy and yellowed, it reminded Ella of the ruffled caps servant women wore long ago. *How bizarre.*

I'm giving you this cap because it has intrigued me. When I first purchased the château, I found it inside an old trunk in the attic. I looked at it and then returned it to the trunk. The next morning, it found its way to my night-stand. Following that incident, the bonnet wouldn't stay inside the box. I tried locking the hat away, moving the trunk outside, relocating it to another room of the house. Nothing could keep it captured.

Perhaps you will do a better job of controlling the cap. At the very least, it will be fun trying.

All you must do now is sign the appropriate papers. Then you're free to take the key and the cap, and experience everything Château de Maincy has to offer.

I love you.
Daddy

CHAPTER 4

Expectation and sentimentality mingled within Ella as she zoomed away from Paris. Fortunately, the more she drove, the more light-hearted she became.

The Audi she'd rented drove well. She was good driver—no thanks to Adelaide. Claiming Ella would be a dull-minded hazard on the road, Ella's stepmother had refused to teach her. Thank God Mimi had stepped in.

As Ella maneuvered the high-performance vehicle through a maze of country roads, she felt like a capable, independent woman. Rolling the windows down, she breathed in the fragrant summer air. On a deep exhale, she released her ponytail and began to relax. Fifteen miles outside Paris, she decided to stop at a charming café and enjoy a quick meal.

After consuming a bowl of creamy tomato soup and a freshly-baked croissant, Ella got back in the car and neared the château. In all her twenty-three years, she'd never been so happy—or felt so free. After all, how bad could the condition of the estate be?

She got her answer as soon as Château de Maincy came into view.

One glance at its shambled grounds, chipped aqua-blue domes, and crumbling stone bridge standing over algae-filled water, melted Ella into a puddle of anxiety. The estate was sun-bathed and larger than life, yet it emanated a deep sense of "what used to be." Rows of unkempt trees arched over hills filled with weeds—and from the look of its run-down façade and slew of shattered windows, the house needed endless hours of attention.

And infinite stacks of cash to repair and maintain it.

She grimaced. She would go through the four hundred and fifty thousand dollars her father had gifted her in no time. What then? Shaking herself, she remembered that she had nowhere else to go. The Santa Barbara mansion was in foreclosure and whether or not she'd enjoy rising to the challenge of fixing up the estate, she needed to do just that.

Gripping the steering wheel tighter, she stopped the rental car at a pair of wrought iron gates. The lock had been smashed. Now it dangled open.

As visions of vandals attacking her in the night came to mind, she hesitated. The car hummed softly in place. Forcing herself to get out of it, Ella swung the gates apart and then drove the Audi past them. Eventually, she pulled into a courtyard centered by a stone fountain. The driveway's gravel crunched under the weight of the tires. Slowly, she brought the vehicle to a halt beneath a portico supported by vine-wrapped columns.

It's a shame the estate has fallen into such disrepair since it was built for a king. Well, at the very least, Jean-Daniel had been a distant heir to the French throne.

Drawing herself up, Ella tried to shed some perspective on the situation. She wasn't a difficult person who threw a tantrum when presented with a task. Like *some* people she knew. She would handle this setback and do something right for a change.

She murmured, "If I'm stuck at Château de Maincy for years . . . if I run out of money, am forced to eat fruit from the groves, and am left with a ghost as my only companion, it will be light years better than living with Adelaide, Hope, and Charity." There, she'd said it out loud, even if no one was around to hear her.

After she yanked her bags out of the car, she glanced up at the house's dilapidated façade. It seemed to be calling to her. Amid a tranquil breeze, Ella moved toward the house's double doors. The hair on her arms stood on end. Blinking against a sensation that she'd finally come home, she unlocked one of them. Once she stepped in, a charged silence greeted her. If that odd sensation wasn't enough to layer goose bumps on her arms, a tremendous sense of déjà vu did.

Winded with emotion, she moved deeper into the château's interior. Vastly spectacular, it was lined with hand-carved wallboards, gorgeous crown molding, domed ceilings, and twelve-light chandeliers.

She set her bags on the floor and flipped a switch to see if one of the chandeliers turned on. *Thank goodness!* The place was wired for electricity.

Noting that the grandiose foyer spoke of days gone by, she traced a scrolled, silver-leaf staircase that rose above the foyer and stretched to an airy second floor. When she lifted her chin higher, she saw that it even ascended to a third level.

Excitement flooded her. All of the elements in the house were faded and damaged, but nonetheless, their historic value intrigued her. The house may be old, but it belonged to her.

"Hello!" Ella let the greeting sail up to the rafters. Delightfully, it echoed back at her.

She chuckled and turned her head to the right. It was strange. The layout of the house already felt familiar. A large library sat off the main hallway. Her brief glimpse into the room allowed her to see large pieces of furniture draped in dust sheets, floor-to-ceiling bookshelves, a mahogany mantel etched in gilt-bronze mounts, and once-plush Persian carpets.

Throughout the years, she'd taken an interest in antique furniture. Since Adelaide had accumulated so many fine pieces which she'd refused to sell, even at the end, the opportunity to study them had presented itself. Still, Ella's real interest lay in cuisine. Unfortunately, it was a career she'd been forced to abandon because of Adelaide. Her resentment had really built at that.

Ella's smile returned. At least she could cook magnificent meals here for herself.

Since she hadn't fully entered the library, she looked down another long hallway. A door stood ajar at its end. She snatched a glimpse of a farmhouse sink, open cupboards, and copper pots hanging from racks.

The kitchen.

What was it Adelaide always said when she was considering purchasing a property? *"The kitchen is the first room to show the age of the house."*

Curious to see how modern this kitchen was—or if it was even usable, Ella strode in that direction. As she passed the drawing room, she halted. Eerie goose bumps blanketed her arm. Drawn to the room, she felt as though she'd been in it before.

Under a sudden trance, she entered. Icy stabs of déjà vu assaulted her. The ornate furnishings and draperies were extremely familiar. *Perhaps*, she considered, *I've seen the room in one of Adelaide's real estate or decorating magazines.*

Taking a few steps forward, she noticed a huge blank spot on the east wall. The area's wallpaper not only showed a variance in color, it outlined a missing, life-sized painting or tapestry.

How odd. Why had the work of art been removed? Where was it now?

An unrelenting force drew her closer to the blank spot. Her inquisitiveness grew. If the missing object was indeed a life-sized painting, it must have taken forever to complete. She wondered about its subject. A landscape? More likely, it was a portrait.

Prodded to start a hunt, she went through several rooms on the main level. She searched the front parlor, the back parlor, and the music room. Her favorite was the ballroom. Stepping across the threshold, a spark met her toes. Wide-eyed, she noticed that rays of sunshine cast a sparkling aura over its faded parquet floor. A glittering chandelier hung in the center of the gold-toned room and anchored the enormous space.

When the chandelier caught a beam of sunlight, Ella received another spark. She put her hand to her warm cheeks. She could almost hear strains of a quadrille and the drone of chatter as if she were at a party.

Not at a party. She rephrased the thought. *A ball.*

Eyes blurred, she slipped into a trance against her will. Suddenly, she was wearing a stunning ivory-colored costume and falling into a waltz with a debonair nobleman sporting a mask. The nobleman pulled her tightly against him. Other guests wearing masks looked on.

It was a masquerade ball! More scenes flashed before Ella. A warm wind gusted into the room and then—

Exiting the trance, she realized the hair on the back of her neck was standing on end. Why in heaven had she experienced that?

Her father had written that Ella had been here before. Yet she had no conscious memory of that visit. *Perhaps*, she thought as she rubbed her arms, *the atmosphere of this house is too seductive to resist.*

Still reeling from the vision, her attention shifted to a longcase clock in the corner. Its shattered face was visible through a hinged glass panel that hung ajar. The top of the clock bore a large, vertical gash.

How odd.

Ella stepped closer. The open door revealed that the timepiece had been frozen at twelve o'clock. She touched the immobile hands— and in the bright light of the room, she noticed that the clock's maker had etched his name and creation date into a groove bordering the clock's pendulum.

Montbleu—1703.

Suddenly, Ella remembered standing in front of the longcase clock, precisely like this. But how could that be? She *must* have re-pressed memories from her visit here as a child. But she couldn't ex-plain the vision of herself dancing with the handsome man.

Once she confirmed that a life-sized painting wasn't hanging in the ballroom, she made her way up the grand staircase. Inexplicably, she felt drawn to where she was going. When she reached the second floor of the house, she studied a wall of faded frescoes that depicted late seventeenth-century French life. When something told her to go on, she padded to the third floor landing.

There must be an attic in this house. A place where items are stored.

A palpable hush filled the corridor ahead of her. Then a charged stream of energy rushed through the hall. Since all the curtains were drawn over the arched windows, the corridor stood dark and shad-owed. Ella should be doing so many things. Unpacking. Cleaning. Deciding which bedroom would be hers. But a sense of urgency prompted her feet to continue.

What will I find in this part of the house? Glimpses of the valiant but very dead vicomte?

Gulping, she opened door after door and peeked in. She gathered that she was in the servants' quarters because many of the rooms con-tained single beds with stark furniture. Ella opened what appeared to be a storage space, with an additional staircase leading up to an attic. Creeping up those stairs, she surveyed the articles on the landing. Broken mirrors and pieces of furniture draped in white sheets lay strewn about and tangled strings of cobwebs swathed the wood pan-eling.

A glowing beam of sunlight angled into the room. Ella's pulse sped. In the corner, she spotted an item covered with a black cloth. The article reclined against the far wall—and appeared to be larger than she was. Pushing the curtains open, she allowed more sunlight to bathe the space. Hands quivering, she moved back to the draped item and pulled away the black cloth.

The painting's gilded frame was stunning. On it, Ella located the nameplate.

Jean-Daniel Girard—Vicomte de Maincy
1678–1703

Slowly, as though her life was being altered with every centimeter, her stare ascended to the nobleman's astonishing face. Instantly, the world fell into a compelling hush.

Jean-Daniel Girard was tall, muscular, and inarguably handsome. In fact, his good looks were so striking that Ella could barely breathe as she gazed upon them. More than that, she knew she'd seen his face somewhere before. While she racked her brain about where she'd seen the stunning man, her gaze roamed over Jean-Daniel's solid body, penetrating aquamarine eyes, and angular face. He could be described as classically handsome. The epitome of male beauty, really. And thankfully, that classic quality helped him transcend the fanciful clothing and wig he wore.

Ella took a step in and studied him some more. True to subjects painted in that era, he wasn't smiling. Rather, he seemed pensive and a bit melancholy. However, she could tell from the laugh lines bracketing his generous mouth that he had grinned often.

Incredibly lifelike, Jean-Daniel seemed capable of emerging from the painting right then and there. Ella's skin tingled.

Her gaze drifted to the adorable dog sitting at the vicomte's feet. A splendid example of a hound, it possessed a gleaming brown-and-white coat, an open mouth, and a protruding tongue. Oddly, the *dog* seemed to be smiling.

"I can tell you loved your master," she murmured.

Mesmerized by the man in the painting, Ella stared at his face for what seemed like hours. The more she analyzed it, the more she noticed a "lost soul" quality. She crossed her arms. No, that wasn't it. Rather, there seemed to be something underlying the vicomte's solemn face. As if he weren't solemn at all. As if he possessed a sense of un-finished business.

To die so young . . .

She finally looked at the portrait's backdrop. A vivid depiction of Château de Maincy surrounded Jean-Daniel. There was a cluster of servants working in the fields adjacent to the splendid house. Wide-eyed bluebirds perched on the tree branches over his wigged head.

So that's the way the estate looked in its heyday.

Stepping closer, she zeroed in on Jean-Daniel's astounding eyes. They seemed to come alive—and for the briefest moment he did as well. If only they were on a first-name basis! The thought exhila-rated her.

While she and the figure in the painting locked stares, a new layer of goose bumps sprang up on Ella's arms. She retreated. Despite the warmth of the room, a chill barraged her body.

"He's quite swoon-worthy, *non*?"

Heart hammering, she whirled around at the voice.

A woman of about fifty extended her hand.

"I didn't know anyone was here," Ella said.

The woman smiled warmly. With a mass of black curls, an oblong face, and keen hazel eyes, she was the management agent Ella recog-nized from the company's website.

"Miss Benoit," the woman spoke in a raspy voice, "you've arrived in Maincy earlier than scheduled. I saw your car outside and have looked for you everywhere."

Ella blushed. "I was exploring." She paused. "You're Pénélope Toulouse, correct?"

"Happy to be of service, Mademoiselle." The agent shook Ella's hand.

"It's nice to meet you." Ella dropped her hand and stared at her shoes. She wasn't very good at introductions.

"We did have an appointment at four thirty, correct?" Pénélope asked.

"We did."

The woman grinned at Jean-Daniel's portrait. "Ah . . . you've found Monsieur Girard. He can take a woman's mind to many places."

Ella laughed. "He's very dashing."

"He may be dashing, but I decided to relocate his portrait before you arrived. You've no doubt heard the rumors, Miss Benoit—"

"Please, call me Ella." She faced the painting, too. "You mean about Jean-Daniel Girard haunting the estate?"

"*Oui.*"

At that moment, two burly men entered the attic. They gave Ella curt nods before fastening their hands on their hips. One of them said, "We fixed the kitchen sink and the leaking pipe behind the refrigerator. Is there anything else, Madame Toulouse?"

Pénélope shook her head. "That's all. Thank you, gentlemen."

They turned to go, but Ella put a hand out to stop them. "Please wait! Can you move this portrait back to the drawing room? I saw an empty spot there and I assume that's where the painting hung before."

Pénélope gave a start. "Return it? Are you sure, Ella?"

"I'm sure. I'm intrigued by it."

The agent frowned. "When your father decided to rent this place to people who obviously placed its historic value above its condition, occupants began complaining that Jean-Daniel's eyes followed them everywhere. Not to mention the 'episodes' renters had with him. Seems Monsieur Girard is prone to moving objects."

Why was Pénélope referring to the vicomte as if he were alive?

"Ironically," the dark-haired woman went on, "the renters claimed they were leasing this place just to see ghosts."

When Ella didn't reply, Pénélope let out an anxious laugh. "Monsieur Girard is quite a prankster." She paused. "A *poltergeist*, in fact."

Ella lowered her voice. "I was trying to convince myself that I believe in ghosts, but I really don't. I'm more concerned about the bad reputation a ghost gives the château."

"If Jean-Daniel decides to show himself often, that bad reputation will just get worse."

Ella felt a little sick to her stomach.

"I must warn you about Monsieur Girard on a different level, Ella." Pénélope gave her shoulder a pat. "Many women find him irresistible."

Ella was tempted to scoff at the idea, but hadn't she just stood and stared at his image for twenty minutes or more?

She turned around to face Pénélope, whose expression was as solemn as someone giving a eulogy. Madame Toulouse wasn't joking about Girard's power of seduction.

Ella was about to ask her more about Jean-Daniel when the shorter burly man cleared his throat. "*Excusé-moi, Mademoiselle.* Do you want the painting taken to the drawing room or not?"

"*Oui,*" Pénélope answered for her. "Miss Benoit prefers it there. So, *tout de suite, messieurs.*"

As the men heaved the painting into their arms, they muttered something Ella couldn't hear. Still intrigued by it, she traipsed after them like a child who didn't want her favorite doll scratched by a meddlesome younger brother.

"It's such a lifelike depiction, isn't it?" Ella asked Pénélope as they followed the men downstairs. "Although I don't know what Jean-Daniel Girard really looked like."

"I can assure you the portrait is a good representation," Pénélope replied. "I've seen other paintings of the vicomte de Maincy in museums. He always seems to stare straight through people with those blue eyes."

The management agent feels it, too. Ella dropped her stare from the portrait. *We weren't really looking at one another. And there is no way he could be as familiar as I thought.*

Once they entered the drawing room, Pénélope steered Ella over to another portrait that hung several feet away from where the workmen were reinstating Jean-Daniel's. "You seem to be unfazed by Château de Maincy's dark history, Ella, so I want to show you another member of the Girard family. This is Colbert Girard—a man just as gorgeous as Jean-Daniel. He happens to be Jean-Daniel's twin brother and the 'bad boy' of the Girard clan."

Ella gazed upon the smaller portrait. Her heart lurched. There was a striking resemblance between the siblings, but Colbert Girard's face housed a menacing side. With dark gray eyes as smoky as the fog that rolled into Santa Barbara and skin more olive than his brother's, he sported a larger nose. He wore a black, curled wig and his clothes were simpler than his brother's, but considering his muscular build, narrow waist, and penetrating gaze, there was no denying Colbert oozed sensuality. Just like Jean-Daniel.

"They're fraternal twins," Ella remarked.

"Yes," Pénélope cocked her head. "Though the term didn't exist in those days. To Colbert's despair, he was born seventeen minutes after Jean-Daniel. That's why he's described as the unfortunate spare, whereas his twin was the revered heir. It became a bone of contention with him."

Ella hadn't lived in France at the time of courts and kings. Nor did she understand sibling rivalry. The truth was she would have killed to have had a real sister with whom she could have grown close.

"As I said, the phrase 'fraternal twins' didn't exist back then," Pénélope jabbered on. "Still, people knew the Girard brothers were as different as day and night. Colbert was cunning and cruel. Jean-Daniel, on the other hand, could charm an éclair away from a pastry lover. Colbert resented his brother and ended up fighting with him continually. Some say he even had a hand in Jean-Daniel's death."

"What happened?"

Pénélope shook her head. "No one knows for certain. Legend has it that the trouble began as soon as *she* came to Château de Maincy."

"Who?" Ella raised an eyebrow.

"Her name isn't recorded anywhere. Apparently, she was a scullery maid at this very château."

"Why did this maid cause so much trouble?"

"Jean-Daniel fell in love with her and their affair caused quite a scandal."

Ella's pulse rushed. *Lucky girl.* The falling in love part, not the causing a scandal part.

"It was a time of political peacefulness, but 'peaceful' did not describe the relationship of the Girard brothers." Pénélope grasped her leather briefcase tightly. "Louis the fourteenth was the king of France at the time. His style of rule incorporated absolute monarchy—with no say from Parlement. The concept worked very well for France and Jean-Daniel was a true fan of Louis's."

"Louis the Fourteenth was known as the Sun King, right?"

"*Oui.* He did much good for the nation. In fact, France was the pre-eminent power of Europe." Pénélope paused. "Jean-Daniel thought he could learn a lot from Louis and was ecstatic when he was invited to Versailles to be a courtier."

"I assume Colbert felt differently."

"Correct. He hated the thought that Jean-Daniel would have the chance to rise even higher in social rank. The brothers had many arguments on the subject."

Ella shuddered. She would hate to see Colbert mad.

"Shortly thereafter," Pénélope said, "Jean-Daniel was found floating in the lake just outside that window." Pénélope indicated which one by a wave of her hand.

"The vicomte drowned?"

"It was deemed a suicide. But when Jean-Daniel's body was retrieved, the gash on his head caused speculation. Some people suggested he'd slipped and fallen into the lake accidentally. Then there was the theory that someone hit him on the back of the head and left him to drown in the lake."

"Such a tragic story." Ella took a final look at the Girard twins before Pénélope guided her out of the drawing room.

"Fortunately for you, it's all in the past." The agent exhaled.

"I suppose." Ella frowned. She couldn't put the house's dark history *completely* behind her. After all, she was going to be living here amongst it.

"I presume you haven't seen much of the house yet. I'll take you on a tour."

"Thank you, Madame Toulouse. I'd like that."

"Call me Pénélope."

During the journey around the house and its grounds, the agent offered a lengthy commentary. Eventually, Ella tuned her out and concentrated on the state of things. As she glimpsed the château's severely outdated kitchen, nine bedrooms that smelled of must, nineteen terraces (she counted them), and highly-neglected wooded parklands and gardens, her sense of "what had been" returned.

As the women strolled back to the foyer, Pénélope said, "I wish you'd been greeted by a smaller list of repairs, Ella. But remember, Rome wasn't built in a day."

"Right." Ella nodded. She wasn't terribly fazed because she was still comparing her situation to living with Adelaide and her two stepsisters. Nothing could be worse.

"I assume there's running water. And what about the Internet?"

"The house has under-floor water pipes and electricity. But be careful. The wires were installed in the thirties and can only handle low-voltage usage. As for the Internet, you can have someone come and install a satellite for you." She passed Ella a card. "I also want to give you the names of some local contractors."

Reaching into her briefcase, she pulled out a sheet of paper and handed it over.

"Is there air-conditioning?" Ella asked. "I notice it's very warm in here."

Pénélope shook her head. "No air-conditioning, I'm afraid."

Ella hadn't thought so.

As Pénélope rearranged the scarf she wore around her neck, Ella peeked at the window above the front door. The sun had begun to set. Despite the warm temperature, a shiver ran down her spine. Suddenly, she didn't want to be alone in an empty house. The truth was she wasn't used to being alone. Adelaide had always been there to command things.

Pénélope smiled, showing crooked teeth. "You look a little flushed, Ella. Are you all right?"

"I guess I'm a bit overwhelmed."

"It's a large estate, but I promise you'll get used to living here."

Whether she'd sell the house after fixing it up, Ella couldn't say. It depended on how much she enjoyed residing here. It also depended on how much of a nuisance this "phantom" became.

She thought about prompting Pénélope for more information on Jean-Daniel, but decided to keep their first meeting to business. "Before you go, Pénélope, can you tell me how far the nearest village is?"

"It's a twenty minute walk," the woman replied. "You can head through the olive grove and around the parkland. There is a path."

"Oh, good. Sounds like a short drive by car."

"Yes." Pénélope frowned. "But the majority of the villagers are very old. You'll make a better first impression if you go there on foot. At least at first."

That made Ella smile. "Do they keep up with who's staying here at the château?"

"They do, indeed."

"You said there have been renters?"

"Yes. Your father set up a monthly maintenance fund with us to take care of things. The money ran out long ago, but I still honor my dealings with him since I knew he'd left the estate to you."

"Thank you." Ella gave her a shy smile. "I appreciate that."

"Although my services are no longer needed, I'll stop in and check on you. As a favor to your father. He was a wonderful man."

"You've been a big help, Pénélope."

Pénélope grinned and waved the thought away with her hand.

"Before you go, I have one last question," Ella said. "Who owned this place before my father bought it?"

"That's a fascinating story. He was a famous Romanian magician named Dragomir Starkov. At the beginning of the twentieth century,

Mr. Starkov rose nearly to the level of Harry Houdini's fame—until he performed his final illusion on top of New York City's Woolworth Building. Rumor claimed this magician was in league with the devil. Allegedly, with his demonic powers, he made himself and his beautiful wife *disappear*."

The estate had a more sinister past than Ella had thought. She cocked a brow as she walked Pénélope to the door.

"Your father told me that when Mr. Starkov lived here, he lost two objects that were very precious to him," the agent said before she left the house.

"Two objects?"

"An Egyptian amulet and its matching bracelet. Starkov and your father never met, but through written documentation, Starkov claimed the jewelry went missing and was never recovered."

"Never?" Ella asked as she gripped the door handle.

Pénélope smiled furtively. "Interestingly, the objects are said to have magical powers. Between restoration projects, perhaps you can entertain yourself by hunting for them."

CHAPTER 5

Holy Christ. It's her.

Trapped inside the portrait, Jean-Daniel watched Ella talk to the management agent.

She is as beautiful as ever. Remarkable!

Like a delicate pink rose shimmering in the morning dew, she had stood before his portrait, looking him directly in the eye. Jean-Daniel had given no response outwardly. Ghosts didn't. They couldn't sense the softness of someone's hair. Or feel the warmth of an ocean breeze, or taste food. But inside, Jean-Daniel was overcome with every emotion a former lover would experience.

If his heart could still beat, it would have pulsated urgently.

Do you recognize me, Ella? He yearned to call out. *Do you remember me at all?*

How could she? She was a different person now. She may be a version of his Ella, but surely she had no memory of her old life.

Jean-Daniel struggled to breathe . . . fought to move inside the painting. He wanted to burst out of it and paint Ella a banner that read, "It's me. Your lost love!" But he could do no such thing. She had returned. He needed to be happy with that for the time being.

While he watched her, she tucked a lock of hair behind her ear. *I remember her doing that!* A thrill rippled across his chest.

I also remember that small birthmark on her collarbone. My God!

Never had he wanted to explode out of the painting so badly. If it were possible, he'd rush to Ella's side and hold her. He burned to tell her that she must come back to him.

But his jaw was locked, frozen in a stoic expression.

Standing there like a wax figure, Jean-Daniel decided he would have to communicate with Ella in alternative ways. If she used any sort of electricity, he'd feed off that. Ghosts sucked up electromagnetic energy and radio waves and internalized those sources for stimulus.

Also, he might be able to move things if more energy was used. *Telekinesis*. He was pretty sure that's what people called it today.

If Ella plugged in a hair dryer or bought a TV, he'd be forever grateful. And if she hooked up her computer, who knew what he would be capable of?

The reality was he'd been able to emerge from the painting before electricity was installed, but those occasions were few and far between during those years. Here in the twenty-first century, it was a different world. A world full of technology and new sources of currents. For those advancements, he was tremendously grateful.

Jean-Daniel watched Ella talk to Pénélope in the foyer. *Damn*! If he could touch her right now, he'd let her know what he felt, through his kisses. Their love had been so astonishing when he was alive that he had anticipated her reappearance for centuries. She'd come to Château de Maincy once, as a child. Her blue eyes, bowed lips, and gleaming blond hair were unmistakable then and now.

Desperately, Jean-Daniel needed her to travel back in time. Back into his arms to set the wheels of change into motion.

It was a long shot, but if Ella could find the enchanted amulet and bracelet the house's previous owner left behind, she might be able to enter his portrait. Jean-Daniel was the only one who knew it was a portal to different dimensions.

He watched her shoot him another shy look from the foyer. Then he panicked a little. If she didn't come to him through the painting, what they had would never be. It was twisted. Convoluted. And could prove difficult. But he had been very good at persuading people to do things when he was alive. He refused to lose that ability as a ghost.

Luckily, his memories of Ella attested to the fact that she'd been at the château in 1703. In this modern era, she seemed as coy as ever. She also possessed the same clear voice and gentle demeanor Jean-Daniel had come to pine for. Back then, Ella had been an unlikely choice, considering his vicomte status. But isn't that what he'd loved about her?

Now, he'd do anything to revel in those lapis-blue eyes again. To converse with her. To caress her arms and skim his fingertips along her porcelain face.

He searched her features for any indication that she recognized him. To his great disappointment, she averted her gaze.

Raw frustration gripped his insides.

Trying to steady himself, he tried to look on the bright side. At least she had instructed those pinheads to restore his painting to its former location. She must have felt *something* when she gazed upon it.

Jean-Daniel watched Pénélope Toulouse leave. Once Ella shut the front door, she returned to her observation spot in front of the portrait.

"I guess it's just you and me now, Monsieur Girard." Pursing her bow-shaped lips, she inclined her head.

Inwardly, his stomach fluttered. *How I remember kissing those soft lips . . .*

She drew in a sharp breath. "We aren't completely alone. We can't forget about your evil-hearted twin, Colbert."

Rage coursed through Jean-Daniel at the name. He hated that Ella had no choice but to look upon Colbert's portrait. Jean-Daniel's contempt for his brother ran deep. Why hadn't Colbert been a normal, supportive sibling? They were twins, but Jean-Daniel had a hard time believing that himself. He and Colbert were as different as the sun and the moon. As opposite as summer and winter. And Colbert had possessed a habit of not only betraying him, but violating Ella.

Jean-Daniel was appreciative that he couldn't see his brother's face. Colbert's painting hung on the same wall as his, and not being able to see it was a godsend. His sibling had been nothing but abrasive, jealous, and bitter. And Jean-Daniel didn't want to spend eternity staring into the face of a traitor.

I'm also glad I can't see the window hovering over the lake. The scene of my murder.

Some people claimed that a person who dies under horrible circumstances is doomed to a state of limbo. For Jean-Daniel, leaving behind a great many regrets added to that torture. He hadn't taken anything seriously centuries ago—until he met Ella. Unfortunately, he died before he could *show* people how much he'd changed.

That was hard enough to live with. (Ha! Another "dead" pun!) But if Ella were to return to 1703 to prevent his death they could celebrate their love longer than the few days they'd shared.

Jean-Daniel hadn't bumped his head and lay there to drown, as some imbeciles claimed afterward. Knowing the identity of his murderer caused him a unique type of torment.

Ella's cell phone interrupted his thoughts. A crackle of energy sparked inside him at each chord of pop music. Ella answered the third ring with a graceful swipe of her fingers.

"Hello."

A pause.

"Mimi! It's so good to hear your voice!"

A pause.

"Yes, I got here a few hours ago." Ella roamed the room, her head down, her phone at her ear, her arm tucked beneath her breasts.

Those breasts, Jean-Daniel reminisced. *Plump. Not overly large but ripe and firm. The most beautiful I've ever seen.*

And her legs. Toned. Tanned. Like nothing he'd seen until she had arrived in the eighteenth century.

She was wearing baggy clothes—which was an odd fashion choice, he had to admit—so he couldn't see her curves. But he could attest to her beautiful figure. And if he could have an erection, he would have a champion one from the memory of it.

Picturing her glorious figure brought him back to the only time they'd made love. In the silence of his grand bedchamber, he'd laid her across silk sheets. Once he had peeled every article of clothing off her magnificent body, moonlight had illuminated her lovely face . . .

If my family and my friends could see me now. They had always asserted that Jean-Daniel didn't have it in him to forge a deep emotional connection with a woman.

He gave an inward grimace. He'd been a rogue before he met Ella. As he watched her chat idly on the phone, he remembered how he had enjoyed the company of many eager females, and he wasn't proud of those meaningless liaisons. Then Ella had appeared to knock some sense into him. She'd turned him around—made him an entirely new man by showing him that life wasn't to be wasted. And he couldn't thank her enough for it.

Unfortunately, he'd reached that new level of purpose just before he'd been killed.

"I got the checkbook from the bank," Ella told Mimi as she plopped down on a sheet-covered divan. "But I don't know how far my father's money will go. This place needs a massive renovation."

Dust particles assaulted her. She coughed and flushed an adorable shade of pink. Grinning inwardly, Jean-Daniel watched her pert nose quiver before she sneezed.

"You're right. Rome wasn't built in a day," she went on. "That's what Pénélope Toulouse said."

A pause.

"Yes. She seems nice enough."

Mimi must have been chattering away because Ella listened and met Jean-Daniel's stare. Since she was sitting in a distant corner of the room, he was forced to gaze at her at an odd angle. When they locked eyes, her tawny eyebrows drew together. She didn't speak for a moment. Then she got up and moved closer to the portrait.

At this close distance, Jean-Daniel could hear her friend raise her voice. "Ella? Are you there?"

"Sorry, Mimi. I'm here."

"What is it?"

"I . . . I don't know. It's just strange—"

"What's strange?"

"I was sitting on the sofa a moment ago. The man in the paint-ing . . . his eyes followed me. I could swear it."

"What man? What painting?"

"There's a huge portrait of the château's original owner hanging in the drawing room. I have the feeling he's watching me."

"You must have jet lag." The caller laughed gently.

"I could swear his eyes followed me, Mimi. You know I wouldn't just say something like that."

Mimi's voice took on a different tone. "Maybe you want to see things. Amid all that rich history, I mean."

Ella shook herself. "Maybe . . ." As she moved away, she kept her eyes glued to Jean-Daniel's. Then she stopped abruptly. "His eyes did it again!"

Ella's friend said something Jean-Daniel couldn't hear. Mean-while, Ella dragged an armchair over to the painting. She was so pe-tite that the portrait towered over her.

"Wait a moment, Mimi," she said. She set the phone on the floor. Standing on the chair's cushion, she stretched an arm up toward Jean-

Daniel's face. A moment later, her feet pierced right through the silver cushion. She fell back with a less-than-graceful *thud*.

"Ella!" the voice from the cell phone cried.

Ella brushed herself off and chuckled into the phone. "I'm okay. I was just seeing if there was a slot in the painting—where the nobleman's eyes are."

Her friend went on to say something else and Ella laughed more heartily. It was the most melodious, the most incredible sound Jean-Daniel had heard since 1703.

"You're right! I must be losing it," she continued. "Creepy paintings don't have eyes, right? This isn't the Haunted Mansion ride at Disneyland."

Ella hesitated, then gazed at the portrait again. In the meantime, Jean-Daniel studied her up close. Her blond hair lay in luminous waves over the right side of her face and her stunning eyes glimmered with excitement.

If only he could reach out and touch her. If only he could smell her sweet scent. He recalled the fragrance of vanilla.

She tucked her hair behind her ear again. And when her lips curved into a smile, it sent that little surge of warmth through him again. He wanted her to stay this close to him all night. When and if he emerged, he could hover next to her.

To his displeasure, she pushed the chair out of the way and stepped back. "Thank goodness no one saw me topple over. I'm just as klutzy as ever."

Jean-Daniel didn't know what "klutzy" meant. To him, Ella was nothing but naturally beautiful, caring, and intelligent. And he had been pierced by Cupid's arrow the moment he saw her.

Of course, when they ran into each other that fateful day outside the château, he'd been an ass. His usual flirtatious self.

"All right, Mimi," Ella said with a sigh. "I'm going to sign off."

She gave the painting a final glance before she flipped the light switch and left the room. That's when Jean-Daniel was one hundred percent certain he maintained inner emotions despite a lack of outer physicality. After all, his heart ached. And when he heard Ella mutter, "I should stay away from the debonair Monsieur Girard," it broke in two.

Light-headed and dizzy, Ella emerged from the drawing room. As she strolled into the foyer and retrieved her luggage, her top lip began to perspire.

This is so odd!

She didn't feel sick, exactly. It was as if she'd been dazed by the same sensation she'd experienced in the ballroom.

The figure in the painting had such a profound effect on her—though she couldn't say why. She'd certainly gawked at handsome men in magazines before. Heck, she even purchased *People*'s Sexiest Man Alive issue every year for kicks. But no male, in person or in a photograph, had ever made her this jittery.

Trying to shrug it off, she clasped the handle of her rolling suitcase. After she slung the carry-on bag over her shoulder, she made her way to the foot of the staircase. Passing a stunning commode with a marble top, she tried to busy her mind with the amusing fact that nowadays the term "commode" was reserved for toilets. But even that didn't work. Something—an unknown force—was commanding her to abandon her luggage and rush back to the drawing room.

She stopped, the wheels of her suitcase squeaking to a halt behind her. Nighttime had fallen. She'd be wise to resist the urge to re-visit the painting since the house sat steeped in shadows.

As she stood there debating what to do next, a cold draft blasted over her. The hair on the back of her neck prickled and she felt a brush against her leg. Crying out, she hoisted the suitcase in her arms and raced upstairs.

Reaching one of the bedrooms, she rushed in and locked the door. She hadn't run that fast since her seventh grade track meet!

Okay, that was really weird. Something had touched the back of her leg just now. She'd swear to it. But there had to be a good explanation for what happened. Right?

Breathing in heavy rasps, she let her luggage fall to the floor. Why couldn't she catch her breath? She jogged every morning and was in decent shape, but an unearthly amount of adrenaline clutched her lungs and wouldn't let go.

Urging herself to calm down, Ella flipped on the lights. She wasn't about to go downstairs again, so she might as well become familiar with her new bedroom. A pair of French "aux Putti" wall sconces illuminated the splendid space. Despite its musty smell, it boasted magnificent elements, such as lovely ceiling-to-floor curtains, a nine-light chandelier, and a spectacular bed. In fact, the bed was her favorite feature of the room. Its front pilasters ascended to meet a domed tester adorned with a blue silk canopy trimmed with tassels.

The bed seemed fit for a princess. A thrill filtered through Ella and did battle with the sensation that she was being watched.

Humming a little melody, as she often did when she wanted to distract herself, she lifted the coverlet off the bed and shook the dust out of it. Choking, she leaned over and smelled the sheets. Thankfully, they didn't smell terribly stale. Even if they did, she was too scared to go back downstairs and wash them.

She proceeded to fold the coverlet over an armchair. All the while, her heart thumped louder than usual. She tried to concentrate on readying herself for bed. The luxurious king-sized mattress was a far cry from her twin-sized version back home. Hope and Charity always had fancy bedclothes layered with plump pillows to match their wallpaper.

But right now they would be extremely jealous.

Ella smiled. Were they having fun feeding Cupcake and Creampuff? Were the dogs snarling at them like they did with anyone who wasn't Adelaide?

Ella suppressed a giggle. Then she said aloud, "To hell with it." She was all alone! Letting out a long, healthy laugh, her shoulders shook and she fell back on the bed. It was a laugh at her stepsisters' expense—something she'd never done before. Something she thoroughly enjoyed.

She laughed until her stomach hurt. *That* was long overdue.

After a moment, Ella heard a soft "pop." Sitting up, she wiped her eyes. Glancing around the room, she noticed that an ivory candle had fallen from a sconce to the floor. Frowning, she stood and picked the candle up. It wasn't broken. Surely it would have snapped if a strong draft had blown it over.

Without dwelling on the incident, she replaced the item and took another look around the room. *Good. No portraits to creep me out.*

She busied herself with unpacking, although the awareness that someone was watching her remained—despite her best efforts to brush it aside.

Once Ella had set her beloved copy of *Wuthering Heights* on the nightstand, she shut the lights off and climbed into bed. Unable to relax, she stared up at the canopy.

Had her dad slept in this room? Had *she*, when she was a child?

She wanted to remember being here with him, but she couldn't. If her father had indeed brought her here, she'd probably forgotten the visit completely.

Her youth had been short-lived—which was a painful truth. But her best recollection was sitting on her father's lap as he'd read her stories. It had fueled her love of literature. And when they began preparing meals together, her love of cooking had been born.

But it had been a long time since she'd baked bread with her father. Or heard the sound of his voice as he read *Alice in Wonderland*.

Sadness, as rich as the musty air around her, surrounded Ella. "I'm going to restore this place to its former glory," she whispered into the darkness. "It's what Dad would have wanted."

CHAPTER 6

Ella woke up to a brilliant morning. Practically jumping out of bed, she hurried to the window. What a glorious day! Tree branches swayed lazily in the breeze. Birds flitted from hedge to hedge. And golden sunshine shone over the green gardens and bounced off the crystalline lake.

The lake where Jean-Daniel drowned.

She frowned. *What a way to kill a mood!*

Turning away from the window, she refused to let lurid thoughts of tragic deaths and ghosts faze her on this cheery morning. Now what was it she was going to do first? Wash the sheets.

Stepping into a pair of fuzzy, camouflage-patterned slippers, she yanked the sheets off the bed. Still wearing the tank top and shorts she'd slept in, she carried the bundle down to a tiny laundry room on the first level.

Assuming the space had once been a butler's pantry, she glanced at the washer and dryer. They must have been installed in the seventies! Both were pea-soup green and had outdated knobs. But, thankfully, the washer possessed an enormous drum.

After she added some towels, she looked for laundry detergent. There wasn't any. That brought out a sigh. She had no choice but to go into town to stock up on groceries, cleaning supplies, and soap.

She grimaced some more. Pénélope had advised her to go to town on foot. At least for her first visit. How many grocery bags could she carry back?

Ella left the washing machine's door open. Once she entered the hallway, butterflies tumbled in her stomach. The drawing room was only a few feet away. Should she sneak a peek at Jean-Daniel?

No. She didn't want to relive the odd sensation he'd sent up her spine yesterday.

Resisting, she turned on her slipper's heel. As she trudged up the stairs, her hands trembled. Not looking at the painting was like refusing a slice of freshly-baked cake. What was it about the dashing vicomte? He'd been dead for over three hundred years, but he seemed more alive and fearless than most men. Especially Christopher Vanders, Ella's last boyfriend. He'd been Adelaide's oncologist. For a while, anyway. As soon as Adelaide caught wind of the attraction between him and Ella, she'd switched doctors. Christopher stopped calling Ella after that.

Apparently, the guy had no guts. Either that or Adelaide had sent some pretty nasty threats his way.

While she changed into her workout clothes, Ella snatched a glance of herself in the mirror. She traced the tiny tattoo on her right hip. She'd had it inked there several years ago, but had immediately regretted it.

Thankfully, no one would know of its existence unless she wore a miniature bikini in public. Which she would never do.

In the shape of a fleur-de-lis, the golden tattoo had been inspired by Ella's affinity for French culture. Which went back to her father's influence.

"That was a tough time in my life," she murmured as she tied her running shoes. When Adelaide got sick, Ella missed her prom, never went to a party, or had any friends. Then she was forced to drop out of culinary school. Cut off from everything she desired to do, she'd rebelled. Well, she got a miniscule tattoo. That'd been the extent of her crazy behavior.

Ella smiled at the thought. In the brightly-lit room, she felt a surge of vitality. *Now it's time to resurrect the part of me that died when I settled in to help Adelaide.*

She stretched for her run and then left the house through the back door. As she descended one side of a magnificent twin staircase, she marveled at how artfully a string of arching vines threaded over its stone wall.

She stopped to smell one of the dahlias.

There was something incredibly enchanting about this tower-topped château. She could see why her father had enjoyed coming here.

Breaking into a jog, she inserted her earphones and loped down a pathway that traversed the lake. Her muscles loosened. Blood began to pulse at her temples as she ran. This was when she did her best thinking.

Which rooms in the château should I renovate first? Perhaps the kitchen and the library. Ella was the only person living here, after all. And it's where she'd be spending most of her time.

As she left the lake behind her, her imagination took hold. She envisioned a Provençal-style farmhouse table and new French doors in the kitchen. And on cold winter nights, she could lounge in the library-*cum*-cozy den. How nice it would be to curl up, watch TV, and eat a hearty bowl of French onion soup!

The fantastic truth was she could do whatever she wanted to here.

Her run took her through a lush olive grove—which made quite an impression. Amazed at how plentiful the grove's trees were, Ella considered that she could always sell the olives if her father's money ran out too quickly.

Once she settled into a comfortable stride, she jogged all the way to Maincy. Lined with quaint shops, cobbled streets, and people who seemed pleasant and unhurried, the place was adorable. Just as she'd experienced inside the château, she felt as though she'd gone back in time.

Locating a general store, she wiped her forehead with the back of her hand and entered it. "*Bonjour,*" she greeted the shopkeeper.

"*Bonjour, Mademoiselle.*"

Smiling shyly, she released her hair from its ponytail. As she surveyed the store's goods, she hid behind her hair and kept her earphones in. They were her safety blanket. Her way of ignoring the outside world.

"May I help you?" The shopkeeper found her in the back of the store and spoke to her in English.

Reluctantly, Ella removed her earphones.

He repeated himself.

"I need to stock up on a few things," she replied.

He hesitated. "Are you the new owner of Château de Maincy?"

"I am. How did you guess?"

The brightness in his eyes dimmed. "Pénélope Toulouse informed my wife and I that you'd be coming. I guessed it was you today because you are so . . . *American*."

What about me is so American? My looks? My manner?

She stopped looking for laundry detergent and decided to make a light joke. "Do the French hate Americans as much as everyone says?"

"No. The people of Maincy don't mind that you're here. In fact, we want you to fix that eyesore of an estate."

Ella straightened her posture. "I'll do my best, but it'll take some time, *Monsieur*."

The man grunted. He went on to help Ella locate the things that she'd come in for. Once she'd filled her wire basket with essentials, she met him at the cash register.

"Maybe you can stop those people from coming to Maincy," he said as he loaded her items into paper grocery bags.

"People?" Ella asked.

"Ghost hunters."

"I didn't realize that was a problem."

"They pump money into the local economy, but they're also giving this place a bad reputation."

Ella had had no inkling of the château's reputation before leaving Santa Barbara. Now, she'd be smart to refute it. "I can assure you there's no ghost at the house," she said, lifting the bags into her arms.

"You're wrong. My son and daughter have seen it. People in town have seen it. It mostly comes out at night, you see. But it's definitely there."

"And you don't approve of such things?"

"I might frown upon them, but I don't deny they happen."

Ella was tempted to ask the man what he wanted her to do. Perform an exorcism to rid the château of all specters? Run for the hills herself?

Saying nothing, she returned home. If Jean-Daniel actually haunted the estate, would Ella see his apparition personally? Visions of his aquamarine eyes and muscular frame made her cheeks flush. *Goodness.* He made her gush like a teenybopper at a One Direction concert.

Arms aching, she plopped the groceries on the kitchen counter and unloaded them. Once she'd started the washing machine, she tended to her rumbling stomach with coffee and a croissant. Then she grabbed a bar of soap and trotted upstairs to take a shower.

The tub was one of those old-fashioned models, with elegant, clawed feet and a shower head attached to it by a metal stem. Drawing the shower curtain around her in a complete circle, Ella spent a good fifteen minutes under the warm spray.

Refreshed, she dressed and blew her hair dry. Until the dryer sparked and sputtered a little, that is.

Damned wiring from the 1930s!

Cripes. Would Ella electrocute herself one of these days? She certainly wasn't going to plug her laptop into *this* outlet.

Making a mental note to put electricity repair at the top of her renovation list, she eyed her computer. Time to have the Internet connected. She'd gone one day without it and was ashamed to say she'd sorely missed it.

Extracting the card Pénélope had handed her, she called Pierre DuBois of WorldWide Dish. Apparently, he installed satellite dishes in the area.

After she made an appointment to have DuBois come out the next day, she fixed herself another cup of coffee. Her short-term plan consisted of shopping for quotes from contractors before she began the renovation process.

Wrapping her hands around the warm coffee mug, Ella sighed. She drank it and braced herself for an afternoon of cleaning.

As daytime darkened into night, Jean-Daniel tingled with anticipation. Today, Ella had used her blow dryer and the washing machine. The energy sources had empowered him enough to emerge from the painting. Perhaps if he moved something, she'd be convinced of his presence.

He slipped out and then swiveled to look at Rémy. The dog gazed at him with understanding.

"This is one haunting," Jean-Daniel said kindly, "I must render by myself, old boy."

Such a loyal dog. Rémy had died from a broken heart directly after Jean-Daniel's demise.

Jean-Daniel offered the animal a smile and then stalked toward Colbert's portrait. It had been years since he'd stopped in front of it. Ella's eyes had certainly grown wide when she'd gazed upon it.

Does she remember him more than she remembers me? If she did, she couldn't have good memories.

Jean-Daniel studied his brother's thundery eyes and defiant stance. The twins had never looked or acted alike. What was it Ella claimed they were? *Fraternal* twins?

It was a miracle that they were related at all. Furthermore, it wasn't fair that Colbert's soul hadn't been trapped between worlds. Jean-Daniel heard that the bastard had gone on to live a full life. Unfairly, he'd died a crotchety old man in his comfy bed.

Then again, Jean-Daniel should be glad Colbert wasn't a ghost. He couldn't think of anything worse than sharing eternity with his twin, here at the château. He often cringed at the idea of bumping into Colbert along these hallways. And he rolled his eyes at the nuisance that vying for position as head ghost would be. Callous Colbert always wanted to have the upper hand.

Funny that Jean-Daniel could feel their sibling rivalry even now.

Turning his thoughts to Ella, he traveled up to the house's second level. She had shut off the lights so she must be asleep.

He dissolved through a wall and eyed the servant's cap she'd positioned on her bureau. Jean-Daniel had enjoyed playing pranks with the cap years ago, moving it numerous times when Ella's father had lived here.

Now, he summoned all his mental strength and channeled the cap to his hand. With a ferocious swipe, he threw it to the floor. Then he floated over Ella's bed. As he gazed down at her, her beauty seized him anew. Her glossy hair billowed across the pillow and her cheeks—flushed a cherry-red—glowed enticingly as she let out a soft breath.

She had kicked the sheets off due to the warmth of the room. Her shirt, scanty by eighteenth-century standards, was bunched up to reveal even scantier underwear. A triangle joined on both sides by a string barely covered her nether hair.

Jean-Daniel cocked a brow. There it was: the golden fleur-de-lis on her hip.

Back in 1703, he'd thought she was wearing some kind of body paint. Now, he knew the design had been permanently inked there. When previous renters had installed a cable dish for the television in the drawing room, Jean-Daniel had watched programs along with them. He'd seen an episode of *Law and Order.* One of the criminals on the show had gotten . . . what was it called? Oh, yes. A tattoo.

Grinning at Ella's nod to French aristocracy, he reached out and traced the fleur-de-lis's outline. She stirred. And when she rolled on her side, the flare of her derriere widened his eyes.

Moonlight flooded the room. Swallowing hard, Jean-Daniel ran his transparent touch along the column of her neck, down to the rise of her breasts. Her chest rose against his touch, although he was sure it was unintentional.

He craved her, there was no doubt. Yet, he couldn't feel sexual stimulation. Hints of arousal came in the form of a thousand pinpricks. Because he'd been such a red-blooded, non-ascetic male while alive, this was the ultimate punishment.

The pinpricks sizzled and spread over Jean-Daniel's body, but he couldn't cool them. Nor alleviate the sensation. There was nothing more frustrating.

His gaze roved over Ella again. He bent his head closer. Unfortunately, he couldn't smell her, either. He'd lost that ability long ago.

As long shadows fell across Ella's face, he studied her pristine features. She didn't seem to be dreaming. Instead, she seemed immersed in peaceful sleep. The house made a settling sound. A little grunt floated from her throat. She rolled onto her back again. The shift moved her panties aside and Jean-Daniel caught a glimpse of her dark blond curls.

As a ghost, he had no choice but to be a voyeur. He had to *imagine* what it felt like to be buried in those curls. To grow hard in her tight depths. Luckily, their real-life encounter years ago helped flesh out his memory.

Observing her some more, Jean-Daniel concluded that the settling noise had set something off in Ella. Her brows furrowed and she thrust her head from side to side.

She's having a nightmare.

Jean-Daniel lowered himself to the bed and stroked her hair slowly. He wished to God he could feel the satiny quality of her tresses. Resolved to watch her, he noticed that her concerned expression disappeared. In fact, she let out a soothed little purr. At the very least, his caress had calmed her.

As expected, Jean-Daniel's closeness caused a cold draft over Ella. How could he tell? Goosebumps rose on her bare arms—and her nipples hardened into peaks.

Will she awaken? She must be tired from her journey here, but part of him wanted her to open her eyes. He longed to look into her lapis-blue irises and see them dilate. Tilting his mouth into a smile, he also longed to cup the roundness of her breasts and lower his mouth to her sweet nipples. He remembered how they'd tasted.

A desperate urge to edge his hand between her tanned thighs rolled over him. If he did that, however, Ella might flee the château without returning. He'd seen people "freaked out" before—as Americans called it.

Jean-Daniel decided to steal a soft kiss . . . one that would leave Ella still asleep and dreaming of more. Leaning over, he dropped his mouth to hers. He recalled her lips being enticingly moist. He'd have to settle for that memory, too.

Ella sighed. Reaching up, she wrapped her arms around his neck. He deepened the kiss. Her soft moans filled the room. Then her eyes flew open as her hands passed right through him and dropped to the mattress.

CHAPTER 7

Ella leapt out of bed. "Is somebody there?"

Like a frightened animal, she wedged herself into a corner of the room.

"I'm here!" Jean-Daniel's mouth formed the words, but only the ghost of Rémy could hear him when he spoke. He wanted to tell Ella not to be afraid. He also wanted to cry out with joy because she'd actually *felt* him. He couldn't feel *her* of course, but the contact was definitely progress.

He didn't want her to be scared out of her mind, however.

The bold connection, though it had been brief, was enough for now. Time wasn't on his side, but still, he must reveal himself little by little.

A ball of frustration, Jean-Daniel floated through the wall and returned to his painting.

Fear pounded Ella's heart like a bass drum. Somebody had touched her a moment ago. No, they'd actually *kissed* her.

Could it have been a dream?

Absolutely not. The sensation had been too vivid. Plus, it had provoked such a visceral reaction that she couldn't have imagined it. She pressed two fingers to her mouth. The kiss hadn't been gentle, friendly, or platonic. Rather, it'd been sensual and carnal enough to leave an imprint of fire on her lips.

With a hand clasped over her heart, she flipped on the lights. Her eyes darted about. Nothing but stillness—and that damned charged energy—met her search. Taking in a deep breath, she inhaled the scent of milled sandalwood soap. How odd! She'd showered earlier with the flowery soap she had purchased in town.

Sinking into the bed, she looked down at her trembling hands. Her attention shifted to the servant's cap lying half-hidden under the bed skirt. Hadn't she set it on top of the bureau?

She checked the window. It was closed and locked. No draft could have lifted the cap and blown it to the floor. As she picked up the cap and returned it to the bureau, her hands trembled more violently. Needing some water to soothe her dry mouth, she donned her robe. *Think, Ella. You need to see if someone's broken into the house.*

Grateful that she'd brought along a mini-flashlight, she grabbed it out of her handbag. Then, picking up an iron poker that sat by the hearth, she went downstairs slowly.

"Don't fail me if I need you," she warned the weapon. Over the years, she'd developed a habit of speaking to inanimate objects. Partly because there was no one else to talk to. Partly because inanimate objects couldn't insult her.

It took a while for Ella to search the château. There was nothing spookier at night than a big, empty house. As she moved from the kitchen to the drawing room to the ballroom, she imagined ghosts of all sorts beckoning to her. She pictured them moving with spectral slowness, reliving their pleasant and not-so-pleasant experiences inside the château.

Feeling as though the apparitions were dancing and laughing around her, she pulled the collar of her robe together.

As she found herself in the ballroom, Ella padded to a huge mirror. God, she looked awful. Her face, as white as snow, reflected her sense of alarm. She hadn't discovered any signs of forced entry. Then again, the château's broken windows presented an open invitation to trespassers.

Standing there, Ella's appearance changed. Suddenly, she was dressed in the same ivory-colored costume she'd envisioned before. Sparkling wings adorned her back, and her dress gleamed in the candlelight while a ball took place around her.

The vision flashed away. She stood in her frayed dressing gown again. *Jesus!* The flashlight shook in her hand. She was really losing it. Maybe she should try the anti-anxiety medicine Hope took on a regular basis and raved about.

Ella rushed out of the ballroom. To her relief, nothing seemed amiss in the rest of the house. The lights were still off, the front door was still locked, and Jean-Daniel was still standing in his portrait, exuding gallons of sensuality. One look at his hulking image managed to quiet her rapid pulse.

Chiding herself for thinking there'd been an intruder, Ella strolled toward the painting. With a tilt of her head, she shone the flashlight directly at it. The intense beam exaggerated the raised brush strokes on the canvas and caused Jean-Daniel's aquamarine eyes to shine.

"Am I infatuated with you?" she whispered under breath. "Apparently, I am."

She stared at Jean-Daniel and she couldn't help but smile. Maybe he had been the one to visit her in bed.

Remembering the ghostly contact, she set the poker down and touched her lips. "Do you want to know what I was dreaming, Monsieur Girard? First, I dreamt that my wicked stepmother came back to life and was trying to snatch the château's deed from me."

Playfully, she studied Jean-Daniel's expression for any reaction. "I know. Insane, isn't it? But I won that battle. Afterward, you were there to celebrate with me. You whipped off your waistcoat and your wig and drew me against your bare chest. I could feel you getting pretty excited, you know. Then, as your warm breath feathered across my face, you—"

She stepped back. "Well, you can imagine the rest."

Ella's glance roved over his square jaw and his laugh lines. "I wish we could have a conversation."

She was groggy, there was no doubt, but she could have sworn a tiny smile tugged at the corner of Jean-Daniel's lips. Her pulse accelerated again. She tried to quell the fire that burned inside her but she couldn't. As a result, exasperation and attraction mingled within her. Was there anything more perfect than he was? The bulk of his muscular calves were visible through his stockings and his shoulders were wider than a mountain's base. And that mouth. It conveyed every lustful thought in the book.

"No doubt women used to swoon at your feet," she whispered. "Offering themselves to you without condition."

Jean-Daniel was so good-looking that Ella was tempted to touch herself. She skimmed her hand down her stomach and trailed it to her panties. Then she gave an inner shake. She couldn't do it. She *wanted* to be free. She wanted to let loose and enjoy sinful pleasures, but she'd been with only one man. A boy, really. In high school. And it hadn't been a good experience at all.

He'd called her a whore before he abused her. And she hadn't spoken up. It was her fault. Well, that's how it felt, anyway. She'd never possessed an assertive personality, but inside, she was full of imagination, creativity, and passion—traits Adelaide never caught wind of.

At this point in Ella's life, she'd repressed her womanly emotions far too long. She yearned to be held by a man, to be fawned over and adored. She also wanted to fall in love and have someone love her back. "Doesn't everyone deserve that?" she whispered.

Jean-Daniel seemed to agree with her. Well, she *imagined* he was nodding his head.

Face flaming, Ella played the flashlight over his entire body. She liked to think he was looking at her with rapt attention.

Raising her brow, she asked, "Pardon the bright light, but you won't judge me, *Monsieur*. Will you?"

His eyes glimmered, but of course he didn't speak.

She pouted. "No, go ahead and judge. I'm talking to an oil painting."

She could have sworn she heard a distant, faraway laugh.

"In my defense, being alone in this house is cutting me off from society." She'd felt the same way back home and it wasn't what she bargained for here.

Ella almost thought Jean-Daniel's expression turned sympathetic. Shrugging, she shut the flashlight off.

When she turned away, a soft noise sounded behind her. Flipping the flashlight back on, she moved it over the room's elements. The clock on the mantel stood immobile—and the carpets lay smooth and untouched. Then she saw a candle lying on the floor. Just like the one that had fallen to the ground in her room.

She glanced at the scrolled candelabra on a nearby table. One of its candlesticks was missing. Ella jerked the flashlight to the picture window. It was closed—just as the windows had been in her bedroom. The air hung around her, warm and thick, stealing away the possibility that a draft had coaxed the candle to fall.

How did it get there?

This place was really starting to spook her.

Like a grenade exploding through the house, the longcase clock in the ballroom chimed the hour. The bellowing gongs filled the silence. Ella counted twelve chimes.

Midnight. *The witching hour.*

Frightened, she sank into a chair and clenched its arms. The clock was broken—frozen in time at twelve o'clock. Wasn't it? Yes! She knew it because she'd strolled up to it in the ballroom at four o'clock in the afternoon.

Would the timepiece chime mysteriously at noon and at midnight every night? But she'd been in the house at noon today and hadn't heard chimes. *Good God. Midnight must have played a very important role in this house.*

Every ounce of sleepiness escaped Ella. Soon the sensation that someone was hovering over her returned. She stared into the darkness. *If an intruder is really here, I'll stay up and catch him.*

She glanced at Jean-Daniel, eyes round. "At least I have a good view of you from here. And *you* have a good view of the hallway. Will you help me keep watch?"

His solemn expression comforted her.

Minutes stretched into hours. All the while, Ella gazed into Jean-Daniel's eyes—until she couldn't keep hers open anymore.

Bang. Bang. Bang.

Incessant knocking came from the front door. Ella woke in a panicked state.

"Mademoiselle Benoit! It's Pierre DuBois from WorldWide Dish."

"Damn it!" she muttered as she pulled herself out of the armchair. She'd overslept.

More banging.

"One minute, Monsieur DuBois!"

"We had zee appointment, did we not?" came his muffled voice.

Tying the sash of her robe into a knot, she answered the door. *"Bon matin, Monsieur."*

"Bon matin, Miss Benoit. *Vous parlez Français*, eh?" Unfortunately, his under-bite made his French difficult to understand.

She perused the large man's appearance. He wore dirty overalls, a striped shirt that hung out of them at the sides, and sported a bad haircut that emphasized a cowlick. From the heat of the day, his face beamed a bright red.

"I speak French," she said in English. "But I'm a little rusty."

He grinned. "It is no problem. We'll speak English."

"Ah, good." She paused. "I'd invite you in, but I'm afraid I overslept. Do you mind waiting out here while I get dressed?"

"Take your time, Miss Benoit. I can eat my breakfast in ze truck."

His crumb-covered clothes gave her the impression that he'd already dug into his breakfast.

"Thank you," she replied. "I'll be back in a jiffy to let you in."

"Jiffy?" He knitted his brows.

"In a minute."

"Ah, *très bien*."

Ella dressed hastily. Ten minutes later, she was motioning DuBois out of his ramshackle truck and into the foyer.

"What a magnificent château," he said as his eyes roamed the place.

"Thank you," Ella replied. "But it needs a great deal of work."

"A project with passion. That's what ze people need in their lives."

Ella was still shaking away the fog of her deep sleep, but she smiled at his wise philosophy.

"This way, *Monsieur*." She directed him farther into the house. "I'm not sure how installing an Internet satellite works, but I'll fix some coffee and you can tell me."

DuBois followed behind her, his work boots making heavy clomps on the tile floor. "It's pretty simple, Miss Benoit. I pick a spot on ze roof, hook up ze dish, and you'll be good for ze go. Ah, one more thing. Do you have a wireless modem?"

"No," she admitted. When she turned to face DuBois, he was grinning broadly.

"Just happen to have one in my truck," he said. "It will cost you seventy-five Euros, but modems are hard to find in ze countryside."

"If that's what it takes—"

"*Oui*. It is what you need. Then you will be able to use your laptop anywhere in ze house."

"Great," Ella remarked.

She fixed some espresso and offered Pierre a cup. He sipped at it. Some dribbled down his chin. Because he didn't seem to notice, Ella offered him a napkin.

"Don't you get nervous living out here all alone?" he asked.

She's been nervous last night but she wasn't going to admit it to a stranger. "Not really."

Pierre laughed. "You are braver zan I. At night, I turn on all ze lights, snuggle with my stuffed bear, and fall asleep to ze neighbors arguing in ze apartment next door. Lots of noise. Zat is what I like."

Ella drank her coffee in order to suppress a laugh. The man looked like a giant teddy bear—and the idea that he actually slept with one amused her.

"I should not have admitted that, right?" Pierre asked. He proceeded to do an impression of himself, scared out of his mind.

Ella was soon chuckling out loud. Pierre joined in.

"Ah," he said, "nothing like to laugh first zing in ze morning." He adjusted the straps of his overalls.

"Nothing," Ella said before she put her cup in the sink.

She liked Pierre. He was jovial and easy to talk to. And he was a local. Did he know much about Château de Maincy and its mysterious ghost? She was tempted to ask him about Jean-Daniel since she couldn't get her mind off the subject.

I'm actually engaging in conversation? Goodness! Her shyness seemed to be leaving her here. Maybe she could thank the sense of freedom she'd gained. Or maybe Jean-Daniel's influence had something to do with it. He made her feel energized and alive.

She turned away from the sink. "Mr. Dubois, I pretended to be brave before. I'm actually nervous living here alone. Do you know why?"

"Pierre, *s'il vous plaît.*"

"Pierre," she repeated.

He cupped his chin with his hand. "You're scared because of ze vandals?"

She shook her head.

"Rodents? Dry rot? Asbestos poisoning?"

Yikes! She hadn't considered *those* horrible things. "No," she replied.

"Hmm . . . I know why you are scared."

"Why?"

"Zis place is haunted."

Ella felt the color leave her face.

Pierre crossed his arms. "When I was a kid, my friends and I tried to break into zis house. We saw ze flash of white inside one of ze windows. Zat is when we ran."

Ella reflected on the flight attendant's words. Danielle claimed that as a child, she had tried to get close to the house, too.

"I suppose it's strange for you to be inside now, Pierre," she said.

"It is. *Très bizarre.*" He paused. "Have you personally seen ze 'activity'?"

"Well," Ella lowered her voice "I've seen a candle and a hat land on the floor without any prompting. And I felt a brush at the back of my legs." She wasn't going to tell him about her visions of dancing at a ball. Or the ghostly kiss. Pierre would have her committed.

"Zat is all?" he asked.

She nodded.

"Zat may not be a lot for some of ze people, but it would be enough to scare me." Pierre gave a shudder. The motion sent his double chin into a waggle. "I would be—how do you Americans put it? Freaked out."

"I *was* freaked out."

"Zis house is old." Pierre glanced around. "I suppose a lot of people died here."

A new shiver raced down her spine. She knew Jean-Daniel had met a violent death at a young age—and reportedly, his spirit had come to haunt the château following his demise. But she wanted to know more. Had he suffered much? Did anyone really know if he was murdered—or if he committed suicide?

Maybe the dashing vicomte wanted to stick around and protect his house. Ella's pulse pounded and she met Pierre's stare. "May I show you something?"

"*Sûrement,*" he replied.

She led the dish installer into the drawing room and indicated Jean-Daniel's painting. As Pierre studied it, he crossed his arms over his enormous belly. "*Merde.* It is so lifelike."

"I agree."

Ella tried to discern whether or not Pierre felt a sinister vibe coming from the portrait. But as he analyzed it, he didn't show any indication that he did. "Zis nobleman seems very regal. And calm."

While Jean-Daniel's expression *was* calm, it made Ella's insides buzz like a horde of bees. She said, "He's the vicomte who supposedly roams these halls."

"Ah," Pierre replied quietly.

She asked Pierre to walk across the room with his eyes glued to Jean-Daniel's. "Do you feel as if his eyes are following you?"

Pierre tested the theory several times. "*Oui!*"

Thank God! Ella thought. *I'm not going crazy.*

"It's creepy, *bien sûr*," he said, "but I assure you there's an explanation."

An explanation? Excitement roared through her.

"Zis is a painting technique."

"It is?"

Pierre nodded. "It is called *trompe l'oeil. Mon mére* told me about it when I was a boy."

Ella waited patiently for him to continue.

"When my parents took me to *le Louvre* Museum to see ze *Mona Lisa.* Her eyes followed me—just like what is happening here. I was 'freaked out.' *Mon mére* said that when something flat is painted with enough life, it will look alive from any angle."

Deciding that this made sense, Ella relaxed a little.

Pierre smiled. "I could stand here and talk about art all day, but I should get to work."

As the rotund man went to gather his equipment, Ella frowned at the painting. "You're extremely handsome, Jean-Daniel, but you're not going to make me lose my mind. Now I know you're not really following me with your eyes."

At that, she swore she saw Jean-Daniel's expression dim.

Minutes later, she heard a faint "thump" and then movement on the roof. She pictured Pierre reaching the spot he'd picked out for the dish. To confirm this, she emerged into the bright sunlight. Once she stood in front of the house and shaded her eyes with her hand, she saw Pierre's gigantic ladder propped against the château's east side. She also saw that the hefty man was trying to keep his balance next to the slope of a tall dome.

Ella put a hand to her heart as he teetered around the eaves. Pierre was large and lumbering. The structure was ancient and weak. He might—

"No!" she yelled as he crashed right through the roof and into the house.

CHAPTER 8

Setting into action, Ella hurried through the front door and up the main staircase. She had a general idea where Pierre was: in the east wing's attic.

Her mind sped as she took the stairs two at a time. Calling his name, she got no response.

As alarm coursed through her, she reached the staircase's topmost landing and was greeted by the same eerie hush she'd encountered before. Since all the curtains were still drawn over the windows lining the hall, the corridor held the same forbidding atmosphere as before.

Tamping down her fear, Ella hurried toward the attic. She called out, "Pierre! Are you all right?"

Still no answer. *My God.* Was he dead?

Shaken, she plowed on. Hopefully, the jovial man was alive and had suffered no injuries.

Trying not to picture the worst scenario, she reached the attic door.

"I am in here." She finally heard Pierre's muffled voice.

Ella exhaled. Climbing the second set of stairs inside the room, she found Pierre half-submerged in an explosion of furniture. He looked like a chubby child wedged in a circular pool float.

"Sorry, Miss Benoit. Now you see why I was named clumsiest kid in primary school?"

Vastly relieved, she smiled. "Are you hurt?"

"I do not think so."

"Can you move?"

"I will try."

With a great deal of effort and without much finesse, he took Ella's hand and pulled himself from the rubble. Remnants of a chair fell away from his body along with the shattered planks of a trunk. Because he was coated from head to toe with white plaster, he looked comical—like one of the Three Stooges.

Grinning sheepishly, he tried moving all his limbs. "Thank ze stars. Nothing is broken."

"What a relief!" she said.

Just then, lightning slashed across the sky and dark clouds gathered over the large hole in the ceiling. They looked up simultaneously.

"*Zat* is not good timing." Pierre grimaced.

"A downpour could soak the attic!" Ella cried. She'd been here two days and already the house was in disaster mode. The feeling that she could never do anything right clawed at her like a lion.

"Do not to worry," Pierre assured her. "I have a cousin who will patch zis up in—how do you say—a jiffy?"

"A cousin?" Ella echoed.

"*Oui.* He is a handyman. Do you want me to call him?"

"Please," Ella replied as she surveyed the damage.

"*Bon.* If you agree to keep zis our little secret, there will be no charge for ze repair."

Ella agreed. There were plenty of old buildings in France—and if Pierre had been more careful, "zis" wouldn't have happened. Then again, she could have warned him to be cautious.

Perhaps they were both to blame for the accident. If Pierre was willing to fix the hole for free, she was willing to forgive him. Compassion was in her nature.

Remaining silent, she watched him make a call to his cousin on his cell phone. He spoke in French, but she understood the entire conversation:

"I was an idiot," he said. "Fell through someone's roof."

A pause.

"Yes. *Again.*"

Another pause.

"Can you come right now?"

A pause.

"This is not the third time this month, Jacques."

Another pause. "Yes, damn it. I'll install that dish at your girl-friend's house on Sunday. Great! Thanks!" He hung up and smiled. "My cousin will arrive in a half hour."

"Thank you," Ella said quietly. "I just hope the rain holds off long enough for him to patch the hole."

Pierre looked embarrassed. "Mademoiselle, those dark clouds mean we don't have much time. Most likely, Jacques will help me stretch a canvas over the hole. Zen we will come back tomorrow and repair ze roof."

"I guess it's the best I can hope for."

Pierre nodded.

Amazingly, the rain did hold out. While Ella and Pierre waited for Jacques's truck, they cleaned up the debris. Pierre moved in slow motion, which told Ella he was sore. Who wouldn't be a little achy? Luckily, he'd fallen at the low end of the sloping roof. Otherwise he could have plummeted a good fifteen feet and broken his leg.

Shaking her head, Ella scooped up the contents of the smashed trunk. Was this the chest in which her father had found the servant's cap? Intrigued, she sifted through the strewn contents. There was a dulled sword in a sheath, a pair of cracked spectacles that looked like they belonged to another century, a tattered gold gown, and a journal of some kind.

Curiosity rising, Ella opened the brown leather book. She didn't understand a word because the journal was penned in a foreign language. The script, recorded in masculine strokes, seemed hurried.

She sounded out a few words in her head. Was the language Hungarian? Romanian, perhaps?

Setting the journal on the ledge of an old dresser, Ella decided to try and translate it later—if she could ever get the Internet up and running. Maybe the diary would provide clues about Jean-Daniel and his premature demise.

Lightning flashed above her head, followed by a rumble of thunder. Not a moment too soon, Jacques telephoned Pierre to say he was pulling through the gates of Château de Maincy.

Ella stayed to clean up while Pierre trotted downstairs to greet his cousin. Unfortunately, she found nothing else of interest inside the attic. As she eyed the dark clouds overhead again, she puffed out a sigh of relief when Jacques, a slimmer, blonder version of Pierre, stuck his head inside the ceiling's hole. Once she thanked the honest-looking man for coming so quickly, he gave her a nod and set about his work with Pierre at his side.

Through a string of loud arguing, the DuBois cousins managed to stretch a large tarp over the jagged hole. Just as they finished securing it, rain pelted the waterproof canopy. Instead of panicking, Ella breathed easy as she realized the attic would remain dry through the downpour.

She hurried downstairs and met the two men at the portico.

"Mademoiselle." Jacques extended his hand. "I'm glad I could be of service."

"*Merci beaucoup.*" She shook his hand.

He seemed like a nice, hardworking man. She noticed his worn, dry hands and downturned eyes, but that was all she noticed because he and Pierre started another argument. Uncomfortable, Ella turned her attention to Jacques's truck. The sign on its door read, *Jacques à Tout Faire.*

Jack of all trades.

She stifled a smile and then decided to interrupt their arguing. "Jacques, I plan to order new windows, but do you mind patching some of them on the first level when you return tomorrow? I'm happy to pay you."

After she received an affirmative answer, she said goodbye to the cousins. With a wave of their hands, the men got into their respective vehicles and drove away. If Jacques did a good job fixing the hole in the ceiling and repairing the windows tomorrow, Ella would ask if he knew a licensed electrician. She wanted to get an estimate on the house's re-wiring.

When she entered the château and shut the door behind her, the familiar charged atmosphere rolled and rattled around her as it usually did. But thanks to the pitter-patter of the rain, it didn't seem so profoundly powerful at the moment.

Resisting the urge to gawk at Jean-Daniel's portrait, Ella climbed the stairs. In the silence, she stared down at her shoes. A vision flashed before her. Her shoes changed from leather flats to wooden clogs—and her baggy trousers transformed into a dress and apron.

This is insane! Grasping the banister, she nearly turned around and ran out the door. Telling herself to breathe, she managed to calm down. She'd never done any drugs. So why was she seeing things?

The visualization dispelled itself a second later, but she was left with a drumming heart. Beads of cold sweat popped up on her brow. Had she played dress-up in the château as a child? Or did the romantic side of her *want* to see these fascinating things? They seemed so real.

Telling herself she had to have the worst case of jet lag in history, Ella continued up the stairs. She reached the attic. Once she picked up the journal, she settled into an old chair and flipped through it. Although she couldn't understand the words, she got the general mood of the diary. Emanating a sense of urgency, the entries were penned in hard, harsh strokes.

She shuddered. The thought that a dark magician who may have been in league with the devil *and* a melancholy ghost with unfinished business had resided in this house at the same time boggled her mind.

Snapping the diary shut, she stood. As she turned to go, she heard it. A soft clawing noise.

Ella remained immobile. Tiptoeing around the room, she strained to hear. Where had the noise come from? *Behind the old dresser.*

Gulping away images of ghosts and goblins, she crept to the ancient piece. There it was again. Soft scratching—quiet enough to give her goose bumps . . . loud enough to draw her attention. Holding her breath, Ella crouched down and looked behind the dresser. In a sudden, terrifying movement, sharp claws reached out and swiped at her. She managed to avoid getting scratched but she teetered off balance. In an ungraceful leap, she fell and twisted her ankle.

The action freed the creature that had been wedged behind the dresser. My God! What had swiped at her? Some sort of wild animal? *Where is it now?*

Her foot throbbed and her heart raced. Besides pressing her hand to the pain in her ankle, she remained still. A moment later, a fluffy-tailed stray cat bounced on her legs.

"I was afraid of *you*?" She laughed. Paranormal activity? She didn't think so.

Without pausing to apologize for its attack, the wily calico scurried off Ella and headed down the stairs. She pulled herself to her feet. With great effort, she limped after the cat and kept it in sight until it made its way between a pair of wallboards and scampered outside.

"And I was just going to offer you some milk." She put her hands on her hips and chuckled. "I can't believe a *cat* scared me half to death!"

No doubt the furry feline was the creature that had brushed against her leg the first night she was here. Most likely it had stolen in when she unloaded her luggage. The animal, however small, had established free rein over the house at that point.

Shaking her head, she limped deeper into the foyer. "Thanks for knocking the hat and candles to the ground, *Monsieur Chat.*" From a window, she saw the feline run across the front portico. A frown replaced Ella's smile. She doubted the cat had made her see her clothes change. Nor did she think the animal had kissed her.

Jean-Daniel found glimpses of Ella's battle with the brown, black, and white cat amusing—until she deemed the animal the "ghost" of the château.

He stood inside the portrait, fists clenched. Clenched in his mind, anyway. Concern and frustration rolled over him at the miscalculation. He had summoned so much energy to communicate with her—in complicated ways, and in ways that were merely rudimentary.

A lot of good it did.

Jean-Daniel had very little energy at the moment because Ella was using so little electricity. But he didn't blame her. Instead, he blamed the ancient wiring *and* that bumbling idiot who had delayed her Internet installation.

Jean-Daniel wished he could clarify things for Ella. Tell her that the clock (not the broken one) was ticking. That they only had until midnight on the anniversary of his death to reverse the events of that night. Otherwise, they would have to wait until next year to try again. Perhaps Ella wouldn't be at the château a year from now.

Jean-Daniel grimaced inwardly. As a ghost with nothing to do but count the days, he knew that the anniversary of his death was less than two weeks away.

Instead of expressing the direness of the situation to her, he remained a tense, frozen figure inside the painting. Discontent behind his stare, he watched Ella hobble toward the kitchen. When he couldn't see her anymore, he listened to the rain thrash the drawing room's windows. As lightning crackled dangerously close to the house, Jean-Daniel sensed Rémy's energy next to him.

That's just what we need! Lightning! The rawest form of energy.

After Ella used the microwave and ate something, Jean-Daniel felt a charge swell within him. He observed her limping across the hall. Once she made her way upstairs, she started a shower.

This is my chance.

Determined to send Ella a solid message—one that would persuade her of his presence and the need he had for her help once and for all—he waited for another lightning slash. Determinedly, he slipped out of the portrait and ascended into the bathroom. It was strange being out of the painting during daylight hours.

As he hovered in a corner, he watched her undress. The sight of her firm curves, tight *derrière*, and toned arms aroused him. He wet his lips.

Damn. There was that sizzle of energy again! But no erection. Just a prickling force field that played over his entire body. Not that a ghost could make use of an erection, anyway.

He held his breath as she unsnapped her bra and slid it off. *Mon Dieu!* Her sweet breasts and her lovely pink buds were as delectable as he remembered. In one elegant motion, she lifted her long hair off her shoulders and swirled it into a charmingly messy chignon. Then she peeled her underwear off and turned away from him in another, graceful motion.

Merde. If he were alive, he would take her straight to bed to make mad, passionate love.

If she knew who I was, that is.

God, he thought, *please know me when you travel back in time.* It would make their lovemaking happen that much sooner.

Ella took the next few minutes to rub her swollen ankle. Then, humming a little melody, she stepped into the shower. To Jean-Daniel's delight, she closed the curtain only partway. As she grabbed a bar of soap, a broad smile spread across her face.

"She's probably thinking of that damned stray cat," he muttered to himself.

His view of her became blurred by an onslaught of steam. The mirror and the windows fogged up, but Jean-Daniel felt no variance in the room's temperature. Even if he were in the midst of a bitter snowstorm or was stranded in a desert, he wouldn't sense hot or cold.

Still, temperature wasn't what he wanted to feel. He wanted to feel Ella.

Struck by how feminine she was, he stepped forward and reached a hand inside the shower. His fingers passed through the water's droplets, causing no interruption in the stream. Slowly, languidly, he traced his touch along the slope of her back. Instead of trying to make contact, he kept his fingertips a few centimeters away.

Still humming a tune, Ella swiveled around and soaped up her breasts. The incredible mounds were close to Jean-Daniel. He studied their beautiful teardrop shape as they glistened with rainbow-infused bubbles.

With his index finger leading the way, he outlined her erect areola but stayed just shy of it. He didn't want to frighten her more than was absolutely necessary. What he was about to do would unfortunately do that.

Withdrawing while she shaved her legs, Jean-Daniel looked around the misty bathroom. This place used to be his dressing room. Where he'd taken his last bath preceding his murder.

Shaking away the unsettling memory, he glanced at the mirror. Yes. There was sufficient steam on it for him to leave a message. Summoning enough strength to make contact with the mirror, he wrote three words across it and then retreated. Meanwhile, Ella stopped the water with a firm turn of the knobs.

After she emerged, she wrapped herself in a towel and unloosed her hair. While she gave it a few quick brushes, she moved to the mirror. What she saw stopped her dead in her tracks.

As she mouthed the message left by an invisible hand, Jean-Daniel witnessed the rise of cold prickles on her skin: *Revenez à moi.*

"Return to me," she translated in a shocked voice.

CHAPTER 9

Ella whirled around, studying every corner of the bathroom. No one was there. The fragrance of milled soap waved over her—as it had in her bedroom. Her mouth went dry.

Pulse stuttering, she called out, "Who are you? Where did you go?" She'd hoped the cat was the culprit that had played some of the tricks on her. But that'd been wishful thinking.

She sunk to the floor. Could it be? Was there really a ghost at the château? If so, she was all alone with it.

Any ordinary person would run. Flee to the village, never to return. But Ella was no ordinary person. Besides the fact that she had nowhere else to go, she'd never had anything to call her own. Now the château was hers. She wasn't about to let anyone or anything drive her away. Not even a ghost!

"Whoever wrote that message has been here for a long time," she whispered, her body chilling. "I know it's you, Jean-Daniel."

Empowered by the knowledge, she stood.

Return to me. She re-read the message before the steam evaporated. Again, the command spun fright and excitement through her. She desperately wanted it to be the handsome eighteenth-century vicomte who'd written it, and not his intense brother, Colbert.

He's watching me right now. She wrapped the towel tighter around her body. It was almost as if Jean-Daniel could emerge from his painting at will and watch her whenever he wanted.

While she swiped at the air, her eyes darted around the bathroom. She must look like an idiot, but she wanted evidence of him. So people wouldn't think she was crazy. So she didn't consider *herself* crazy.

Unfortunately, nothing but emptiness greeted her swings.

Sensing that the phantom was no longer in the room, she scooted out of the bathroom. Pulling on a tank top and shorts, she sped downstairs. While she hurried to the drawing room, a cold breeze assaulted her along the corridor. Was Jean-Daniel moving directly in front of her? She wished she could see him, feel him, and speak to him. But she couldn't do any of those things.

Entering the drawing room, she could have sworn she saw a flash of white move to the painting. The transparent light melted gracefully into the portrait—positioning itself directly over the depiction of Jean-Daniel.

There was an unnerving stillness.

The contact—and his journey around the château in the daytime—exhausted Jean-Daniel. Glad to be inside the sanctity of his portrait for once, he settled into his frozen state.

What would Ella make of the message he left? If possible, he would have written a paragraph. A story describing the night of the ball. Of how he drowned in the lake. Of how the blow to the back of his head landed him there.

But as it stood, he'd struggled intensely to manifest his finger against the mirror and write just the simple message. He was extremely fatigued.

Still, he held out hope that Ella would learn more. People had so many resources today including the Internet and public libraries. Surely Ella's curiosity would prompt her to research what happened to him.

The bad part was the events of that night were mostly secrets. Unrecorded and undocumented for anyone's eyes.

The longcase clock chimed midnight. It was a sound that struck panic in Jean-Daniel's heart, even after all these years.

He wished to God he could stuff cotton in his ears.

* * *

Ella didn't sleep at all that night. Early the next morning, she decided to call Mimi. It was nighttime back in Santa Barbara and Ella had a feeling her friend was home.

When Mimi answered on the second ring, she cried, "Thank God I caught you!"

"Ella? Are you all right?"

"I think so."

"Your voice sounds shaky."

"Mimi, there are some strange things going on here."

A careful pause. "What things?"

"I'll tell you—if you promise not to put me in a straitjacket."

"Can't promise anything," Mimi joked.

Ella revealed the details of the cap being tossed to the ground, the candles suddenly appearing on the floor, the brush against her legs, her visions of being at the château long ago, garbed in different clothing, the ghostly kiss, and the most recent shocker: the message on the mirror.

A long pause stretched across the miles. Finally, Mimi asked, "Have you been dipping into the good wine, Ella?"

"No! Please listen. I'm having incredible déjà vu. More than that, there's a presence here."

Mimi exhaled. "The sense of déjà vu can be explained by your visit to the château as a child."

"About that. Why didn't you or Walter tell me I came here as a kid?"

"You were so young, we didn't think you'd remember."

"Well, this place sure feels familiar."

"Memories can resurface if triggered by a catalyst."

"Sounds plausible," Ella said.

Mimi paused. "For argument's sake, let's say there's a ghostly presence. Do you think this entity is harmful? That it could be malicious?"

"No. I feel as though—" Ella's voice drifted off. Dare she say it?

"As though what?"

"As if the ghost is *beckoning* me."

"Beckoning you?" A pause. "And what is this ghost's name?" Mimi's voice took on the tone of someone conversing with the criminally insane.

"Jean-Daniel Girard, the former vicomte de Maincy."

"The nobleman in the portrait you told me about?"

"Yes."

"I admit that the writing on the mirror is really strange," Mimi said. "But I think it can be explained."

"How?"

"If a message was written long ago and the mirror was never cleaned, it's possible that the message might appear many years later—via steam from the bath."

"Mimi, I heard a squeaking sound. Like someone was writing the message right then and there."

"I can't explain that. But what could a three-hundred-year-old ghost be beckoning you to *do*, Ella?"

"I know it sounds crazy. A real stretch. But I think he wants me to go back in time to be with him."

"That's preposterous!"

"Considering the visions I'm having, of going back in time, I could swear that's his intention." Ella paused.

"Even if it's something you're deliberating, *how* would you do it?"

She sighed. "I really don't know."

"Listen to yourself, Ella. Maybe Adelaide's death and inheriting Château de Maincy have been too much for you."

"It isn't that."

"What, then?"

"I need to learn more, so I have a favor to ask."

Mimi swallowed hard. "Wait, Ella, I think I should fly there so we can talk."

"Please. Just hear me out."

Mimi exhaled. "Okay."

"Inside the attic, I found a journal written in a foreign language. Do you think you could have one of your friends at the college translate it for me?"

For years, Mimi Brimhall had been a professor at a community college outside of Santa Barbara. She'd been in the philosophy department before she retired, but she still kept in contact with her former colleagues.

"All right," she said. "Scan the pages and I'll email them to Stanley Kellogg."

After assuring Mimi that she didn't have to fly to France to help her calm down, Ella hung up. Then she decided to fetch the journal.

Before she could climb the grand staircase, a knock at the front door stopped her.

Pierre and Jacques were back! She could finally get the Internet hooked up and do some research on the mysterious Jean-Daniel.

Flushed, she let the cousins in and turned her attention to details of the roof repair. Pierre, who seemed relieved that the rainstorm was behind them, helped Jacques patch the roof seamlessly. The job took hours. Afterwards, Pierre installed a shiny new satellite dish without incident. He even presented Ella with a wireless modem, free of charge.

Ella thanked him, although her thoughts were elsewhere. After the cousins patched the windows on the first level, the trio stood outside. Ella asked Jacques if he could recommend a licensed electrician. He said that he was one, and asked what she needed done. Surprised, Ella requested his estimate for re-wiring the house. Jacques, whose bland expression didn't tell her if he was overwhelmed by the prospect or excited about it, surveyed the entire château. He proceeded to give Ella what she thought was a reasonable price.

After he promised to round up a team of workers and complete the job within the month, she agreed to hire him.

It was almost dusk when the DuBois cousins departed. Realizing she'd skipped breakfast and lunch, Ella changed her clothes and drove to Maincy. In town, she was lucky enough to purchase a printer/scanner combo. Next, she contemplated buying food at the local market, but when she spotted a quaint restaurant on the corner, she decided to treat herself to dinner.

More than that, it was probably a good idea to be away from the château for a while.

A hostess escorted her to a table. The rumbling of her stomach accompanied them. Trying to relax, Ella sat and sipped an excellent French wine inside *La Rose Café*. A waiter delivered savory *coq au vin* with sweet potato fries and a cold salad topped with a delicious vinaigrette dressing.

As she ate, couples at the tables surrounding hers engaged in quiet conversation. Some were even snuggled up closely and feeding one another.

To be in France, eating and drinking with the man you love. Who wouldn't be in heaven?

Ella felt very alone. That is, until an American family with two shy teenage boys entered the café. When she heard the loud-mouthed parents using poor French and taking forever to order, she smiled. *I guess Americans do stand out here.*

After stocking up on food and other groceries, she headed back home. It was ten o'clock before she arrived. The car wheels squealed as she brought the vehicle to a halt in front of the dark château. Her skin tingled. The thought of further contact with Jean-Daniel's ghost jolted her usually calm demeanor. It wasn't that she felt afraid, exactly. Instead, she was anxious—as if her every sense was heightened. As though seeing those words written on the mirror made her realize that she hadn't begun living until now.

Once she entered the house, she turned on a few lights. To her dismay, the bulbs flickered violently before they finally stayed on. Glad that Jacques would update the electricity soon, Ella put her leftovers and groceries inside the refrigerator. Then she eyed the box that held the new printer/scanner. It took her awhile, but she managed to hook the device up to her laptop. Now both items sat on the kitchen table, which seemed an adequate location for the time being.

An hour later, she'd scanned the pages of the journal and emailed them to Mimi. As soon as she finished, the kitchen lights began to flicker again.

Damned wiring from the 1930s! It was becoming her motto.

Ella was ready to get upset about the age and condition of the house all over again when she glanced at the light switch. It was moving up and down! Fingers quaking, she inched toward it. The switch stopped moving, but then she heard a creaking noise. She crept around the corner. Had it been it a window opening? Yes, because a refreshing breeze carrying an outdoor scent filled her nostrils.

Nervously, she followed the breeze to the ballroom. Casting a glance at the longcase clock made her heart hammer. She shifted her eyes to the French doors. They stood ajar.

As she was about to close them, she heard another noise. Wheeling around, she gasped as footsteps sounded and something touched her ear. The chandelier above her clattered loudly as it swung to and fro unexpectedly. Then the French doors banged against the wall on a sudden gust of wind, sending the curtains that framed them off the ground in a dramatic billow.

Terrified, Ella took a step backward. "Show yourself," she said hoarsely.

Fear stabbed her skin like icy slivers. Compelling herself to walk through the French doors, she exited the ballroom very slowly. There on the terrace, bathed in moonlight, hovered the ghost of a man. The apparition was eerily transparent—and garbed in the same clothing as Jean-Daniel wore in the painting!

Ella halted in her tracks. Fright curling within her, she stood behind the specter as it stared out over the gardens.

If only I could the see the ghost's face! Then I could confirm it's Jean-Daniel.

Speak to it, she told herself. *This is your chance. Don't be afraid.*

Clearing her throat, she said, "Hello."

Hello? Good God. She couldn't come up with something better than that? At the very least she should have said *"Bonsoir."*

Floating at least a foot off the ground, the phantom turned to expose its profile. Ella gulped. It *was* her mysterious vicomte! She would recognize that aristocratic nose and those sculpted cheekbones anywhere.

Could this really be happening? In a moment of panic, she pressed her eyes closed and then flung them open. There was no denying Jean-Daniel's presence. He faced her and her pulse drummed. Amid the surreal atmosphere, she took a minute to study him. Without a hint of color, a whitish haze illuminated his face and body. He appeared ethereal but his strong chin and muscular outline were still visible.

Jean-Daniel slid his cool gaze over her. Then he smiled. Deep grooves framed his lips and to Ella's surprise, dimples materialized.

How can I be afraid of a ghost with dimples?

She locked eyes with him. Exhilaration bursting through her, she asked the obvious, in French. "Are you Jean-Daniel Girard?"

He nodded.

Skin prickling, she put a hand to the doorframe. If anyone had told her a year ago that she'd be standing here talking to a centuries-old ghost at a French estate she'd inherited, she wouldn't have believed them.

"You're trying to tell me something, aren't you?"

The ghost nodded again. Slowly, it turned and pointed to the lake.

"Is that really where you died?" she asked, surprised at her boldness.

His expression turned sad. A moment later, his image wavered and began to disappear.

The longcase clock chimed midnight. Slowly, as he melted away, Jean-Daniel mouthed, *"Sauve moi."*

Save me.

"No!" she cried. Lunging forward, Ella tried to touch the apparition before it faded into nothing. She steadied herself by leaning on the terrace's low railing. Disbelief encircled her along with questions about her sanity. But only for a minute. She knew what she'd seen and it had been a genuine ghost. More importantly, it had been *Jean-Daniel's* ghost. If the vicomte was this dashing in the afterlife, she could only imagine how charming he'd been when alive.

Ella studied the spot over which he'd hovered. There was no evidence of him, no sign of vapor or ectoplasm. Yet she knew what she'd seen.

The unique experience made her feel heady. Special. Hot-cheeked. Touching a hand to her flaming face, she looked up at the starry night sky. Where had Jean-Daniel gone? Ghosts certainly didn't go back and forth from earth to heaven. Did they?

Going off the thought that the vicomte was trapped at Château de Maincy for eternity, Ella gazed over the edge of the terrace. Pity filled her heart. Jean-Daniel couldn't walk into the fields beyond and visit the town. He could never zoom away in a car and leave his fate behind. *Eternity.* Ella knew what it felt like to be imprisoned by something—and forever was a mighty long time.

Standing on unsure legs, she gazed at the kidney-shaped lake below. Its surface rippled under a warm breeze. Jean-Daniel had pointed to the body of water. "Save me," he'd said.

My God. How could he think it was possible for her to travel back to the night he died? The plea was beyond ludicrous. Besides, her luck had just begun to change. She'd started a new life here at the château. A life with purpose. A chance to do something right for a change. Was she willing to give all that up for a man, rather a ghost, she didn't know from Adam?

But wasn't that the irony of the situation? Ella felt like she *did* know him. He hardly felt like a stranger from the past.

Hurrying inside, she switched on the lights and made her way to Jean-Daniel's portrait. His aquamarine eyes glowed lucidly—like two white-blue ice caps in the Arctic Ocean. He stared back at her as he always did, but this time his glance penetrated deeper into her soul.

Fixated on his image, she stood there for a long while. Overwhelmed, she lay on the sofa. Something was drawing her to him. She was no longer afraid; she simply wanted to find out what happened to him.

The dark of evening shifted to a purple glow and signaled the first rays of sunrise. Finally, Ella fell asleep. In her dream, she became encompassed with the feeling that—although it had been centuries ago—she and Jean-Daniel had slept together in the same room before.

CHAPTER 10

Numerous rounds of coffee helped Ella stay alert at her laptop the next day. She checked her email, which disappointingly wasn't as full as she'd assumed it would be.

She tucked a lock of hair behind her ear. One email came from Mimi, about how much furniture they'd sold at auction. Then there was one each from Hope and Charity. As always, Ella's stepsisters didn't mince words. They asked again for money.

Ella didn't respond.

After hours of perusing history-based sites on the Internet, she confirmed the information about Jean-Daniel that Pénélope Toulouse had divulged to her. In addition, she learned some new—and very interesting—tidbits about his death.

Apparently, Jean-Daniel *did* fall in love with a mysterious servant girl back in 1703. Some sources claimed that the scandalous union was the catalyst for his premature death. Others claimed Jean-Daniel's rivalry with his brother was to blame. During that time, the French government was a very glamourous thing to be part of. Louis XIV was the powerful and highly-revered king of France. Jean-Daniel had been invited to be a courtier at his palace at Versailles. As Jean-Daniel was a distant cousin of Louis, he was to receive preferential treatment there, more so than other courtiers. But accepting the position meant he would have to take up residency at Versailles and leave Maincy. His brother, Colbert, was extremely jealous at this elevation in Jean-Daniel's social status. Hence, Jean-Daniel's association with the esteemed Louis XIV caused an even greater rift between the brothers. They began to fight about it constantly.

Just when their disagreements began to escalate into vicious rows, Jean-Daniel wound up dead during a grand masquerade ball held at Château de Maincy in the summer of 1703.

Gracious! There was *a masquerade ball that night,* Ella thought. This was getting very uncanny.

When she read on, she discovered that Louis XIV had made some unpopular decisions late in his reign. These decisions included an edict that chased many Protestants out of France plus a war with a divided Spain that put a strain on France's finances. Had anti-royalists crashed the masquerade ball in order to kill Jean-Daniel? Did his twin have a hand in his drowning? Or did Jean-Daniel take his own life when his shameful affair with the servant girl went awry?

Ella rubbed her weary eyes. She wished she could find the answers to those questions on Wikipedia.

No such luck.

All she knew was that the deceased vicomte had pointed to the lake at the stroke of midnight. And there must be a reason for that.

On the bright side, Ella found a series of paintings and photos on the Internet that captured Château de Maincy's decline through the years. Because the images were displayed chronologically, they highlighted the estate's deterioration. The last set of photos showcased the house's cobweb-draped hallways and smashed windows, thus emphasizing its haunted personality.

At least there was evidence of what the place had looked like in its prime.

Next, Ella discovered that the television show, *Ghost Chasers,* had filmed an episode at Château de Maincy. Once she located the episode on Netflix, she watched three paranormal investigators agree to be locked in the house all night. Genuinely frightened, the investigators ended up fleeing the ghost-riddled château right after midnight.

Ella could relate to their fear. That's how she'd felt when she had first come to the house.

But what really captivated her was when the *Ghost Chasers* episode reenacted Jean-Daniel's death. Using actors, the segment gave viewers a visual timeline of the night he died. By playing up the question of murder versus suicide and by showing him floating face down in the bloody, shadowed lake, the scene captured the unanswered mystery surrounding Jean-Daniel's demise.

Adding to the ominous atmosphere was the music that drifted from the open French doors. The lavish masquerade ball took place only steps from the spot where Jean-Daniel died. In a stunning climax, the television show suggested that he took his last breath at midnight.

Ella shivered. She wished she could chalk all of this up to coincidence, but something unearthly was definitely guiding her. Shivering some more, she took note of the date of Jean-Daniel's death. June 25th. *A week and a half from now.*

While her stomach roiled, she wondered if that's why his ghost was becoming so insistent in its communication. But what could the specter want her to do in order to save him?

In the middle of surfing the Internet for more specifics, Ella heard someone enter the house. Fright flooded her, for it didn't sound like a cat. With thoughts of murder and ghosts filling her head, she grasped the edge of the table—until Pénélope Toulouse swept into the kitchen. Apparently, it wasn't in the Frenchwoman's nature to telephone before a visit. Or to ring the doorbell when she arrived. Ella would have to get used to that. Or she could remember to lock the front door.

"As you are one of my favorite clients, I wanted to stop by and check on you. This house can be a bit spooky—especially for someone living here alone." Pénélope clasped Ella's hands.

Even though the agent was being kind, Ella was reluctant to rehash her scary episodes. She gave a half-smile. "I'm fine."

Pénélope raised an eyebrow. "Are you sure?"

Ella nodded.

"I'll be truthful. It was Pierre who told me how out of sorts you are."

Pierre is more observant than I thought. Then Ella put the mental brakes on. "Wait a minute, why have you been speaking to Pierre?"

Pénélope shrugged. "His mother and I are best friends."

Thus your recommendation of him.

"You look pale," the woman said. "As if you've seen—"

What? A ghost?

"I promise you I'm fine," Ella said.

"No." Pénélope shook her head. "I can tell something is wrong."

Ella invited her to sit at the outdated kitchen table. "Pénélope. I assume that with all the paranormal accounts associated with this house, you believe in the supernatural."

Once Ella located a hint of affirmation in the woman's hazel eyes, she went on in a rush. "I've witnessed strange things at the château myself."

The management agent listened carefully as Ella described every chilling incident she'd encountered, including the moving light switch and the astonishing message on the mirror.

She ended with, "I've seen him. I've *seen* Jean-Daniel's ghost."

Pénélope remained expressionless. "And?"

Part of Ella was relieved that Pénélope appeared unfazed. The other part of her wished the woman would leap enthusiastically out of her seat. "... *and,*" Ella continued, "Jean-Daniel is trying to tell me something. Something concerning his death."

"Tell you something?" Thankfully, Pénélope kept sarcasm out of her voice. "I didn't think ghosts could talk."

Ella cleared her throat. "What I mean is he stood on the terrace and indicated the lake below."

"Of course he did. *Mon Dieu!* What a horrible demise. To suffer a head injury and then drown in the water's depths."

"Doesn't the fact that Jean-Daniel had a head injury rule out suicide?" Ella paused. "Who strikes himself over the head and waits to sink to the bottom of a lake? Why not just drown yourself?"

"Maybe Jean-Daniel's death was an accident." Pénélope suggested. "Nevertheless, it's a mystery that remains unsolved."

"Yes, it is." Ella pursed her lips.

"This is why you are so upset, eh? I suppose seeing a ghost will do that to a person."

Ella nodded. They fell into silence until she asked Pénélope if she'd like a cup of coffee. Once she fixed it and handed the cup over, she sipped at her own java in order to avoid peeking at the entrance to the drawing room. She felt Jean-Daniel's presence roll over her even now. It was becoming harder and harder to shake him from her mind. And to avoid standing in front of the painting for hours.

Pénélope crossed her arms as her coffee cooled. "Now you see why I had the vicomte's portrait stored in the attic. I think it's time we returned it there."

"Put it back?" Ella shook her head vehemently. "Out of sight, out of mind was not a tactic that would work with her. She was trying too hard to abandon the motto she had lived by: *Don't let it show. Then no one will know.*

Pénélope's expression turned dire. "You don't understand, Ella. Every time I cover Jean-Daniel's portrait and place it in the attic, the disturbances stop. That's why I believe the painting is the vicomte's portal to the modern world."

As soon as the management agent spoke the words, a loud banging split the air. Ella and Pénélope exchanged startled glances. They leapt out of their seats. Following the sound, they raced into the drawing room and gasped simultaneously. Jean-Daniel's painting rumbled and clanged against the wall. If anything else in the room had been moving so violently, Ella would have assumed an earthquake was taking place. Incredibly, nothing but the portrait shook.

"Try to steady it!" Pénélope yelled.

The women sprang toward the shifting painting, each clutching a section of the frame on one side. Ella caught a glimpse of Jean-Daniel's eyes, which seemed to be looking at her even from this sharp angle.

As the painting convulsed, it was difficult for Ella to hang on to it. Her hand penetrated the backing and ripped it open. She shouted an expletive while the portrait bounced away from the wall and crashed to the ground. It narrowly missed her feet and Pénélope's. Two glittering objects spilled from the ripped backing. One was a necklace with Egyptian markings. The other was a bracelet forged of the same material and in the same style.

"You've found them!" Pénélope cried.

"Them?" Ella asked.

"Yes! The necklace and the bracelet the former owner of this house lost. The necklace and bracelet Dragomir Starkov was desperate to recover."

Ella had nearly forgotten the story.

"Help me lean the painting against the wall," Pénélope instructed. Ella nodded.

Together, the women managed to secure the heavy portrait. Next, Ella bent over and picked up the pieces of jewelry. They were extremely heavy and appeared to be very valuable. The necklace showcased a brilliant lapis stone hung by a thin silver chain. The stone bore ancient Egyptian markings. The gorgeous bracelet opened and closed with a clasp and possessed hieroglyphic indications similar to the ones on the necklace.

Both objects stunned her because they seemed to have fallen into her lap. "What do you know about them?" Ella asked Pénélope.

"They were unearthed by a British archaeologist during one of his nineteenth-century excavations in Egypt. The objects are said to have magical powers. I think it's a good thing they've gone missing until now." Pénélope paused. "The magician who misplaced them had a connection with the Dark Arts."

"You told me that before."

"Yes, but what I didn't tell you was how scared the Dark Arts make me. I'd be extremely careful with these objects if I were you. They might be cursed."

"Good advice," Ella murmured. She didn't dare don the pieces of jewelry. The man they had belonged to frightened her, but they also radiated energy identical to the kind that filled the house.

Pénélope eyed Jean-Daniel's painting. "That portrait has a mind of its own. Are you sure you don't want me to help you take it to the attic?"

Ella suspected that it might not stay there. "No, thank you. But maybe we can try to hang it again."

"*Bien sûr.*"

The women managed to hook the painting on the wall, though they couldn't do anything about its cracked frame and ripped backing.

"I discovered something yesterday that might be important," Ella said once they'd plopped onto the sofa, exhausted.

"What?"

"A journal. I came across it in the attic. It's written in a foreign language . . . perhaps Romanian."

"It may be Dragomir Starkov's diary," Pénélope said excitedly. "If you're able to translate it, you might learn more about the amulet and the bracelet."

"Maybe." Ella set the pieces of jewelry on a side table and glanced at the painting. Jean-Daniel was definitely sending her clues for a reason. She felt his pleas down to the bottom of her soul.

Pénélope stood. "I'm not sure staying here alone is a good idea."

"I'll be fine," Ella said. "I'm not afraid anymore. Just curious."

"Promise you'll call if you see the ghost again?"

"You have my word."

"Very well." Pénélope paused. "If you change your mind, there's more than enough room at my place. I just went through a divorce and my sons are grown."

Ella walked Pénélope to the front door. "I appreciate the invitation. Have a good night."

Pénélope gave her a hug. "Have an *uneventful* night."

After Pénélope departed, Ella eyed the setting sun through the overhead window. She'd noticed that Jean-Daniel's ghost showed a preference for coming alive at night. Well, tonight she would be ready for any form of communication he wished to initiate.

Moving to the portrait, she locked eyes with the dashing vicomte. She could swear his pupils dilated and his crystal-blue eyes sparkled. *What is he thinking as he stares at me? Is his spirit locked in that portrait whenever he isn't visible to people?*

She had so many questions.

"Please send me another clue tonight," she spoke in a hushed whisper. "Tell me *why* you want me to return to you."

Jean-Daniel remained motionless. But the energy inside the drawing room pulsated with unspoken words. She sensed that Jean-Daniel was frustrated. That he was desperate to communicate with her.

Being trapped inside a painting, unable to communicate, must be hell.

"Do you want me to learn the details of your death?" she asked.

A shadow shifted across his impossibly handsome face. As he met her stare, heat sparked between them hot enough to burn.

My room. That's where he likes to visit me.

After giving him a smile, Ella put the necklace and the amulet inside a credenza and then left the drawing room.

Yes! Inwardly, Jean-Daniel swelled with happiness. Ella had acknowledged his presence and had gotten the gist of what he wanted her to do. She'd even found the enchanted Egyptian jewelry.

That had taken a good deal of energy. But it was worth it.

Ella was a smart girl. Jean-Daniel had realized that immediately when their paths crossed for the first time in 1703.

As she went upstairs, his thoughts turned to the day the amulet and the bracelet had been left inside the backing of his portrait. Dragomir Starkov's wife had just gotten wind of Starkov's mind-boggling powers. To break the hypnotic trance he'd cast over her,

Rose Starkov had taken the amulet off and hidden it along with the matching bracelet.

Pénélope Toulouse spoke of a curse, but Jean-Daniel couldn't care less. He was already cursed in this hellish state of limbo.

Things couldn't get much worse.

In fact, when Jean-Daniel saw how agonized Dragomir Starkov had been when his wife fled, he knew that if the magician could have found the amulet and the bracelet, surely he would have taken advantage of their powers to get his wife back.

Jean-Daniel wished he knew precisely what those black magic powers were, but he had an inkling that they could help Ella enter his portrait.

Scooping up her laptop, Ella trudged toward the stairs. A few minutes later she reached her bedroom and set the computer on the bed, leaving it on while she washed her face and brushed her teeth.

Unhurriedly, she changed into her pajamas. Once she disappeared into the bathroom, she turned on the water at the sink. As Ella reached for the toothpaste, her thoughts turned to her father.

Had *he* seen the ghost of Jean-Daniel? If so, how many times?

Perhaps he never saw it, Ella considered. She didn't think Jean-Daniel had been overly naughty when her father visited here. Laurent Benoit probably wouldn't have bequeathed a dangerous place to his daughter.

Jean-Daniel.

Ella's instincts told her he'd been a brilliant ray of sunshine when he was alive. Full of mischief and fun. A man brimming with dynamism and a zest for pleasure.

She didn't know how she knew these things. Truth be told, it was a stretch for her to believe that Jean-Daniel was anything different than a dull vicomte with a tragic history. In fact, when Ella encountered his ghost, it had moved with a gloomy air, showing no signs of being a prankish poltergeist. But then he'd smiled at her. His charismatic grin and those damn dimples revealed his true personality.

As Ella leaned over the sink, the edge of her camisole lifted and the small of her back became exposed. Suddenly, a feathering sensation swept across her skin. She straightened up and stared in the mirror. There was no one there. Still, she sensed a body, strong and hard, pressed against her backside.

A cool touch ran along her arm, as if someone was using the back of their curled fingers against it. She spun around and stared into the dim light of her bedroom. It appeared empty as well.

Senses whirling, she turned off the light switch in the bathroom and scurried to her bed. She had hope. Jean-Daniel had touched her just now. Maybe if she slept, he'd come to her in her dreams.

She could only hope. As she settled under the covers, she noticed that the computer screen was flashing brightly. Swiveling the laptop around to face her, she gasped. Typed across its screen were the words: REVENIR À 1703. JE T'AIME.

Come back to 1703. I love you.

CHAPTER 11

Ella stared at the computer screen. Time froze. The incessant beating of her heart was the way she knew she wasn't inside a vision.

How can Jean-Daniel love me unless we've met before?

Astonishingly, they seemed to share a passionate history. Now he wanted her to come to his aid. And the reason involved his death. She knew it, but how could she possibly alter his fate?

Within the stillness of the moment, everything that used to be important to Ella fell away like a wilted flower petal. Gaining her stepmother's approval, making her father proud, even fixing up the dilapidated château became insignificant. Replacing them was a rushing sense of purpose.

Jean-Daniel had clearly answered Ella when she'd asked, "Why do you want me to return to you?"

She ran her hands through her hair. Studying the computer screen again, she shook her head. This was crazy. Unbelievable. Impossible. She knew nothing of time travel except what she'd seen in the movies. Didn't one need a huge machine outfitted with gadgets and buttons to travel backward through the decades?

Well, she didn't have a magic machine. Nor could she speculate as to how to time-travel without one. She didn't even know if there were official reports of anyone *succeeding* in such a journey. Maybe information could be found on the Internet.

Grateful for the strong satellite connection Pierre had supplied, she settled in bed with her laptop propped on a pillow. Surfing numerous websites turned up nothing useful. She ended up reading accounts of people who claimed to have been abducted by aliens and transported back to the sixties—when they were young.

Rolling her eyes, Ella let out a yawn. The searching was making her extremely sleepy. Without finding anything earth-shattering, she let her eyes drop. Soon she was fast asleep and dreaming of Jean-Daniel.

Ella stood in a room where long curtains flew off the ground on wisps of hot, summer air. Jean-Daniel walked toward her as he slipped his shirt off his shoulders and down his back. He was alluringly ripped. Removing his wig, he revealed shaggy, caramel-colored hair. Ella's fingers itched to run through the tresses, but Jean-Daniel wasn't yet close enough to her. Walking slowly—exaggeratedly so, in fact, as things often seem in a dream—he gave Ella the chance to study his every handsome feature. Finally, he stood before her.

She smiled shyly.

"This is going to be amazing, *mon coeur*," he said in a husky rasp.

Ella's pulse stuttered wildly.

She trailed her hand up his bare washboard stomach and curled her fingers around his biceps. His muscles were hard, taut, and lined with fine veins. She loved the sight of them. Tilting her head to the side, she lifted her chin as he brought a crushing kiss down on her mouth. She rose on her tiptoes to greet it.

Jean-Daniel's lips were moist and warm and his breath was sweet and scalding.

He was like no man Ella had ever seen. Passionate. Soul-binding. Exquisitely good-looking. And kind-natured, she could tell.

He ran his fingertips along her jawline and she melted against him. Jean-Daniel had the most astonishing effect on her—and she had no inclination to resist that effect.

"You've come to me," he whispered. "As I asked you to. It makes me very happy."

He grasped the back of her head and released her bun. Thrusting his tongue forward, he collided it with hers. The tangled contact prompted a stirring between her legs. With a hungry grunt, he scooped her off the marbled tile and marched with her to an ornate bed fashioned with plum-colored drapes. Ella could hear a party taking place just outside the door.

"Won't someone discover us here?" she asked urgently.

"Maybe," he replied as he hovered over her like a massive gladiator. "But their closeness will make our encounter even more exciting."

God. If a woman could fall in love with a man based solely on his sensual voice, Ella just had.

Deftly, Jean-Daniel laid her down and peeled away her dress—a simple servant's garment made of muslin that spoke of the eighteenth century.

"You're beautiful," he murmured. "Beyond magnificent."

Ella was embarrassed, acutely aware of the tepid breeze blowing over her bare skin, making her nipples stand at attention.

Jean-Daniel pouted. "Don't be shy. I enjoy the sight of you."

Bending over her, he offered her another kiss, this one traveling from her mouth, down the length of her neck to her collarbone. His lips seemed to burn hotter and hotter as they fell on her skin. Ella moaned.

"Let me explore your glorious body . . . please?" he asked charmingly. She nodded—and in an instant that made her jaw drop, Jean-Daniel buried his head at her breasts.

"So ripe. So perfect," he uttered.

The sensation of his tongue licking in circles moistened her womanly parts. Sucking in a breath of ecstasy, Ella let her head drop back. As she did, her golden hair flowed over the pillow.

"You have the most beautiful locks I've ever seen." Jean-Daniel coiled her hair in his fingers. "The color of sunshine in the morning."

Ella closed her eyes, savoring the comforting feeling of his strokes through her shoulder-length mane. She opened them as he gently lifted her head to his chest. He wanted her to taste his nipples, too. Pressing her open mouth to the flat surfaces, she lapped at his salty skin bronzed from the sun. His pebbles hardened right then and there.

"God, yes." Cupping her face in his hands, he plundered her mouth again. Between forbidden kisses, he murmured explicit comments about how much he wanted her.

In the middle of his kisses, Ella studied him. She watched his strong jaw work under the movement of his lips and she loved how his caramel hair lay boyishly across his forehead. She knew their liaison was sinful, but she didn't care. Not only was Jean-Daniel built like an Adonis—his personality was completely irresistible.

At his urging, she rolled over and spread herself across the bedsheet.

"Your backside is fit for royalty," he said softly. "Your *ass*." Jean-Daniel slid his palms up her thighs, taking time to caress her skin at every inch. He fondled her buttocks with a deep grunt before fueling the excitement between her legs with his fingers.

"That feels amazing." Ella's voice caught.

All at once, Jean-Daniel glided his velvet hand from the crease of her bottom forward to her core. Then he entered her with two fingers. Shifting, she intensified the friction. When she glanced behind her, she was able to watch his face as he brought her to a pinnacle with his handiwork. He grinned because she let him know her climax was astounding . . . as incredible as the seas parting, as magical as the best illusion, and as fulfilling as the deepest kiss.

He slipped his hand under her breast. While he tweaked her bud to a point, he said, "You're ready for me, but I won't take you yet."

The words feathered lust up Ella's spine and unraveled her desire for him like one unties a bow. She bit her lip as he continued to tease and provoke her nipple with a twist of his fingers. Lolling her neck to the side, she closed her eyes to relish the moment. Jean-Daniel eased her hair out of the way while he pressed hot kisses along her bare nape.

"I know we're not supposed to be together, Ella, but you've become my everything," he whispered. "And I intend to make you mine right now." In one impulsive, heated moment, he drove his manhood inside her, and—

Ella stirred in her sleep. A part of her brain recognized that she was dreaming. She snapped open her eyes. Cutting the dream short, she glanced around at the dark bedroom. Cheeks heated with lust, she looked beside her.

My God! There was an indentation on the sheets next to her!

Reaching out, she swept her hand across the area to see if anything solid met her touch. The space was empty. Yet a spark—as warm as her cheeks and as strong as her want—made her jump.

She felt a jolt of electricity . . . palpable evidence of contact. Any girl in her right mind would run if she thought she was in bed with a ghost. But Ella didn't mind. She *wanted* Jean-Daniel to sleep next to her. She desired to be with him in any form because that was the kind of connection they had. Not entirely physical, their bond stemmed from a force too irresistible to ignore. *Love?* Perhaps.

All she knew at this point was that she was being pulled by a relentless and commanding hand. And it more than suggested that she and Jean-Daniel had fallen for each other in another century.

Dawn gave way to late morning. Groggy-eyed, Ella finally awoke. Erotic dreams as real as anything had kept her in a deep REM sleep. She felt exhausted, but in a good way.

Jean-Daniel's spirit—whether it was corporeal or alive in her mind—had taken control of her.

How does one become obsessed with a figure in a painting and then subsequently become obsessed with that figure's ghost? She didn't know. She just knew that she *was* obsessed—and because Jean-Daniel reciprocated the attraction, she must do something about it.

Shaking away her grogginess, Ella grabbed her computer and stared at the screen. The haunting plea from Jean-Daniel was typed across it again. Tingling, she saved the message in a file. Then she visited more websites that spoke to the possibility of time travel.

Astrophysicists, history professors, and researchers alike claimed that it wasn't possible. At least journeying to the past wasn't. Some proposed that transporting to the future may be. Under Albert Einstein's Theory of Relativity, they asserted, one might be able to venture years ahead . . . if one traveled faster than the speed of light.

"I don't want to see the *future*," Ella muttered.

She searched more and discovered another roadblock, from an expert who insisted that traveling back in time violated a fundamental rule of logic. According to him, cause always comes before effect. Therefore, one can never go from the present to the past.

Growing disheartened, Ella watched a YouTube video that actually poked fun at the idea of time travel. A roving reporter asked people on the street what they'd do if they could accomplish the phenomenon. One person said they'd ask out Marilyn Monroe, another said they would play the lottery because they would already know the winning numbers. Yet another interviewee said they'd marry somebody other than their ex-husband.

Ella chuckled at the last admission just as knocking sounded downstairs. Who had come to call?

Grabbing a robe, she hurried out of the bedroom. Beyond the glass at the front door stood Mimi Brimhall. She was the last person Ella had expected to see!

Yanking the portal open, she flung her arms around her friend. "Goodness! I'm so happy you're here!"

"I wanted to surprise you." Mimi laughed and squeezed her back. As always, she smelled of sweet perfume and face powder and Ella rejoiced in the familiar scents.

Ella pulled away with a smile. "I can't believe you came."

Mimi patted her arm as they passed through the front door. "I got worried during our last phone conversation," she said. "That's why I hopped on the next available flight."

"You're the best." Ella grinned.

Mimi wheeled her suitcase across the threshold. Once she stopped inside the foyer, she surveyed the château with awe. "This place is re-markable." But then her face fell. "And a huge task for one young woman, I might add."

"I *have* been a little overwhelmed. That's why I haven't done much work on it yet."

"I can understand your anxiety. Besides, it seems this dashing Jean-Daniel Girard has been distracting you."

You have no idea. "I'll tell you about him once you've had a chance to relax."

Chattering on about the house, Ella showed Mimi to her room. Ella dressed and then suggested they meander out to the orchard. Ella pulled lemons off a tree and made lemonade, then they settled on the sun-bathed veranda off the drawing room. It was the spot where Ella had seen Jean-Daniel's specter.

"How are Hope and Charity doing?" Ella asked, shading her eyes from the sun.

"You mean how are they coping without you?"

Ella laughed.

"They are a mess, to be honest." Mimi crossed her legs. "But that's what you get when you depend on other people all your life."

Before Hope and Charity had moved to New York City, Ella had done everything for the girls—from laundry to cooking their meals and making their beds. The girls must be going through withdrawals.

She and Mimi drank their lemonade and basked in the landscape's golden glow. Thoughts ran through Ella's mind. As they always did lately, they involved Jean-Daniel. Had that towering cypress tree been here when he was alive? Did he enjoy the outdoors as much as she did? Did he fill the château with this much energy when he was alive?

Eventually, she brought the conversation around to her attempts to find out how to time travel.

"You probably think I've gone off the deep end, right?" she asked Mimi.

Mimi set her lemonade glass aside. "No. But I am concerned that you're infatuated with someone who's dead."

Ella raised an eyebrow. "Is there an academic term for somebody like me, professor?"

"Love-struck." Mimi smiled. Her eyes crinkled kindly at the corners. "Show me this Jean-Daniel."

The women rose and passed through the French doors. A warm breeze followed them. Once they stood in front of the portrait, Mimi donned the glasses she kept handy, on a neck-chain.

"This painting is incredibly lifelike," she commented. "The vicomte seems as though he could reach out and touch you."

He has. "Mimi," Ella said, "he wants me to travel back to the time he was alive but I don't know how."

"Are you sure that's the message he's conveying?"

"I can show you the words he typed on my computer." Ella's tone housed no irritation. Only eagerness.

"All right."

After Ella fetched her computer and Mimi read the message, Mimi went a little pale. "Go back to 1703? And furthermore, he *loves* you?"

"Crazy, isn't it?" Ella asked, sheepishly.

"I guess that's why he wants to communicate with you so much." Mimi got lost in thought. Finally, she said, "Let's look at the painting once more. Maybe we can figure something out." Minutes later, she patted perspiration from her upper lip. "My, my. He's quite handsome." Her lips quirked. "If I were twenty years younger . . ."

"Mimi!" Ella chortled.

"All right. Let's concentrate."

They studied the portrait for several more minutes but nothing new struck them.

Mimi stepped back. "Have the locals given you information about Jean-Daniel?"

"Yes. The management agent, Pénélope Toulouse, told me all about his life and his volatile relationship with his brother. Her story is confirmed by historical accounts on the Internet." Ella indicated Colbert Girard's painting on the same wall as Jean-Daniel's. She hadn't looked at it since the first day she'd arrived here.

Mimi moved to Colbert's image. "He's quite handsome, too."

"He was, but he was the black sheep of the family."

Mimi nodded firmly. "I can tell. His eyes are dark and stormy. I'm sure he was nothing but trouble in his day." She paused. "What else did Ms. Toulouse say?"

"She tried to get me to store Jean-Daniel's painting because he's a mischievous poltergeist. A spirit who uses his painting as a portal to the modern world—" Ella gasped. "That's it!"

"What's it?" Mimi asked, rejoining her in front of the vicomte's portrait.

"Maybe the painting is also a portal to the *past. That's* how Jean-Daniel wants me to go back to him. Through his painting!"

Mimi's brows shot up. She moved closer to the portrait and swept her hand over its bumps of paint. "This canvas is solid, Ella." She lifted one corner of the frame away from the wall. "And there is nothing but solid plaster behind it."

Ella knew that all too well.

Mimi returned the portrait to its normal position. "How do you expect to—" Now *her* words cut off. "Look here!"

She waved Ella forward and pointed to the painting's upper left corner—to a tiny group of servants working in the fields. The servants were depicted in a much smaller scale than the vicomte, indicating distance. "That girl looks just like you!"

Ella had never taken more than a glance at the field workers before. Squinting, she focused on the servant Mimi had indicated. "I can't tell."

"Use my glasses. They're like a magnifying lens."

After Ella donned the spectacles, she noticed that the servant girl wore a cap just like the one Ella's father had left inside the safety deposit box. And though the girl's face was partially shrouded by the bonnet, the female servant was about the same age as Ella and resembled her greatly.

Disbelief washed over Mimi's face. "This woman has your nose, your mouth, and your blue eyes."

"Could I *be* her?"

CHAPTER 12

Nausea edged up Ella's throat. Hands trembling, she handed the glasses back to Mimi. It appeared Ella had been here at the château in 1703. Thus her visions of a past life. Thus the possibility that she and Jean-Daniel had fallen in love. But how could that be?

Mimi shook her head. "We are talking reincarnation, Ella. I don't know if that's even possible."

"It doesn't seem *plausible*," Ella agreed. "Yet so many strange things have happened to confirm it."

Mimi put her hands on her hips. "It's simply a coincidence that you look like that girl. Don't you think?"

Numbly, Ella shrugged.

"This is getting too weird for me. Let's take a break from talking about ghostly messages and time travel."

Good suggestion, Ella thought. Being without electricity and running water was one thing, but the idea of giving up her current life to be a servant girl in the past didn't appeal to her in the least. She'd been a servant in the Santa Barbara mansion too recently.

Mimi frowned. "If Hope and Charity catch wind of this crazy talk, they'll have you committed, Ella."

She winced. Mimi spoke the truth.

Mimi directed her to the sofa. They sat and looked up at Jean-Daniel's painting. Both took in a sharp breath.

Damned if Jean-Daniel isn't staring at me right now, Ella thought.

"You know I'm a philosophy professor," Mimi said. "I believe that destiny can be a guiding force beyond our control. But I'd hoped you'd find a man to love in *this* century." She pulled a handkerchief from her blouse pocket and dabbed her forehead with it. Ella was perspiring as well.

"I've always wanted someone to need me and love me desperately," Ella said softly.

Mimi went on. "If Jean-Daniel died a violent death, you'd be in danger if you did manage to time travel."

It was something to consider. Ella's hands shook until she locked eyes with Jean-Daniel. *Gad!* The spell he cast over her was astounding. She crossed her arms. "It's mind-boggling how a man can exude so much charisma from a painting. Imagine what Jean-Daniel was like when he was alive!"

"Believe me, I have." Mimi laughed.

Ella, on the other hand, shuddered against the familiar electric charge filling the room.

They sat there in silence for a long while. Finally, Mimi said, "Ella, you may be tempted to try and visit Jean-Daniel in the eighteenth century, but you might never return to this era. Even if you do, your life might not be the same."

Ella faced her. "Traveling back in time for a handsome stranger sounds romantic."

Mimi smiled forlornly. "Your father put many romantic notions in your head, didn't he?"

Sadness grabbed hold of Ella. "I don't even know how I'd accomplish it."

"Speaking of your father," Mimi said, "I have something for you. Wait here."

Excited, Ella watched Mimi hurry upstairs. After Mimi returned, she held a beautiful sapphire pouch bearing the Benoit Footwear insignia. Then, hugging the pouch to her chest, she sat.

"Walter, Hope, Charity, and I are preparing for an estate sale. That's why I was going through Adelaide's things. This bag sat stashed behind a pile of sweaters at the back of her closet."

Ella's heart thrummed. She'd never seen anything as lovely as the pouch. Usually, shoes came in the typical cardboard box—and her father's line of footwear was no different.

Laying the bag on her lap, Mimi opened the drawstrings and removed a pair of glass slippers. They were absolutely stunning. When Mimi held them up, they shimmered against a beam of sunlight that showcased their transparent quality.

"I've never seen anything like them," Ella said.

"I don't think your father made a duplicate pair since."

Taking the glass slippers from Mimi, Ella studied one of them from various angles. It possessed a curved Rococo heel and a sharply pointed toe, but what she loved most about it was the circle of jewels planted at the center of its vamp.

"I acted like I hated my father's fashion lines, but I actually knew every style in them," Ella said.

Mimi arched a brow. "I assume this particular shoe was never featured in stores, magazines, or on the runway."

"You're right."

"Well, I don't know as much about Benoit Footwear as you do. That's why I'm glad the pouch contains a note."

"A note?" Ella's eyes widened.

Nodding, Mimi withdrew a message—hand-written on one of Laurent Benoit's stationary cards. Ella read it in a hushed whisper:

> *January 5, 1997*
>
> *My darling Ella,*
>
> *These shoes are meant for you. They are a one-of-a-kind design, inspired by you, my little princess. I intend to give them to you on your wedding day. To ensure they stay a secret until then, I've asked Adelaide to hide them away for me.*
>
> *I suppose it's your big day, or you wouldn't be reading this note. Please know that I love you and wish you nothing but the best as you venture into your future with your true love.*
>
> *Please wear these magical shoes fit for a princess . . .*
>
> *Love, Daddy*

A tear slipped down Ella's cheek. She had been seven years old when her father wrote the note. It was incredible how he had correctly estimated her adult shoe size. Bittersweet poignancy stung at her emotions.

"Don't cry, sweetheart." Mimi handed her a lace handkerchief.

"My father was the most thoughtful man in the world. And he won't get to see me on my wedding day."

"If you wear these shoes," Mimi said, drawing her into an embrace, "I'm sure he'll be with you."

Mimi hugged Ella for a long time, then urged her back to a sitting position. "Your father referred to the slippers as magical. Maybe they can dispel this pesky ghost and help you find true love with someone who is *alive*."

"Maybe they will." Ella smiled forlornly.

"And maybe your future will be found in this historic place."

"It would be funny, wouldn't it?" She stood. "Speaking of magic, it's my turn to show you something."

Mimi stayed put as Ella went to a credenza nestled in a corner of the drawing room and extracted two objects. She brought them to Mimi.

"What are these?"

"An ancient amulet and bracelet left behind by the former owner of this house."

"They're amazing," Mimi took the objects and examined them. Then she handed them back to Ella. "Where did you find them?"

"They were hidden in the backing of Jean-Daniel's painting."

"That's extraordinary!"

"What's more," Ella sat down "Pénélope asserts that these pieces of jewelry might have magical powers."

"More magic?"

Ella nodded. "Dragomir Starkov, the man who owned the château before my father, was a famous illusionist. An illusionist who dabbled in black magic."

Mimi shuddered. "This is getting stranger by the minute."

Lost in the beauty of the objects, Ella fell silent.

Mimi took Ella's hand. "Listen to me. You need to stay away from Jean-Daniel's portrait. And if these items stem from black magic, you need to lock them away in a safe place."

* * *

An hour later, Ella and Mimi were sitting inside *La Rose Café*. Ella's enthusiastic description of the *coq au vin* had persuaded Mimi to try it. Their lunch entrees arrived and over a bottle of delightfully dry Chardonnay, they discussed the journal pages Ella had sent to Mimi for translation.

"Stanley Kellogg is a brilliant professor, but it's only been two days since you sent the pages to me." Mimi took a bite of chicken.

Ella frowned. "Mimi, the pages may contain relevant information about the amulet and the bracelet."

"Do you promise not to wear them?" Mimi asked her.

"Yes."

"Good. I'll give Stanley a nudge when I return home."

A sliver of panic slid up Ella's spine. "When are you leaving?"

Mimi laughed. "Day after tomorrow. I promised Walter I'd be there for the estate sale."

"I'll miss you." Her voice caught.

"What is it, Ella?"

"I don't know if I can handle renovating the estate on my own. Maybe I'm in way over my head."

Mimi patted her hand. "You *can* do this, Ella. Your father's spirit is on your side. Besides, you've faced worse. Being treated like a slave by Adelaide and her two selfish daughters, for one thing."

Ella grimaced. "A slave is right."

Mimi chattered away as they ate. Then she noticed how good-looking their waiter was. "Now, why can't you turn your attentions to a guy like that?"

"Like what?"

"A man who isn't imprisoned inside a painting."

Ella gave a halfhearted chuckle.

"Let's get down to brass tacks," Mimi said. "You swear not to try to travel back in time, right?"

"I swear."

"Good. No one knows if time travel is possible, but there are thousands of people who go missing every year. I don't want you to be one of them." Mimi paused.

"And I swear I won't wear the Egyptian jewelry." Ella read her mind.

Mimi put a hand over her heart. "Thank goodness. You understand that I'm only looking out for you."

"Of course."

Mimi tsked. "As far as renovating the estate, never give up hope that you can accomplish anything, my dear."

As they left the restaurant, Mimi's words intrigued Ella. Perhaps Mimi was right. Perhaps there *were* no documented accounts of anyone successfully traveling back in time simply because those people had never returned. Up till now, Ella had been tossing around the idea of trying to time travel. She'd envisioned going back temporarily, possibly seeing Jean-Daniel in the flesh, helping him with his problem, and then returning to the present.

What if that wasn't the case? *What if I get stuck in the past permanently—never to realize my dreams in the present?*

They strolled back to the château. A warm gust of summer air rippled over Ella. All of her concerns paled at the thought of seeing Jean-Daniel alive and in the flesh. In fact, without the excitement and distraction of Jean-Daniel's mission, she had no real aspirations. Well, fixing up the estate and finding true love, but those were long-term goals that stretched into the distant future. Besides, if she wanted to find true love in 2015, she'd need a warm-blooded, corporeal man to do that with.

On Thursday, Ella followed Mimi to Paris, both of them driving their respective rental cars. Once they arrived in the vibrant city, they visited the Eiffel Tower and a small portion of the Louvre before Mimi's plane departed. It was something both of them had always wanted to do.

Next, Ella returned the rental car and gave Pénélope a call to ask her if she could pick her up from the train station in Maincy upon her return.

Ninety minutes later, Ella was saying goodbye to Mimi at the airport's security checkpoint.

"Good luck, my dear." Tears misted Mimi's eyes.

Emotion clogged Ella's throat.

"Remember to be brave. And to take your life here one day at a time. You've always felt that nothing you do turns out right, Ella. But I know this will. *This* will be your dream come true."

Ella smiled. "Sometimes I think you're my guardian angel."

The twinkle in Mimi's eye returned. "How do you know I'm not?"

CHAPTER 13

Behind his placid image in the painting, Jean-Daniel scowled. That Mimi woman had seemed kind enough, but she'd given Ella the wrong advice! He'd almost gotten Ella to a willing state. Hell, an eager state.

Would she listen to her friend, or would she follow his persuasive pathway? Jean-Daniel thought he knew the answer to that. Ella had known Mimi a lot longer. At least, that's what she *believed*.

Anger bubbled inside him. Ella should be returning from Paris at any moment. And he planned to contact her as soon as she did.

Headlights streamed into the room and car wheels crunched over the gravel driveway. Jean-Daniel sucked in a breath. *Here she comes!*

Fidgeting sounded at the door. Then it swung open and in walked two shadowed figures. Since the arching entryway of the drawing room partially inhibited Jean-Daniel's view, he could barely see them. But he *could* hear the figures speaking to one another.

"It's a good thing Mimi won't be here," said the first girl.

"Yeah, she's flying back to the States today, right?"

"Right. And it's a *really* good thing I found this spare key among Mother's things. My guess was right. It does open the front door!"

The girls huddled and snickered. Then they let their luggage drop from their hands with a loud *clunk*.

"Ella!" they called out.

Once they stepped forward, Jean-Daniel gazed upon their unpleasant features. If he could have cringed, he would have. *Étrange!* In all of his 338 years, he'd never seen such unattractive women. The sense of misery they wore on their faces made their features even more unpleasant. One of the women possessed a slack chin and bulging, bloodshot eyes that made her look like something in a horror film. The second was very plump and sported wiry blond hair as bristly as a porcupine's.

Ella walked in the front door. "Hello?" she said cautiously. "Is someone here? I saw a car in the driveway."

When she flicked the light switch on, she gasped at the sight of the two girls. "Hope? Charity? What are you doing here?"

"Ella! Our favorite stepsister!" Sarcasm coated Hope's voice.

For the love of God, Jean-Daniel thought. *These are Ella's stepsisters?* "Step" was right. The girls didn't have a drop of Ella's beauty. But wait. Hadn't he seen them somewhere before?

The girls went to embrace Ella, but she stiffened. "I want to know what you're doing here. Don't you have Adelaide's estate sale to attend to?"

Hope waved the thought away. "Mimi has the matter in hand. Besides, we're here to see you."

"You never wanted to spend time with me before, so I doubt this is a social call."

Brava, Jean-Daniel observed. Ella was starting to show signs of the backbone she had displayed in 1703.

Charity glanced around at the château's vast interior. "This place is amazing. But it doesn't look like you've spent that much money fixing it up."

"I've only been here six days." Ella frowned. "Speaking of money, how did you afford plane tickets to Paris?"

"We charged them," Hope answered. "But racking up our credit cards isn't something we want to do anymore."

"What do you mean by that?" Ella fumed.

"Didn't you get our emails?"

"Yes." She raised her chin defiantly. "I chose not to answer them."

"Is there somewhere we can sit and talk?" Hope asked. "Jetlag's got the better of us, so go make some coffee."

Ella's resentment, which had no doubt been welling deep in the pit of her stomach for years, exploded into the open. "In case you haven't noticed, I'm no longer your servant girl. I own this house. It's mine and you're guests in it. If you were civilized, well-mannered guests, I'd gladly fix you some coffee. But you're not. So get out."

Jean-Daniel wanted to clap. Ella couldn't have handled the situation better!

"Get out?" Charity's eyes grew dark. "Some sister you are. You have more than enough money. Why don't you share it?"

"Because I don't have to." Ella's hands curled into fists.

"Oh yes you do. We met some shady people in New York City." Hope's gaze narrowed enough to make Ella shudder. ". . . people who can assure this house goes up in flames."

"You wouldn't dare!" In an instant, Ella reverted back to the scared girl she'd always been. Jean-Daniel assumed that Hope and Charity had a way of frightening her. Bullying her.

"My father wanted *me* to have the money," she said softly.

"You're heartless, Ella," Hope sneered. "Didn't I always say she was a brat, Charity?"

Charity crossed her arms. "Yes you did, sister."

"It doesn't matter what you think." Ella's voice quivered. "I upheld my promise to care for your ailing mother. Now our lives are separate and I don't have to take care of *anyone* anymore."

"We need money!" Hope stalked toward her. "If you won't give us some from your trust fund, at least give us the glass shoes your father left you."

Ella gasped for the second time that night. "How do you know about those?"

Hope shrugged. "We helped Mimi clear out Adelaide's things. We were with her when she discovered them. It's my guess they'll fetch a fortune at auction."

"You can't have them!" Ella shouted.

"What are *you* going to do with them? Wear them here in the countryside for *no one* to see?"

That drew out a wicked laugh from Charity. "Yeah, no one!"

Ella seemed at a loss. Jean-Daniel assumed that short of calling the police, she didn't know how to make Hope and Charity leave.

It was time he took action.

The front door creaked open with a preternatural moan. When it slammed shut, Ella's blood froze. Hope and Charity spun in alarmed circles.

"Wh . . . what was that?" the Benoit sisters screeched.

It's Jean-Daniel! Goosebumps layered Ella's arm. She could feel his presence at her side, prickling and twitching with energy. From the corner of her eye, she saw a flash of white move to the drawing room. She followed it. The room was pitch black since the curtains were drawn, but she knew her way.

"Turn on the lights, Ella!" Hope screamed as she followed behind. "I can't see a thing!"

Ella watched in awe as an unseen force lit five candles. That same force placed the shoe pouch containing the glass slippers into her hands. Then the credenza door unlocked and out floated the amulet and the bracelet. The bracelet came forward. Without thinking, Ella grasped it. Next the amulet found its place around her neck.

Fright churned inside her. She'd promised Mimi she would never put the objects on. What dangers would they render?

Before she knew it, the servant's cap landed in her hands, too. All the items she held started to glitter and shimmer. Had their magic powers been jump-started?

"Someone's pulling my hair!" yelled Charity.

"And someone's yanking on my purse!" Hope added in a panic.

Suddenly, the curtains swooshed open. The candles went out, but moonlight flooded the room. The girls watched in horror as Hope's red lipstick floated from her handbag and flew to the mirror above the mantel. Tilted at an angle, the lipstick penned something in French: *Sortir demi-soeurs!*

Get out stepsisters!

"What the hell kind of prank is this?" Hope flashed a grim look at Ella.

"It's no prank, Hope. This house is haunted, so I suggest you leave it immediately."

"You can't tell me what to do!" Hope lunged at her, her long red nails leading the way.

Ella stood in front of Jean-Daniel's painting. The ball of light she'd seen before flashed in front of her and then landed on the painting. She realized that Jean-Daniel had re-entered the portrait. As soon as he did, he reached a ghostly hand out for her. Time seemed to freeze. Knowing that her next action would change her life forever, she quickly debated. Should she stay or should she go? Ultimately, her immense curiosity and sense of "this is meant to be" won out.

Barely avoiding Hope's razor-sharp swipe, Ella took the apparition's hand and leapt into the portrait.

Once she penetrated the canvas, streams of light surrounded her. With a whizzing noise, the drawing room disappeared. Terrified, Ella spiraled through a churning wormhole at lightning speed.

Where was Jean-Daniel? Whether the trip was being fueled by science, magic, or by a ghost's fantastical purpose, she couldn't tell.

Her head spun and her vision blurred. Landing on her stomach with a *plop*, she opened her eyes. She saw that she was outside somewhere. Tall stalks of wheat walled her off from a new world. Pulse pounding violently, she flipped over and sat up. Gone were her baggy trousers and shirt. In place of them, she wore a gray servant's dress made of muslin.

"This is insane!" She scrambled to her feet to confirm that she was in the fields beyond Château de Maincy. She'd lost her shoes on the way, and her toes pressed into the cool dirt. She was frightened, but more than that she was excited. Was she experiencing what only a handful of people had accomplished? Pushing her shoulders back, she realized that she had no urgent desire to go back to her old life. Certainly, she had no desire to face money-hungry Hope and Charity at the moment.

Château de Maincy stood like a towering beacon before Ella. It looked so different. Its domes glimmered with fresh blue paint and its grounds appeared lovingly manicured. This couldn't be happening! Yet every detail was incredibly clear and astoundingly real. The wheat was soft against her fingers, the sun's heat beat down on her causing palpable discomfort, and the breeze that flitted by swayed the loose tendrils of her hair.

Being here seemed impossible, even inconceivable. But here Ella was in 1703!

Dazed and almost overcome, she felt her mouth go dry. How long would she be here? Would she ever be able to get back to the present day?

Jean-Daniel's ghost! It had transported her here, but she wanted to see the living, breathing Jean-Daniel.

Grappling with her new reality, Ella cradled the pouch that held the glass slippers. Too scared to take off the Egyptian amulet in case doing so might whisk her back to the twenty-first century without having seen her vicomte, she placed the bracelet inside her apron pocket along with the pouch. She stood again and gazed at the château.

Perhaps I am the servant girl in the painting.

She decided to plop the cap on her head, just in case. At least she'd possess an immediate identity here that might help her avoid being thrown in jail for trespassing.

Where was Jean-Daniel? She was desperate to see him. After all, his firm yank had propelled her here.

Anticipation rose inside her as she shaded her eyes. Approximately a hundred yards away, three female servants were busy placing bundles of cut wheat into baskets. None of them made eye contact with Ella.

To her right, a brilliant sun hung over the horizon. Was it the end of the workday? She hoped so.

To her left, a magnificent field of lavender radiated a vivid purple color. Had the stalks been planted just to make oil for Jean-Daniel's bath?

What was he really like? She assumed she'd find out soon.

One of the servant girls lifted her head and stared straight at Ella. Although the girl shouted something, Ella was unable to hear her at this distance. Panicking, she spun away from the château and hurried into the woodland.

She'd only just gotten to eighteenth-century Maincy and she needed time to get her story straight.

Rays of sunshine shone on oaks and European beeches. Running her hand along a fat tree trunk, she huffed out a ragged breath. She would stay safely hidden here until she decided to show herself. She had a lot of thinking to do.

Ella treaded over a bed of mushrooms nestled in the shadows of the forest. She'd never ventured this far away from the château in the present day and the woodland was beautiful. But that wasn't what she was thinking about. A bullet whizzed by her head. With a loud crack, it pierced the oak behind her. Heart clamoring, she bolted out of sight, stumbling and scraping her shin along the way. She pressed her back to a large oak while the thunder of horses' hooves rang in her ears. When she dared peek out, she saw a gorgeous brown stallion outfitted in regal finery. The creature galloped toward her, a muscular man seated erectly on its back. The man shoved his musket over his shoulder by way of its strap. Then he let out a furious "whoa!" as he yanked his stallion to a stop.

It was Jean-Daniel! Ella hadn't recognized him for a moment without his wig, but it was definitely him. She was ready to jump out and reveal her presence, but the sight of his aquamarine eyes in person buckled her knees.

As he dismounted, his forearms flexed. He acted as though he were looking for something.

Ella gathered her courage. She nearly took a step forward when an adorable hound dog came bounding around the corner. The dog yapped to get his master's attention.

Laughing, Jean-Daniel bent to pet it. "Good boy, Rémy! You had the fox's scent but I have lousy aim!"

Rémy barked in agreement.

"When we hold the official hunt next week, you'll be ready."

Hanging its tongue to the side, the brown and white dog panted eagerly.

"It's the dog in the painting," Ella murmured.

Jean-Daniel jerked to his feet. "Did you hear that, boy? We aren't alone."

Rémy let out a string of barks and circled the tree. Ella thought her heart was going to fly out of her chest. Trying not to breathe, she pressed her back to the tree trunk again. She wanted to talk to Jean-Daniel, touch him, but now she felt panicky.

Twigs snapped. Grass rustled. Then there was a hand on her arm.

CHAPTER 14

Jean-Daniel pulled Ella from her hiding place. She hung her head low, disguising her face with her cap.

"I don't believe it," he said. "A servant this far inside the hunting park?"

The hunting park? Cripes! She could have lost her head to a musket ball!

Rémy sat on his haunches and cocked his head to the side. Meanwhile, Jean-Daniel put his hand under Ella's chin. Because her eyes were downcast, she couldn't help but notice he wore snug-fitting breeches the color of California sand and black, knee-high boots polished to a high shine.

Slowly, he lifted her chin so they could lock eyes. She couldn't believe she was standing a foot away from him. He, in return, sucked in a breath as sharp as hers.

"My God . . ." his voice trailed off. "You're beautiful."

Words escaped her. She was angry with him because he'd almost killed her just now. But seeing him in the flesh was more magical than she could have envisioned. Adding to the enchanting moment, he thought *she* was beautiful.

Apparently dumbstruck, he shook his head and backed away. "Pardon me. I didn't mean to be so bold."

His touch had electrified her. Her senses swam with excitement.

Summoning all the courage she had, she asked, "Do you know me, sir?"

Unfortunately, Rémy yelped loudly at the same time. Jean-Daniel hadn't heard her, but did he recognize her? Something, whether it was familiarity or pure attraction, swept over his face.

He put his hands on his hips. "What is your name, girl?"

Apparently it hadn't been recognition.

She gulped. "Ella."

"Ella, is it? Ella what?"

"Umm . . ." She was stammering like a scared child!

"I've never seen you before, girl. Where did you come from?"

If she hadn't flung herself into his portrait so swiftly, she could have planned this with greater forethought. Now what explanation would she offer?

While she contemplated what to say, Jean-Daniel stood so close she could smell him. He emanated a raw fragrance—a mixture of perspiration and expensive, musk-based cologne, she surmised. And she liked it.

Jean-Daniel widened his stance. The position highlighted his thick arms. It also showcased his substantial manhood. Ella had no complaints about the tight-fitting pants men wore in the past.

When she locked eyes with Jean-Daniel again, her entire life seemed to come around full circle. She wanted to explain how far she'd journeyed to be here, yet he didn't know her.

That's when her heart plummeted. She didn't know what she had expected. For the two of them to fall into each other's arms immediately? Now she had no idea how to return to the future. And there was no possibility of asking him for advice.

"Ella is a pretty name for a very pretty girl," he said. "But I asked you where you are from."

"Let's just say I don't belong here," she replied honestly.

Jean-Daniel looked taken aback. Then he appeared amused.

"She *does* belong here," said a voice out of nowhere. "This girl is on loan from Madame Fouquet." A middle aged servant with rotting teeth rushed forward. The woman pushed her way to the bullet-pierced tree so that she could clasp Ella's arm.

On loan? How primitive! Worse, it reminded Ella of her servant status with Adelaide. *Should I click my heels three times like Dorothy and wish to go home?*

This sure felt like Oz.

Rémy barked even louder.

"Ah, she's here to help with my ball," Jean-Daniel seemed to understand.

"Yes, Monsieur," the woman said. "She isn't a field servant at all. I don't know what she's doing out of the house."

Puzzlement lit Jean-Daniel's eyes. His stare roved over Ella. Then he said, "Release her, Madame Yvette. She's bleeding."

Astonished, Ella stared down at her bare feet. Blood had trickled onto one from her leg, but she hadn't felt a thing until now.

Jean-Daniel knelt. He raised one eyebrow and the hem of her dress simultaneously. Once a deep gash across her shin was revealed, he stopped lifting.

"When I heard the gunshot," Ella explained, "I stumbled and fell."

"I'm sorry I frightened you."

Madame Yvette cleared her throat impatiently.

Jean-Daniel stood. "Return to your duties, Madame," he instructed sternly. "I shall take this girl to the house myself."

"That's highly unusual, Monsieur le vicomte."

His eyes narrowed. Their color morphed from a clear aquamarine color to a tempestuous sapphire. "She's bleeding. Are you being insubordinate?"

"Not at all, Monsieur."

"Good," Jean-Daniel said steadily.

Red-faced, the woman disappeared. Jean-Daniel turned to Ella and posed another question. "Why didn't you mention you were hurt, Mademoiselle?"

"I had no idea I was, Your Majesty."

Jean-Daniel let out a hearty laugh. It was the most magnificent sound Ella had ever heard. Still, her face flamed and she felt like an idiot.

"Why are you laughing at me?" she asked sharply. No one knew her in this century and she was determined to show some *chutzpah* here.

"No need to call me 'Your Majesty' my dear," he said. "I'm only a vicomte." Ella grimaced. Her French was rusty, which made spot-on translations of titles difficult.

When Jean-Daniel stepped in again, attraction as intense as a blinding light washed over his handsome features. "You have a beautiful face, Ella. But besides that, there is something I like about you. Maybe it's the feisty way you speak."

No one had ever said *that* to her before.

He placed his open palm to her cheek. His hand wasn't soft, like a pampered nobleman's might be. It felt strong and weathered, making Ella guess that he enjoyed spending a lot of time outdoors. It's probably why he'd been painted in front of the château.

"Now that we are alone—" He wet his lips.

A wizened old man bouncing about on horseback interrupted the exchange. The white-haired gentleman pulled his animal to a halt and climbed off of it arduously.

"Let me rephrase that." Jean-Daniel threw Ella a dashing smile. "Now that Hervé has joined us . . ."

"Monsieur le vicomte!" Hervé frowned. "I insisted you stay with me on this training hunt. You know my rheumatism is acting up."

"Sorry, old friend," Jean-Daniel faced the courtier. "But as part of his drills, Rémy was leading me to the fox."

"Fox?" Hervé looked around for the animal. "I don't see any fox."

"Rheumatism *and* poor eyesight." Jean-Daniel dropped his shoulder and whispered the observation to Ella. "Is that what we have to look forward to in old age?"

She raised an eyebrow.

Teetering on spindly legs, Hervé handed Jean-Daniel his cocked hat. His hands shook as he extracted his *pince-nez* from his waistcoat pocket. As Ella watched the man fidget, she realized he couldn't be any younger than seventy.

Hervé acknowledged her with a sour expression. "What are you doing here, Mademoiselle? Get back to your duties."

"Yes, sir." Ella did a curtsy, as she'd seen women do in movies. She began to hustle away when Jean-Daniel stopped her.

"I said I would take you back to the house myself."

"I don't need you to take me anywhere, Monsieur."

If snow had begun to fall over the summer landscape, Jean-Daniel couldn't have looked more surprised. "No maiden has ever talked to me in that manner."

Well, this "maiden" is very confused right now.

"You're taking her back to the house?" Hervé protested. "She looks like a field servant."

"She's on loan," Jean-Daniel explained as he came close to Ella. His unwavering stare fueled her nerves. "But she'll be anything I want her to be here."

Did he just say that? The audacity! Anger percolated inside her— until she noticed how handsomely his eyes crinkled at the corners.

"But right now"—Jean-Daniel glanced at Hervé over his shoulder—"she needs to ready the château for the ball."

"Who is she on loan from?" Hervé asked.

Why were they talking about her as though she wasn't there?

"Madame Fouquet."

The advisor made a face. "Madame Fouquet? That nasty, self-important—"

"Remember your weak heart, Hervé."

"Quite right." Hervé paused. "About the ball, Monsieur. Your mother is insisting that every eligible maiden in the province attend with her mother. She won't have you marrying a commoner without a worthy family. As far as the food . . ."

Ella snuck away in the middle of their conversation. As she emerged from the woods, she could hardly breathe. Oozing charisma, Jean-Daniel no doubt possessed a reckless zest for life. But he was also spoiled and accustomed to getting his way. Could she fall in love with a man like that?

Ella began the long walk to the château. The sun blazed down on her, but she didn't dare remove the neckerchief *fichu* from her neck. It would expose the amulet.

All at once, the pounding of horse's hooves made her turn around. Jean-Daniel—his cocked hat pulled low—galloped toward her. Leaning over the side of his horse, he caught her around the waist and scooped her onto his horse. Her *fichu* came undone and she gave a little cry. Stuffing it back to its original position, she wriggled against Jean-Daniel. He'd planted her firmly across his lap and kept her in place with one arm around her middle. His fingers crept higher. And as the two of them jostled about on his magnificent stallion, he nearly touched the underside of her breast.

"Monsieur, this is uncalled for!"

Luckily, Jean-Daniel hadn't felt the bulge in her apron. Would the glass slippers and the jewelry fly out? Worse, would the slippers break? They were so delicate.

Ella slipped her hand around the apron and hugged the items tightly to her body. Flying across the fields she said breathlessly, "I could have walked!"

"Isn't this more fun? Besides, you're bleeding."

The more they streamed along, the more she felt as free as a child. She nodded.

"Sling your arm around my shoulder," he commanded.

Hanging onto him for dear life, she was aware of her cheek pressed to his. Like a daredevil, Jean-Daniel jumped logs and leapt streams—barely clearing the obstacles. Ella's heart fluttered. Even more so when he prodded his stallion into a lightning-fast run across the field of lavender.

Warm air rushed over her and giddiness rattled through her.

The servants cried out in dismay as Jean-Daniel sent the bundles they'd gathered flying in all directions. Meanwhile, Ella's sense of restraint nearly made her protest. But then she decided that she liked the danger. In fact, it was the most fun she'd ever had.

Jean-Daniel pulled her closer. "Hold tight for this last jump."

A bed of tall, swaying sunflowers lay in wait. Behind the flowerbed stood a low wall, high enough to bring Jean-Daniel's tomfoolery to a halt.

Ella braced herself.

Time slowed.

Bending forward, Jean-Daniel flicked his horse's reigns and took the jump. They soared gracefully over the flowers and landed with a firm *thud*.

Ella sucked in a painful breath. She could swear she'd gotten whiplash. Jean-Daniel, who seemed unfazed, guided his horse to the rear of Château de Maincy . . . and to stables that were no longer part of the estate's grounds in her time.

It was all too disorienting to take in. Ella tried pinching herself, to see if she'd snap out of the daydream. It didn't work. She was really here.

Jean-Daniel handed the reins to a stable boy. Next, he dismounted and helped Ella down. The feel of his strong hands squeezing her waist made her even more breathless. As he brought her gently to the ground, her low neckline grabbed his attention. His eyes settled on her rounded cleavage below the *fichu* and the hidden amulet. Ella was mortified. She missed her baggy clothes and hated the fact that her skin was on display.

To make the items in her apron less noticeable, she stuffed her hands inside the front pockets. Thank God the slippers and bracelet were intact.

"You are a good sport, Mademoiselle." Jean-Daniel removed his hat and gave her a dashing bow. His white teeth flashed.

Head reeling, Ella knew it wasn't the sun causing her dizziness. Jean-Daniel represented adventure, gallantry, and virility. God, was he compelling and persuasive! Would she be here long enough for him to persuade her into sinful things?

Seeing him in the flesh still astonished her. As he spoke, she watched his generous mouth move. "I'll want a bath," he said. "Please draw it in fifteen minutes."

Jean-Daniel looked so delicious that she didn't want him to bathe. His hair was swept across his forehead in damp, shaggy layers. And as the sunlight settled on his forehead, it set off strands of gold and caramel. Two of his shirt buttons had popped open, allowing Ella a glimpse of his muscular chest glistening with sweat.

"A bath?" she managed to utter. "Yes, Monsieur."

"Don't bother to heat the well water on the stove. I need to soak in something cool."

After Jean-Daniel gave her a knee-buckling grin, they parted. Lips downturned, Ella headed up the split stone staircase at the back of the château. Vines of dahlias still provided a fragrant border around it. She stopped and smelled one.

Yes. I am definitely here.

Once she entered the house, it took a moment for her eyes to adjust to the light. Succulent scents of cheese, duck, vegetables, and hot baguettes came from the kitchen.

My God! Lifting her skirts, Ella ventured down the hall. Numerous servants darted from room to room, some carrying trays, some transporting cleaning supplies. No one took note of her.

Luckily, she knew her way around, but the château looked so different. It glowed with brand new fixtures and *boiseries*—intricate wood paneling—along the hallways.

Everything gleamed with freshness and spoke of the finest things.

Jean-Daniel demanded those fine things, she was sure. And right now he was demanding a bath. Her mind went blank. How does one "draw" a bath in the eighteenth century? She couldn't just twist the faucet and wait for the water to come pouring out.

He had mentioned a well . . .

At the risk of looking ridiculous, she needed to inquire.

Voices coming from the end of the passageway urged her closer. Ella was about to turn the corner when a woman popped out and barred her way.

"Are you the girl on loan?"

With a head full of gray hair and kindly blue eyes that wrinkled at the corners, the woman was the spitting image of Mimi! Ella wanted to reach out and give her a hug, but she didn't dare. *Don't you recognize me, either?!*

"Are you Ella?" the woman repeated.

Ella wasn't certain if she *was* the servant on loan from Madame Fouquet, but she decided to go with that story. "Yes," she stammered.

"Heavens, child! I've been looking for you everywhere. You were supposed to report to me directly."

"I'm sorry." Ella studied her bare feet. Would the woman notice she was missing her shoes?

"I'm Madame Manard, the head housekeeper. As you can see, this house is in pure chaos and I don't do chaos very well." Her face flushed. "You're here to assist us with the vicomte's ball, correct?"

"The vicomte's ball?" Ella said as apprehensive tingles flew up her spine. *No one knows what kind of fate lies in wait for Jean-Daniel.*

Would she be here long enough to try to reverse his destiny? Part of her hoped she would. Part of her feared that, as well.

Madame Manard's mouth pouted in a sympathetic gesture. "Have you been told nothing?"

Ella shook her head. She took a moment to study Madame Manard. The lady was a reincarnation of Mimi. Rather, Mimi was the reincarnation of Madame Manard.

Ella's head hurt. It seemed there was an identical set of people in this century—people she knew and admired. She only hoped there were no clones of Adelaide, Hope, and Charity.

"The vicomte's mother is organizing a ball," the housekeeper explained. "The lavish party will provide a chance for her older son to find a wife. I think it's time he grew up, too. But don't repeat that."

"I won't."

"Good girl. Anyway, Madame has invited every maiden in the province worth her salt. The ball will take place in ten days. There is much to do."

"I'll help with whatever is needed, after I draw Monsieur a bath."

Astonishment lit Madame Manard's face. "When did you meet Monsieur le vicomte?"

"Just now. At the rear of the house." Ella didn't dare tell the housekeeper that they'd actually met in the hunting park.

"Drawing the vicomte's bath is Julie's duty." Madame Manard indicated a pale, thin girl on her knees washing the baseboards. "But you're much prettier." Smiling, the housekeeper seemed to put two and two together.

Ella cleared her throat. "Since I'm new here, can you tell me where to fetch the water?"

"Of course. Come with me."

Ella picked up her skirts. That's when Madame Manard noticed her lack of shoes. "What on earth happened to your clogs, my dear?"

"I lost them."

Madame Manard put her hands on her hips and let out a sigh. "I may regret this, but you may have my extra pair."

"Thank you, Madame."

"Wait here." The woman disappeared for a moment only to return with a pair of clogs and a large bucket. She handed Ella the clogs first. "Here you are."

"I'm grateful."

"My goodness, child!" Madame Manard looked down again. "You're bleeding!"

"It's nothing."

Clucking and bustling, the housekeeper fetched some liniment and soap. After she cleaned and bandaged Ella's shin, she took a step back. "There. You're as good as new."

"You're very kind," Ella said.

"You live in Madame Fouquet's house. It's the least I can do. That woman doesn't have a decent bone in her body."

Great.

"Now." Madame Manard led her to bay window. "The well is past the gardens and on the edge of the orchard. Here's the bucket."

Ella's body vibrated with stress. Still, the housekeeper hadn't sent her back to the Fouquet household.

Clutching the bucket, which proved heavy enough empty, Ella hurried outside. She hobbled down the pathway and reached the well. She'd never noticed it in the present day. Maybe it was disguised by overgrown trees and brush. Or perhaps it no longer existed.

She lowered the attached pail by the rope pulley. Water sloshed into it and when she checked the weight of the bucket, she deemed it full. Lugging the heavy bucket up more slowly than she intended to, she clasped it with both hands.

Soon, she was making her way inside the house. Limping from her twisted ankle and shin injury, she grimaced. Up the central staircase she climbed—spilling a good deal of the water in the process. Terror and embarrassment plagued her. Would anyone catch the emotions on her face?

As Ella plowed clumsily on, a sense of déjà vu gripped her. Her clogs. And her hand on the banister. She'd seen the exact images before. In fact, she had lived this moment in the twenty-first century.

Ella was so caught up in the spine-tingling moment that she ran headlong into a man's steely chest. Face flaming, she cast her eyes down and gazed upon a pair of shining black jackboots topped with an ominous devil's-horns insignia.

CHAPTER 15

"Watch where you're going, girl!" the man growled. "I just had my boots polished!"

"A thousand pardons, sir." Ella had heard that in a movie too, but as soon as she said it, she doubted the expression fit the era.

"Look at me." The gravelly command raised the hair on her arms.

She lifted her head and gazed up at Colbert Girard. A wall of muscle, hard planes, and dark clothing, he emanated trouble. With wavy brown hair that touched his shoulders, a vertical dash of facial hair under his lip, and eyes grayer than a sky preceding a tempest, he scared Ella.

Evil calculations and selfish motives splashed across his face. Apparently, he had no desire to hide them.

"I nearly plowed you down, girl."

She took a step back. Water sloshed on the marble stairs.

"I haven't seen you before," he stated flatly.

"I'm on loan from the Fouquet household." She figured she should offer an explanation—regardless of its God-awful nature.

Colbert took a step forward. His boot tip stopped centimeters from her scuffed clogs.

"What are you doing bringing water up the main stairs?" he asked sternly. "Has no one told you there's a servant's stairwell?"

"No, Monsieur le vicomte."

He threw his head back and laughed. The timbre of his amusement seemed the only thing he had in common with his twin. "No need to call me le vicomte. I'm simply a baron."

Would she ever get the aristocratic titles right? It seemed she didn't know how to act in any century.

With one enormous hand, Colbert gripped the banister. As he planted his other hand on his hip, the stance created a wide barrier for Ella. He reminded her of an insurmountable mountain—one mountain climbers may well lose their lives to if they attempted to conquer it.

Silence hung between them. Colbert surveyed her appearance. It became obvious that he liked what he saw. "You're quite a ragamuffin," he said, nostrils flaring. "Still, you're pretty. Tell me you aren't bringing water to my brother."

"Monsieur would like a bath."

"Monsieur would, would he?" Colbert let out another hearty laugh.

"Yes."

"Isn't that just like my brother? He's spotted the new girl before I have. Ahead of me on every account!"

Ella's leg throbbed and her arms ached from holding the water bucket. She just wanted to soak in a bath herself.

"Well, the least I can do is show you to Monsieur le vicomte's apartments."

Just then the clock downstairs chimed the hour. Three dongs . . . three o'clock.

The longcase clock hasn't been broken yet! Disbelief that she'd traveled centuries into the past rolled over Ella anew.

"This way, Mademoiselle," Colbert said.

"Oh, no, Monsieur. Surely, I can find my own way."

"I insist." Colbert gallantly waved his hand and let Ella pass. Of course, he wasn't gallant enough to take the bucket from her.

By the time they reached the second story, the bucket's contents had been depleted considerably.

"My brother's chambers are at the end of the corridor," Colbert said.

"Thank you," Ella murmured.

Greediness surfaced in Colbert's stare. He took a step closer. His warm breath, tainted by brandy, feathered across her face. "You can thank me later."

Ella's high school boyfriend had made the same suggestion when she was seventeen—shortly before he'd forced himself on her. The words made her gut roil. Feeling off balance, she quickly looked away.

Pushing the traumatizing memory from her mind, Ella knocked on the door. Anxiousness enveloped her. She waited and as soon as Colbert disappeared, she heard Jean-Daniel's muffled voice. "Enter."

Striding through the door, she found it a gateway to the wondrous. Every luxury one could possibly possess in the eighteenth century filled the space. A plush, amethyst divan centered the room, surrounded by an ornate desk, two high-backed chairs, and remarkable damask curtains. A grand fireplace fashioned with silver details stood to the right. Beside it on an easel sat the very portrait of Jean-Daniel that graced the château in the present day!

It was incredible to see it here—and Ella nearly dropped her bucket in shock.

Jean-Daniel walked out of his bedroom wearing only a towel. This time, Ella did let go of the bucket's handle—because he was magnificent. Sinewy muscles layered his abdomen and chest and his arms swelled with defined muscles as well. A small, concave belly button topped an alluring line of brown hair that disappeared into the towel. With the shadow of a goatee darkening his chin, he resembled a rugged model in a magazine.

Shooting her a brilliant smile, Jean-Daniel poured himself a glass of red wine. Ella got a glimpse of his back which curved and swayed with definition. Her jaw went slack.

"Do you like it?" he asked.

Her mouth dried. Backing away, she stumbled into the bucket. Even more water sloshed over its side. "Like what, Monsieur?"

"My portrait." He turned around.

"It doesn't really look like you," Ella mumbled.

"Hmm. That's funny. People are saying it is a spot-on likeness."

It doesn't capture your charm.

"In any event, the artist promises to complete it in a few days," Jean-Daniel said. "Which is a damned good thing. Posing for it, as I did this morning, is something I'm growing tired of."

The smell of drying paint seeped into the air.

"Have you ever seen anything like it?" He placed a hand on his hip as he sipped his wine.

Actually, I have.

"What I meant to say is: Have you seen anything so vulgar? My mother commissioned it." He shook his head and padded toward Ella. "It makes me seem very self-important. A pompous nobleman. The truth is, I'd rather do anything but govern."

"I don't think it's vulgar, Monsieur. You are a vicomte after all."

An amused look returned to his face. "You're different from other girls, aren't you?"

"A little."

He came closer. "I like different."

She wanted to wipe a bead of the scarlet liquid from his lip, but she refrained.

He winced as he took another sip. No doubt it burned. "Anyway, I'm trying to convince my mother that my portrait should hang here rather than in the drawing room for the world to see."

Ella knew who won that argument.

"Unfortunately, my mother can be quite stubborn."

Ella started tapping her foot.

He studied her. "You're a nervous one."

"I suppose," she said, averting her eyes. After all, she didn't want Jean-Daniel to catch her ogling his rock-hard body.

Jean-Daniel looked at the bucket and laughed. "What happened to my water?"

"I'm afraid I'm not very coordinated."

"No matter. Find Madame Manard and tell her to have Julie bring more."

"Yes, Monsieur." She turned to go, but he placed a hand on her arm.

"I don't bite, you know."

What Jean-Daniel didn't know about Ella was that she'd never be caught alone with a strange man in an unfamiliar hotel room. And that's what this felt like.

She preferred to get to know him, yet she had no idea if she'd get sucked forward to the twenty-first century before she could. On the other hand, would she return at all?

Seeing him in his towel helped pacify the dilemma. In fact, it had been worth coming here just for that image.

Ella remained with her back to him. She didn't want him to see the self-consciousness staining her cheeks. He came around her. Hot, flavored with the spice of the wine and completely tantalizing, his breath waved across her face.

"You must think me a cad," he said, "drinking at three o'clock in the afternoon and taking a bath when everyone else is working."

"As I said, you're a vicomte. You can do whatever you want."

"Believe me, I do." His words suggested the forbidden. And the way he slurred them confirmed that he was drunk at three o'clock in the afternoon.

Ella moistened her lips. She liked the sight of his rough hands around the tall crystal glass. She also liked the calmness he showed as he swirled the wine in circles.

"I have more than enough fun, Ella. *Too* much fun, my mother says."

Why is he discussing this with me? Where is Hervé?

"You look like you work very hard."

You have no idea.

"I respect that. I can't say that I do the same, but I respect it."

Here was a man who enjoyed an abundance of fun. In contrast, Ella had had no frivolity in her life. At least not since her father had died. Maybe she and Jean-Daniel could find a balance between them.

"A strong work ethic is a virtue," she said. "At the same time, knowing how to enjoy life is an ability everyone should have."

"Very well put." He paused to sip his drink. "So you're suggesting that I work harder and enjoy myself less?"

"Perhaps," she said softly. Who was she to give advice to a vicomte?

Jean-Daniel stepped in. She could practically hear his heartbeat. When she caught a whiff of his natural, masculine scent she nearly swooned. The feel of his taut stomach touching the glass slippers and pieces of jewelry protruding from her pocket spun her mind in circles. *Will he ask about them?*

Thankfully, he didn't seem to notice. Mouth quirking, his supple lips hovered inches from hers. Seeping from his body was undeniable attraction.

Ella longed to run her hands up his toned chest, but that was something she dare do only in her dreams.

"The problem with your suggestion," he continued, "is that life is too short. I feel as if I should squeeze in all the pleasure I can get."

Jean-Daniel leaned in but didn't touch her. Body humming with excitement, Ella thought he was going to kiss her. He tilted his head, but then he stopped and began to study her again. Really study her.

She felt heady under the gaze of his aquamarine eyes. *What is he thinking?* Her pulse thumped.

At this close range, she studied him, too. His slim aristocratic nose dipped slightly into a middle point, his angled cheekbones rivaled a sculpted Grecian statue, and she could see where his dimples hibernated between smiles.

He was absolutely perfect.

Cocking a brow, Jean-Daniel stepped back. "You're different from other girls."

"You already said that."

"So I did."

She wanted to ask how she was different, but she wasn't brave enough.

"You're a very good listener," he said in the husky voice she had longed to hear when he'd been inside the portrait.

She exhaled. "In the past, no one cared what I had to say. That's when I learned to listen."

He smiled broadly. There they were. Those adorable dimples. "I, for one, enjoy talking to you."

"Thank you, Monsieur."

Madame Manard burst in, breathless. "Monsieur le vicomte, Julie is on her way to bring you more water." She hurried over and snatched Ella's bucket off the ground. "Clumsy girl! I followed your damp trail up the stairs and figured you hadn't brought enough."

"It's no matter, Madame Manard," Jean-Daniel said. "She did the best she could."

"I have enough to worry about with the ball drawing near."

Jean-Daniel finished off the last of his wine then slammed the glass on a nearby table. "God damned ball! It's not a good idea to try to make love happen."

That explains why most of the couples on "The Bachelor" don't stay together. Ella repressed a smile.

Madame Manard shook her head. "Madame is insisting."

Jean-Daniel frowned. "My mother may have good intentions, but I'm perfectly capable of finding a wife on my own."

Ella stood before him awkwardly. Did he *want* to find a wife? She held her breath as she waited for him to continue.

Madame Manard wagged her finger. "Are you still here, girl? Find something to do downstairs."

"Yes, Madame." With a sideways glance at Jean-Daniel, Ella headed for the door.

"One moment, Mademoiselle Ella," Jean-Daniel called out. "I'd like my bed turned down at eleven o'clock tonight."

Ella turned to face him. Her glance jumped from his handsome features to the housekeeper's bright red face. Still, Madame Manard said nothing.

After Ella curtsied, she made her way downstairs. With her belly fluttering, she hardly noticed the other servants, intent on their duties. She pushed through the back door in a daze and meandered into the sunshine. Jean-Daniel's image flashed in her mind. Built like a fitness model, he'd been dashing and kind. He'd even listened to her—and had remarked on her beauty in the magical setting of the hunting park.

How could she stay mad at him? Besides, she was here on a dire mission. To save his life.

In spite of the three glasses of wine that Jean-Daniel enjoyed after his ride, he knew he'd been struck by the "thunderbolt." That's what his father had called it. "Love at first sight is rare, my son," he'd said. "If you're lucky enough to find it, don't let it escape your grasp."

As Jean-Daniel watched the new girl disappear from his apartment, he tried to steady his insane heartbeat. She intrigued him. Fascinated him. And he didn't know if he'd ever be the same.

It was all very complicated. Although he'd never set eyes on Ella before today, he felt comfortable around her. As if he'd met her before.

Julie rushed in with more bathwater and Madame Manard drew the curtains, but Jean-Daniel took little notice of them. Instead, he stood in one spot . . . fixated on Ella's image. The girl had the most startling eyes—as blue as a lapis and shaped like a feline's. Her mouth, curved and sensual, spoke illicit things to him, yet it revealed guardedness at the same time. With a creamy pink complexion and a graceful neck, the girl emanated a natural beauty that resonated with him. And certainly the swell of her breasts over her low neckline had called to him in a different way.

Ella enthralled Jean-Daniel physically, but most of all he could talk to her. She'd listened with genuine interest to his complaints. She had even offered intelligent suggestions. Most women twittered and giggled around him. Or they simply agreed with everything he said.

But not her.

Ella seemed older than her years—savvy to the way the world worked. Unspoiled and grounded. Jean-Daniel had been so impressed by her that he'd almost kissed her.

But then he had retreated. Oddly, Ella hadn't thrown herself at him. It made her seem untouchable. And he had never experienced *that* in a woman.

His life was twisting itself into such a knot that he was going to like having Ella around. It would be refreshing to have someone to talk to.

Jean-Daniel stalked to his bedchamber and threw himself on his bed. Landing on his back, he crossed his feet at the ankles and wove his fingers together over his stomach. *Sweet Jesus!* Was he really going to let his mother persuade him into proposing to a woman he didn't love?

If he wanted to keep his title and honor his father's name, he might.

"Why can't I choose my wife?" he muttered, gazing at the ceiling.

According to French law, a vicomte must be betrothed to nobility. He must choose a woman from a respectable family, with roots planted firmly in European soil. A vicomte wasn't supposed to marry a commoner. Or a servant girl, which, he considered after meeting Ella, was a crying shame.

Like two lightning-fast trains passing one another, an event was taking place inside the château three hundred and eleven years in the future.

Ella's cell phone sat in her room. In the emptiness of the house, no one was there to hear it ring.

Mimi left an urgent voicemail message.

"Ella! If you're there, call me back! Stanley Kellogg finally translated the journal pages for you. I'll scan them and send them along in a few minutes.

"In the meantime, *do not wear the Egyptian necklace you found!* It's cursed. Apparently it belonged to an ancient princess who took a forbidden lover . . . a priest in her court. The affair sealed her fate.

The Underworld God, Anubis, cursed the princess, making her kill her lover before committing suicide. Now any woman who wears the necklace—even once—will kill the man she loves and then take her own life.

"The only hope is the bracelet. It was made with the forces of good. But I wouldn't count on it counteracting anything if I were you."

Back in 1703, Ella thought luck was on her side. But she had already worn the necklace on her journey back in time. And she was still wearing it.

CHAPTER 16

"P_{sst!}"

Ella swiveled around. A servant girl, who appeared to be around her age, waved Ella closer.

"I'm Claudia," the girl said. "Follow me."

Ella trailed behind her into the drawing room. Ella knew the room well, but the details were different. She noticed that an enormous tapestry hung where Jean-Daniel's portrait was suspended in present day. And all the furniture shimmered, shiny and new—and void of dust sheets.

"Madame Manard wants you to clean this room from ceiling to floor. Then you must take out the rugs, beat them, and polish the fixtures around the hearth."

Ella sighed. "It's a lot of work getting this house ready for the ball."

"It's imperative that it look spectacular." Claudia paused. "You're a temporary servant, aren't you?"

"Yes."

The auburn-haired girl wrinkled her nose. "Have you ever been in so grand a house, Mademoiselle . . . ?"

"Ella." She couldn't speak about the Fouquet house in contrast, so she said, "This house is certainly grand, but I believe the splendor of the ball will be lost on the vicomte."

"The vicomte?"

"He's against having it."

Claudia's eyes widened. "Where did you hear that?"

Ella searched for an answer. She didn't want to admit she'd heard it from Jean-Daniel's own mouth. She really shouldn't have been talking to him. "Servants gossip . . ."

"Well, they shouldn't be flapping their lips. My mother brought me up in this job, and she said spreading rumors is the kiss of death."

Falling silent, Ella accepted a cleaning rag from Claudia.

"But he *is* impossibly handsome, isn't he?"

"The vicomte?" Ella met the girl's starry-eyed gaze.

"Yes, the vicomte!" gushed Claudia. "He's as nice as pie and as dashing as a king."

He is.

"When some lucky girl marries him," Claudia said, "it'll be a dream come true for her."

"*If* the vicomte decides to marry." Ella said nonchalantly, to hide the fact that her heart was beating faster than wheels spin on a race car.

"He must marry and step up to his duties," Claudia asserted. "If he doesn't, his mother will transfer the vicomte's power to his brother, Baron Girard."

"She can do that?"

Claudia nodded while she helped Ella move some furniture. "When the former Vicomte de Maincy died, his wife, Madame de Maincy, was left in charge. Since her husband had passed on and her oldest son was too young to govern the province, she took over for a while. Now that Jean-Daniel Girard is of age, he's the natural choice to inherit. But if Jean-Daniel shirks his duties and refuses to marry—thus ending the family lineage—Madame has the authority to deem the younger twin the new vicomte."

"If that happens, won't the vicomte be humiliated?"

"No doubt. That's why it's assumed he'll marry—even if he doesn't want to."

This is terrible! Talk about an ill-timed visit. Ella had no idea how long she'd be here. If she stayed, she certainly didn't want to watch Jean-Daniel propose to someone else. Nor did she want to see him marry some unknown girl he didn't love from a neighboring family.

Unfortunately, it was all being planned out for him.

A secret part of her hoped his zest for fun might steer him away from a loveless marriage.

Claudia shrugged. "Apparently, you know little of aristocracy and lineages, but a man born into a title will do anything to honor and keep his social status."

"Ella!" Madame Manard's sing-song voice caused her to whirl around.

"Yes, Madame?"

"The baron is asking for the new girl. He requests you mend his shirt and polish his boots."

Polish his boots? Colbert said they were recently polished!

Fright echoed through her. Colbert Girard was the last man she wanted to be alone with. "Perhaps the Baron's valet can—"

"The Baron's valet is fetching a waistcoat commissioned from a tailor in Maincy."

When Ella hesitated, Madame Manard insisted she go.

"Very well." Face hot, Ella left Claudia in the drawing room and searched for the back stairwell. She wasn't about to get in trouble for using the central staircase again.

Once she reached the second landing, a daunting row of doors greeted her. Which one was Colbert's?

Thankfully, Julie—the thin girl who'd been washing the baseboards downstairs—came toward her carrying a stack of linens.

"Pardon me," Ella called out. "I'm looking for the baron's apartments."

Julie raised a rounded eyebrow. "After you turn the corner, they're the first set of doors on the left."

"Thank you."

Nodding, Julie went about her business.

Ella knocked on the door. As she waited for an answer, her lungs hitched. When no one responded, she turned to go. Then she heard, "Enter, for God's sake!"

Muscles tensed, she stepped into the dimly lit room. She saw no sign of Colbert.

"Close the door behind you," came his voice from deep in the shadows.

Where was he?

Ella shut the door. Slowly, she walked farther into the room.

"I'm in my bedchamber." Shirtless, Colbert Girard was slung casually in a wingback chair. He was harshly handsome—and there was no denying the impressiveness of his geometrically outlined body. With widespread knees, a narrow waist, and a massive torso that formed a *V,* his figure cut the shape of an angular hourglass. Ella could see he was just as muscular and fit as Jean-Daniel. Yet his shifty eyes and brusque manner dampened his attractiveness.

He dangled his shirt toward her. It hung on one finger and Ella wanted to scream. She wasn't a dog being baited by a bone and she refused to give into the wiles Colbert assumed he possessed.

She practically snatched the shirt from him.

He laughed darkly, the hue of his gray eyes descending to a smoky black. "I thought you were a shy one. Now that we're alone, you're showing your spirit, eh?" He spread his knees even wider and flexed his chest muscles.

"No, Monsieur."

"It's tempting to let your guard down behind closed doors."

She took a step back. "I will mend your shirt and have it back to you within the hour."

Colbert seemed displeased. "Did Madame Manard neglect to tell you that I'd like my boots polished, as well?"

Irritation and fright spread through Ella simultaneously. "Where are your boots, Monsieur?"

"Over there."

Ella bent to pick the boots up off the floor. Colbert stood and sauntered toward her.

She gulped. He smelled of expensive cologne, brandy, and raw danger. Her heart drummed and her hands began to shake.

Colbert grabbed her by the arm. "Don't go so soon, my beauty. I'm bored this afternoon. I want to play."

"I'm afraid you'll have to find another playmate."

His lips stretched into a wide smile. In the dim light of the room, he reminded Ella of the Cheshire Cat from *Alice in Wonderland.* White teeth were all she could see for a moment.

"Don't worry, Mademoiselle," he suggested. "If you lack knowledge, I can teach you *how* to play."

She tried to wriggle free of his grasp, but he was too strong.

"What is your name?"

"Ella."

"My lovely Ella, the purpose of a servant is to serve."

He pulled her toward him. The jut of his manhood pressed against her.

Flashes of being overcome by her high school boyfriend seized her. Panic shot through her in hot flashes.

"As you can tell," he growled in that horrible voice Ella had come to hate, "I need servicing."

Scumbag. Brute. Bastard. The words leapt to her mind, but before Ella could spew them, a knock sounded at the door.

"Colbert?" It was Jean-Daniel's voice. Never had Ella heard such a sweet sound.

Colbert released her arm then stepped away. "What is it, brother?"

Ella heard the door click open. A few seconds later, Jean-Daniel marched into the bedchamber.

He eyed Ella and the shirt and boots she held in her hands. After giving her a nod, his gaze flickered to Colbert, who had resumed his seat in the wingback chair. The scene looked perfectly normal.

Had Jean-Daniel noticed Ella's flaming cheeks and shallow breath?

"Join me for a drink in the library?" Jean-Daniel asked his brother.

"Why me?" Colbert retorted. A sneer accompanied the nasty remark.

"I want to discuss business with you. The king's courtiers have contacted me again." Jean-Daniel lowered his voice when he spoke the second sentence. It gave Ella the impression that he wished to discuss a private topic with his twin.

"Very well." Colbert pushed himself out of the chair. "There is nothing much happening here."

Night had fallen by the time Ella crept down the back stairwell and tiptoed to the library. The door was shut, but the sound of flaring tempers penetrated it.

Ella grabbed her stomach. She hated when anyone argued. She was a peacemaker by nature. Regardless, she wanted to know what was transpiring.

Pressing her ear to the door, she listened. Never before had she heard such angry voices. Weren't twins supposed to have a special bond? Best friends for life . . . that sort of thing?

"Jean-Daniel. You are not the courtier type!" thundered Colbert.

"Who are you to say? Your jealousy taints all your thoughts."

"That is not true."

"Admit it. You have resented me since birth."

"You don't know what you're talking about," Colbert ground out.

"Try and see this my way, Col. If I go to Versailles and become a courtier of the king, it will be a two-fold mission. I can learn a great deal about government from Louis. Furthermore, it's a way to represent our province well in the modern world."

"Louis—*Le Roi Soleil*—will have a bad effect on you," Colbert seethed. "Even I have the ability to recognize that!"

"You're wrong," Jean-Daniel said. "Louis has an incredible head for politics. Even you can't deny that under his rule, this nation has become the pre-eminent power of Europe."

Colbert's voice grew louder. "It isn't that. I know you, brother, and you're easily swayed. Soon you'll become a creampuff like Louis. Did you know he stands for hours on end in front of his hall of mirrors? *And* did you know he's recently commissioned fourteen statues of himself. Fourteen!"

"Louis's tremendous confidence is justified." Jean-Daniel's voice grew steely.

Colbert paused. "Don't you agree that the King has a penchant for vanity?"

"Perhaps. But *I'm* not vain, Colbert."

"Then you need to stop thinking of yourself for once. If you take up residence at Versailles, you will be leaving your people high and dry."

"I'm going for the good of the province," argued Jean-Daniel. "Besides, it is a temporary situation—and you'll be in charge while I'm gone. Isn't that what you've always wanted?"

Ella heard Colbert gulp a drink. "No. While you rub elbows with the king of France, I'll be governing a piddling, forgotten province as its temporary head. Congratulations to me."

There was a pause. A chair scraped loudly along the parquet floor. Jean-Daniel began speaking in a softer voice so Ella barely heard him.

She pressed her ear closer against the door as her nervousness escalated. If she were found eavesdropping at the door, she'd be carted back to Lady Fouquet, whoever this lady was, in a heartbeat.

"Colbert," Jean-Daniel said, "why can't you be happy for me?"

Another chair scraped along the floor, and Ella guessed Colbert had flown out of it. She imagined the dark-haired twin scowling. "Try walking a mile in my boots, Jean-Daniel. I've been snubbed at every turn. And now this?"

"If you can't see the opportunity through your jealousy," Jean-Daniel said gravelly, "I feel sorry for you."

There was a crash. Ella cringed. Apparently, some sort of porcelain object had shattered into a hundred pieces. She listened again.

"You're a fool, brother!" Colbert raged. "There has been backlash concerning some of Louis's latest decisions. That makes you unpopular in some people's eyes right now."

A moment of silence ensued. "Are you saying I should protect myself?"

Footfalls in the hallway made Ella feign interest in a plant. Julie walked past her without saying a word.

Tearing herself away from Colbert and Jean-Daniel's conversation, Ella headed for the kitchen. As smells of a lavish dinner assaulted her, her stomach rumbled.

Grateful that she wasn't a kitchen servant, she sat at a large farmhouse table and took her clogs off. They didn't fit properly and were giving her a blister. As she rubbed her feet, none of the other servants spoke to her. Nor did they address her at supper. It was a silent affair—unlike the television programs Ella had watched that involved upstairs aristocrats and downstairs servants.

After consuming a hearty meal, she grew tired. She heard the longcase clock chime nine bells. Must she stay awake for two more hours to turn down Jean-Daniel's bed?

Claudia offered to show Ella to her room—a tiny space they would share during Ella's stay. Ella remembered the room because it was one of the bedchambers she'd stuck her head into the first day she arrived at the château. Located near the entry to the attic loft where she'd gazed upon Jean-Daniel's portrait for the first time, the tiny room contained two twin beds, a wash stand, and a small wardrobe.

After Ella bathed, she lay on top of the small bed assigned to her and forced herself to stay awake. Then again, how could she sleep? While Claudia changed into her nightgown, the auburn-haired girl chattered on about how demanding Madame Manard was and how intimidating Colbert Girard could be.

Of course, Claudia had nothing negative to say about Jean-Daniel. In fact, Ella caught more traces of the girl's infatuation with him as she relayed his daily activities in a dreamy voice.

"Sometimes," Claudia said, "I even spy on him as he rides. He takes off like a Roman god on horseback, with that adorable dog at his heels."

"You spy on him?" Ella tried not to sound judgmental.

"Yes." Claudia lowered her voice. "But I have to be careful. One time I nearly got caught crouching behind a bush. That's when I lowered myself down the well and used the secret passageway."

"There's a secret passageway inside the well?" Ella knew she sounded like a parrot, but the information was fascinating.

Claudia nodded. "The former vicomte created it when he built the château. A trap door inside leads straight to the basement of the house. From there, you can climb a set of stone steps that brings you to a false wall in the drawing room."

"It sounds like a funhouse."

"A funhouse?" Claudia raised an eyebrow in confusion.

"Never mind."

Ella crossed her ankles and stared up at the ceiling. No doubt every woman in the province would spy on Jean-Daniel if she had the chance. Those same women had probably begun to groom and polish their etiquette in preparation for the ball. If a woman looked and acted her best during the dance, perhaps she would ensnare Jean-Daniel with her charms.

Not only would marriage with him lead to a sky-high social status, he was quite a catch. Even the maids were falling for him!

But Ella wasn't jealous. She'd definitely felt a spark of attraction ignite between them during their encounters today. What's more, it was *his* spirit that had pulled her through the painting, bringing her back in time.

She rolled on her side. She mustn't forget the most important reason she was here. To help Jean-Daniel. And she must discover how she could come to his aid.

Inside the ballroom, two flights below, the clock chimed eleven times. Ella looked over at Claudia. The pudgy-faced girl was fast asleep. Sucking in a breath, Ella removed the glass slippers and the Egyptian bracelet from her apron and hid them under her bed. She didn't want to take a chance that she'd shatter the slippers or lose the enchanted piece of jewelry.

Once she got dressed, she crept out the door and made her way to the kitchen. Then she brewed some tea and hurried to Jean-Daniel's apartments. The whole way, her body quaked at the possibility of running into Colbert.

The teacup clattered against its saucer as she knocked on Jean-Daniel's door.

"Come in," he called out.

Pushing through, Ella entered the sitting area portion of his chambers. Jean-Daniel was nowhere to be found, so she walked to his bedroom. He sat on a window seat, cross-legged, with his back to her.

"Monsieur le vicomte," she said softly, "I brought you some tea."

He swiveled around. To Ella's horror, he had a black eye.

"Monsieur!" she cried.

"It's nothing."

Assuming Colbert had given Jean-Daniel the black eye after she left her eavesdropping spot outside the library, Ella was tempted to call the dark twin every name in the book. Yet she wasn't supposed to be listening to the Girard brothers argue at the door.

She set the teacup down by Jean-Daniel's bed and came to stand in front of him. "How did you get that, Monsieur?"

"I guess my brother doesn't see eye-to-eye with my political views."

Still shocked, Ella said nothing.

"It was a joke. Eye-to-eye. Black eye?" He dropped his smile. "Sorry, it wasn't a good joke. Anyway, my eye is throbbing."

"I'll fix that." Ella padded to the dressing room. It was an enormous space, complete with six armoires full of clothes, a basin for shaving, and a glorious claw-foot tub. She picked up a towel, poured some cool water into the basin from a pitcher and dipped the towel in. After she studied an army of bottles sitting by the bathtub, she selected some lavender oil. Pouring a few drops onto the damp towel, she took in the familiar scent.

"Here, Monsieur." Ella handed the towel to Jean-Daniel. "Keep your eye closed. The lavender oil may sting it if it gets inside."

Jean-Daniel did as she suggested. "That feels good."

Ella smiled. At Adelaide's request, she would rub lavender oil on her stepmother's temples when she had a headache. It had soothing properties.

"It smells peaceful."

"Do you pour a few drops in your bathwater at night, as I do?" she asked gently. "It helps me sleep."

"I might if I stopped bathing at three o'clock in the afternoon." He grinned.

She laughed lightly.

"Please sit." He indicated the window seat bench.

Hesitating, she sat stiffly and laced her fingers together.

"As I said, I don't bite."

Jean-Daniel had no idea the effect he had over her. Still, she wasn't ready to reveal her attraction to him. That's why she'd just as soon remain on the opposite side of the bench.

"Did the baron really give you a black eye, Monsieur?" she asked.

"Yes. We had a heated argument." He paused as he set the towel in his lap. "I'll let you in on a little secret. The baron is tempestuous and can be vulgar with women, but he has incredible passion for affairs of state. I may not agree with his views, but in some regards he'd make a dedicated vicomte."

Ella had a whole lot to say about Colbert but it wasn't about his passion for politics, so she stopped herself. "I'm sure *you're* a good vicomte."

"Not that I couldn't be. It's just that I haven't applied myself."

"Did your father give you much advice?" Ella didn't know if she was overstepping her bounds as a servant, but she was inspired to speak openly. After all, Jean-Daniel was doing the same.

"My father died when I was eight," Jean-Daniel said solemnly.

"So did my father."

Jean-Daniel looked astonished. "That's a coincidence!" He ran a hand through his hair. "Eight was a difficult age. I was mature enough to register the impact of his loss. But I was also childish enough to be angry about it."

"That's how I felt. Although I was more sad than angry."

He shifted his position on the bench so that he was facing her directly. "What was your father like?"

Ella squared her shoulders and smiled. "He was smart and loving and artistic. He used to call me his princess."

"I'm sure he loved you very much."

"I think he did. What was *your* father like?"

Jean-Daniel gazed out to the darkened gardens. "He was wise and fair and funny. All the things a father and a nobleman should be—wrapped up in one."

"I have a feeling you have those same qualities."

"Some of them." Jean-Daniel met her stare. Ella tried not to swoon like a schoolgirl under it. "I just need to apply myself more to the business of economics and finance. I'm afraid I prefer other distractions."

"If your brother has a good sense for those things, why don't you consult him about certain matters?"

Jean-Daniel's face was awash with approval. "You're very intelligent, aren't you?"

"Thank you." Now she was sure she was blushing.

"I *would* let my brother advise me; it's just that we have this damned competitive wall between us. Colbert has always been jealous of me. In his defense, it would be hard to have been born the younger twin. But there it is."

"Where you never close? Even as boys?"

"Never. Colbert and I always fought like cats and dogs. Luckily, I'm strong enough to protect myself when he gets angry."

Ella shuddered. She glanced down at the bruise Colbert's grip had left on her arm.

In the moment, she wanted to concentrate on how strong Jean-Daniel was. While he returned the towel to his eye, she snatched a glimpse of his solid physique. A snug-fitting silk shirt tucked into his narrow waistband showcased the muscle-bound chest Ella had glimpsed earlier. His face astounded her in the golden glow of the candlelight. His aquamarine eyes—at least the one that wasn't black and swollen—shimmered with interest in what she had to say while his skin gleamed with an appealing tan.

"Do you have siblings, Mademoiselle?"

The subject roiled Ella's stomach. "Stepsisters. But we aren't close."

"So your father remarried before he died?"

"Yes. Unfortunately."

"My mother may be a royal pain," Jean-Daniel said, "but I love her dearly." He got up and paced the room. "I just wished she'd give up on this ball business."

"Isn't it just a ball?" Ella decided to feign ignorance.

"Not quite." Jean-Daniel shoved his hand through his hair. The gesture made his locks fall across his forehead in shaggy layers. He was boyish and charming and seductive all at once and the combination spurred Ella's heart to beat erratically. "My mother has organized the party as a venue for me to meet marriage-worthy women."

"Is she anxious for grandchildren?"

"My mother has more in mind than grandchildren," he went on.

Ella drew her brows together. "Such as?"

Jean-Daniel sat again. "Family honor and lineage are things you might not be familiar with, but they rule *our* world. My mother insists it's time I grow up and fulfill my duties to the maximum potential."

"And that means finding a wife." Ella spoke the words more to herself than to him. The notion ripped at her soul.

"Yes," Jean-Daniel answered darkly.

Ella leaned forward on one locked arm. He did the same.

"I know," he said softly, "it's difficult to feel sorry for me. I seem to have the world at my fingertips."

"Money and power cannot buy happiness."

"Very well put," he murmured. He met her gaze again. Ella sucked in an anxious breath.

"I've never met anyone like you," he said.

In a slow, drawn-out motion, he lowered the towel and scooted toward her.

"Tell me more about yourself, Ella."

"What would you like to know?"

"What is the most spontaneous thing you've ever done?"

Travel over three hundred years to be with you. She shook herself. "I'm afraid I'm not very spontaneous."

"If you spend enough time with me, that will change."

Her insides tingled. As he craned his neck forward, Ella watched him lick his lips. Would he steal a kiss? Rational thoughts filled her head. Surely it was forbidden for a nobleman to kiss a servant. Still, the distance she'd traveled to get that kiss was mindboggling. And she wanted it more than anything.

Irrational thoughts replaced her rational ones. She could hardly breathe.

His face came closer to hers. It'd been years since she'd been kissed—and she'd never been kissed by anyone like Jean-Daniel.

In a husky voice, he asked, "May I?"

The flames of the candles crackled and wind blew softly against the window. Amid the soft noises, desire sizzled between Ella and Jean-Daniel. She nodded.

Swooping forward, Jean-Daniel pressed his lips to hers. A spark—as magical as Ella's journey through time—heated her every inch. His mouth was warm and moist and when he cupped her chin with his hand, she tilted deeper into it. Moaning, he kissed her gently at first. His tentativeness gave her the impression that he was hesitant to break the rules. But then he traced the outline of her lips with his tongue and darted it inside.

Nothing had ever felt more delicious.

What other woman had traveled centuries for one of Jean-Daniel's kisses? No one.

Powerful, sweet, and purely male, Jean-Daniel gave another moan. The wonderful noise prompted Ella to be bolder than she'd ever been. Senses roaring, she licked across his top lip and savored its salty flavor. Driving herself toward him, she yearned for him to pull her into his arms, where he might do so many things to her.

Fortunately, the single kiss was so satisfying that if Ella died tomorrow she would die happy and fulfilled.

Jean-Daniel pulled away, breathless. "You're a very special woman."

Pulse speeding, she drew back, too.

"Thank you for listening to me," he said.

She smiled. "You're welcome."

"I think I'll be very grown up tonight and turn down my own bed."

"Very well," she replied, cheeks heated.

With that, they parted ways. During Ella's walk to her own bed, she touched her still-scorching lips.

The kiss would remain their secret.

CHAPTER 17

Over the next few days, the palace's buzz about the ball grew. Moving at a rapid pace, the servants hung spectacular new drapes in the ballroom, hosted tailors who'd come to measure Jean-Daniel for a special suit, and accommodated renowned chefs from Paris who had arrived to organize the menu.

Ella got caught up in the excitement, too. Of course, the pace proved overwhelming at times. Adding to her stress were her raw hands. Her calluses had begun to form calluses! Red and chapped, they looked as they had under Adelaide's thumb in Santa Barbara.

While most of the servants were assigned to certain parts of the house in order to perform designated chores, Ella's duties encompassed a wide range of tasks in various locations. Plucking chickens, mopping, light gardening, fetching water, and laundry topped the list. Unfortunately, the one thing Ella hadn't done was cook. Each time she entered the kitchen, she longed to whip up something spectacular.

"I think I've accomplished everything I was supposed to do," she murmured as she made her way to the kitchen. She was looking forward to sinking into a chair when she heard Madame Manard's voice rattle down the hall.

"Mademoiselle Ella! Don't even think about sitting down! It's two o'clock. Time for tea in the drawing room."

"Tea? Isn't that Julie's duty?"

Madame Manard came closer, her beefy face crimson. "That girl has gotten herself into trouble with the baron's valet."

"Bernard?" Ella whispered sharply.

"Yes." The housekeeper paused. To Ella's surprise, she rubbed her chin. "Odd pairing, don't you think?"

Very. Julie, who was tall and thin, hovered over short and portly Bernard. One lacked personality while the other oozed a quick wit. There seemed to be no outward chemistry between them. *Go figure.*

"Anyhow," Madame Manard continued, "Julie is crying in her room so it's left to you to bring tea."

The housekeeper departed and Ella set into action. She warmed a few ounces of milk, poured a few scoops of coarse sugar into a decorative bowl, and then gathered teacups, saucers, spoons, and an assortment of fine cakes. The tea smelled heavenly as she transported it to the drawing room. She wished she could take a sip.

Did people in the eighteenth century know about the benefits of caffeine in the afternoon?

She knocked.

"Please enter," called a pleasant female voice.

Ella stepped inside the drawing room and her eyes swept the space. Jean-Daniel's mother, Madame de Maincy, a fine-boned, middle aged woman with a shining head of chestnut hair, sat primly on a settee. Sour-faced Colbert stood by the mantel, shoulders hulking. Lastly, Jean-Daniel sat sprawled in a chair by the window, one leg over the armrest. Rémy lay contentedly beside him.

Jean-Daniel flashed a brilliant smile. Nerves humming, Ella set the tray down. Pretending to busy herself with the tea, she offered him a secretive smile from beneath her cap brim. Meanwhile, she noticed his black eye had taken on a lighter, purplish color.

"I take mine with cream and sugar, my dear," said Madame de Maincy. "Add nothing to the boys' cups." The noblewoman spoke in a clear, energetic voice. Ella would have liked her except for the fact that she was trying to marry her son off to someone else.

"We aren't *boys* anymore, Mother." Colbert crossed his arms and leaned his back against the wall.

"I spent twelve hours in labor with you and Jean-Daniel." She frowned. "The least you can do is humor me now."

Jean-Daniel mirrored his mother's expression. "For once I agree with Colbert. You must stop interfering with our lives, Mother. About this ball business—"

"I think you'll be pleased with the arrangements I've made," Madame de Maincy said excitedly. "We'll have the best of everything! Oh, and I hear Madame de Vaudreuil's niece has grown into quite a beauty."

"I saw her in Paris," Colbert growled. "She still has knobby elbows and yellow teeth."

"Beauty is in the eye of the beholder," his mother chirped.

After Ella watched Jean-Daniel roll his eyes, she returned her attention to the tea tray.

"Promise me you won't be rude to the girls who attend the ball, Jean-Daniel," Ella heard the noblewoman instruct.

"I'm never *rude*. Disinterested, maybe."

"I beg you to give each girl a chance."

He let out a loud, resigned sigh. "If it means that much to you."

"After you meet the girl of your dreams, brother," Colbert smirked, "I'll take your leftovers. As always."

"We don't talk like that in this house, Colbert!"

"Sorry, Mother." Colbert exchanged an annoyed glance with his twin.

Ella distributed the tea. Madame de Maincy thanked her politely. Colbert flung her a hungry look, and Jean-Daniel beamed at her. When she returned to the tea tray, she was still listening intensely.

The noblewoman cleared her throat. "I only want you to have the kind of marriage your father and I had, Jean-Daniel."

"Your marriage wasn't arranged," Colbert pointed out.

"I want the happy union you and Father had, too." Jean-Daniel set his cup down. "But mine won't be grounded in true love if I don't fall in love on my own."

"Son, you *haven't* found the right girl on your own. That's my point. I want to speed up the process."

"No. You're interfering, Mother."

"It's done out of love." The noblewoman accepted a cake from Ella and bit into it. "This is excellent, my dear."

"Thank you, Madame."

"Now, Jean-Daniel," his mother continued. "It's time to pose for your painting again."

Tuning out the rest of the conversation, Ella made for the door. Before she left, she turned to Jean-Daniel. While no one else was watching, he mouthed, "Meet me outside at six o'clock."

She slipped out the door. Not a minute later, Claudia grabbed her by the arm.

"It's all very exciting!" Rosy-cheeked, Claudia hurried her along the hallway.

"What is?" Ella asked.

"The renowned painter, Michél LeBeau, wants to add a group of servant girls to the background of the vicomte's portrait. He's chosen me, you, and Marguerite!"

Ella's knees buckled. *This is how I came to be depicted in the lavender field!* It was all too strange. "How did Monsieur LeBeau select us?"

Claudia shrugged. "He's been milling about the château this morning, contemplating. You probably didn't notice him."

There *had* been a slew of people in and out of the house in the past few days.

"LeBeau thinks we'll add a sense of *humanity* to the painting," Claudia went on. "Whatever that means!"

Ella stopped in her tracks. It was hot outside. How long would they have to pose? Or pretend to work in the blazing sun?

"Come along!" Claudia said excitedly.

The girls hurried into the bright sunshine. They were joined by Marguerite, a young girl with black hair who didn't seem nearly as excited as Claudia to be part of the painting process. Nevertheless, it was a glorious day. A cloudless sky provided a canopy for billowing breezes and swaying, low-lying trees. A sense of the carefree radiated in the air.

Ella held onto her cap as she followed Claudia to their designated position. Michél emerged from the house, a beret atop his bald head and a paint-splattered smock buttoned over his clothes. Two footmen carried Jean-Daniel's painting behind him. A third lugged painting supplies. Out came Jean-Daniel next, wearing that damned periwig. Ella smiled.

Ears bouncing, Rémy yapped at his heels and streamed across the fields as free as a bird.

Before Jean-Daniel moved to his spot and assumed his solemn pose, he offered Ella a brilliant grin. Claudia gazed at him with adoring eyes. Did the girl think he was smiling at her? Ella didn't want to spoil her fun.

"Yes, Mademoiselles," LeBeau said, cocking an eyebrow. "Concentrate on your work, as you usually do. I want 'natural' today."

Jean-Daniel unbuttoned the stiff collar of his jacket. LeBeau caught him grinning.

"No, Monsieur le vicomte!" the temperamental artist cried. "We've been over this. You are forbidden to change anything about your pose! I am trying to paint with detail and capture a sense of dignity."

Ella couldn't see Jean-Daniel's face, but she assumed he was rolling his eyes.

Once Rémy settled at Jean-Daniel's feet, LeBeau began to paint. "Mademoiselles!" he shouted. "Assume a pose and maintain it like a statue."

Since Ella had no idea what she was doing in the fields, she copied Claudia and Julie. She began to perspire and was tempted to remove her fichu, but she wanted to keep the amulet hidden. To distract herself, she began to hum a little tune. Soon Julie and Claudia joined in and Ella began to enjoy herself as the afternoon stretched on.

So this is what modeling meant in the eighteenth century!

Claudia nudged Ella. "I'm anxious to see what the painting looks like. What *we* look like." The girl cast a glance at Jean-Daniel's backside and sighed. Then she resumed her fixed position.

Ella mumbled a faint response in agreement, but she already knew how the painting turned out in the end.

Bustling like a mother hen, Madame Manard brought lemonade for everyone, including the servant girls. As they sipped it during a break, Ella locked eyes with Jean-Daniel. Had anyone noticed their connection? Her heart sped.

LeBeau painted for several more hours. Ella was starting to feel faint when she heard, "A-ha! I'm finally finished!!" LeBeau held up his paintbrush like a trophy.

"Thank God," she said under her breath.

The girls moved toward the artist and Jean-Daniel. Jean-Daniel came round the easel, but when he looked upon the painting he pursed his lips in disapproval. Before the young ladies could view it, Madame Manard shooed Ella, Marguerite, and Claudia inside.

The girls removed their caps and fanned themselves.

"I know," clucked the housekeeper. "You wanted to see the finished product, but you'll get to view the vicomte's portrait when it hangs in the drawing room, soon enough. Now get to your unfinished work."

A few more chores kept Ella busy until six o'clock. Fortunately, no one saw her slip outside to keep her date with Jean-Daniel.

She ventured to the gardens. Anxiousness fanned over her as she waited for him to appear. To distract herself, she took in the beauty of the lush commons. Blooming jonquils, fragrant roses, and bright azaleas lined the boxwood rows. A half dozen cypress trees swayed hypnotically to the rhythm of the stone fountain while Ella inhaled the fresh air.

Giving a little smile, she sat on the edge of the fountain. A waft of wind blew over her face and relaxed her. She was getting plenty of exercise doing chores, but it had been days since she jogged. She itched to kick off her clogs and go for a run.

If only she had her cross-trainers.

What she was grateful for was the fact that she hadn't been flung out of the past yet. Her time here was still a reality, and she needed to remain here until the night of the ball. She only hoped she'd learn *how* she was supposed to save Jean-Daniel's life.

Unfortunately she couldn't ask him.

Her thoughts flew to their stolen kiss. She'd searched the château for Jean-Daniel everywhere since then, but it seemed their schedules conflicted lately. When he was riding, she was scrubbing the windows. When he was reading in the library, she was scouring pots in the kitchen. And when he was arguing with his brother, she was beating rugs in the courtyard.

Ella had thought about bringing him some evening tea last night, but had decided against it. She'd learned in her short time here that an aristocrat must ask a servant to do something or that servant didn't do it at all. Thus, knocking on Jean-Daniel's door with a cup of tea would be a breach of her duties.

At least she got to see him today.

The thunder of hooves snagged her attention. Like a valiant knight on his steed, Jean-Daniel flew over the fields adjacent to the gardens on horseback. Back straight, he gripped the reins with sure and steady hands. Ella smiled at the concentration washing over his face.

Once he slowed down, he caught sight of her. She tucked a lock of hair behind her ear and waved. A huge smile brightened his handsome features. With a swoop of his arm, he invited her into the woods.

Excitement pinged to every part of her body. She wanted to be alone with him and now was her chance.

Treading deep into the woodland, they said nothing. Jean-Daniel dismounted. When he turned to face her, he dropped his horse's reins.

"What did you think of the conversation I had with my mother?" he asked.

"She definitely cares about you."

He picked up a white dandelion. Twirling it in circles, he blew at its seeds. The seeds shimmered and floated like pixie dust in the waning sunlight. "She cares too much, I think."

"There is no such thing," Ella said quietly. "You're lucky to have her." She hadn't really known her mother, and she'd give anything to reverse the sad truth.

He stepped closer. Ella looked down at her clogs.

"I missed you," he remarked.

She blushed furiously.

Gently, he raised her chin so they could lock eyes. "I enjoyed our kiss the other night."

"So did I." She spoke shyly.

Face full of interest, he studied her. Languidly, he ran the back of his hand along her cheek. "Your skin is so soft. And your face is so naturally beautiful."

She gave him a tiny smile before she cast her gaze away.

"Do I make you nervous?"

"In a good way."

"You're more beautiful than this lovely day," he said kindly.

Her heart soared.

He took in a breath. "I love natural things. I've made it a point to learn a great deal about them."

"You like botany?"

"Yes, I also love animals."

She bent down and plucked at an unfamiliar plant. "What is this bush called?"

"Wood sorrel."

"And that?" She pointed to a flowering plant.

"Lady's mantle." He scoured the ground. "This is Astilbe. Beside it lies a cluster of toad lilies."

"My goodness. You are knowledgeable." She moved to his horse and stroked the stallion's side. "And what interests you about animals?"

"Animals are free to roam the outdoors at whim. No one tells them what to do—at least when they're in the wild. Plus, they're able to choose their mates."

She laughed. "No arranged marriages for them."

He joined her at his horse. "Still, some animals, such as swans, mate for life."

Eyes darkening, he stroked the horse, too. Attraction spread over Ella like a warm blanket. His fingers touched hers and she gave a tiny smile.

"Let's sit in a shady spot and discuss everything under the sun," he suggested.

Ella was beginning to get his sense of humor.

For hours, they jabbered away. They compared their interests and their families, mulled over the state of France, discussed their likes and dislikes, and shared their hopes and their dreams as day turned into night.

A galaxy of stars materialized. Under it, Jean-Daniel lay with his head next to Ella's. They stretched their legs in opposite directions and folded their hands over their stomachs.

"I just saw a shooting star!" Jean-Daniel cried.

"So did I!"

"Make a wish," he instructed.

Ella did.

He raised himself up on one elbow and looked down at her. "What did you wish for?"

She shook her head. "Can't tell."

"Why not?"

She frowned. Jean-Daniel must not know the rule. Was it a modern belief? "If someone tells a wish, it won't come true."

Grinning, he lay on the ground again. "You are definitely smarter than me." He added, "All right. I won't reveal my wish because I desperately want it to come true."

Gazing up at the evening sky, she smiled.

"I could talk to you for hours," he said lazily.

"You just have," she joked.

He let out one of his great big laughs. "So I have, Ella. So I have."

She laughed, too.

When he raised himself up again, he thrust her an astonished look. "I just realized that I don't know your last name."

Her heart lurched. "Benoit. My last name is Benoit."

Just before they parted ways for the night, he said dreamily. "Ella Benoit. The sweetest name ever to roll off my tongue. Say you'll meet me here tomorrow night, Ella Benoit."

She agreed without hesitation.

CHAPTER 18

When Ella rose in the morning, she practically leapt out of bed. She would see Jean-Daniel tonight. He was able to both calm and excite her—an ideal combination in her eyes. She needed a man she could really talk to. She'd held things in for so long that it felt incredible to express herself. It also felt wonderful to be listened to.

While Jean-Daniel's life had been a fairly smooth ride, hers had been bumpy. While he'd never worked hard at any one thing, she'd had no room for triviality in her focused existence. They were fascinated by the other's experiences, riveted by how and why the other one pushed on.

During their conversation under the stars, Jean-Daniel had vowed to start taking life more seriously. Ella, on the other hand, had sworn the very opposite thing.

"My lovely Ella," he said when night had fallen and she'd kept her promise to sneak out to meet him in the woodland. "Tell me more about your passion for cooking."

Jean-Daniel nestled his head in her lap. Smiling, Ella plucked the petals off a flower. "I've always wanted to cook for the crowned heads of Europe."

"I'm not a crowned head, but I'm a nobleman. Do I count?"

"Certainly." *You count more than anyone in the world.*

Gazing up, he moistened his lips. "What would you prepare?"

"I'd start with a delicious hors d'oeuvre. Stuffed mushrooms, perhaps. Then I'd serve some *pôchouse*." Her stomach rumbled at the thought of the fish stewed in red wine. "For an entrée I'd make boeuf bourguignon, and after fixing a salad with walnuts, endive and watercress, I'd whip up a special dessert. Something called a doughnut."

"A doughnut? Sounds fascinating. What is it? A bunch of nuts folded into dough?"

Ella laughed as she stroked his hair. "No, but I promise you'd love it."

"Mmm," he purred. "A meal cooked by you. I'll bet your meat would be succulent and your dessert . . . oh-so-sweet."

His tone is so sensual!

As he reached up and traced the lines of her face, she envisioned his hand somewhere else against her bare skin. Caressing. Teasing. Leaving a fiery imprint.

He continued. "Will you cook for me sometime, Ella?"

"I'd be happy to."

A panel of stars sparkled overhead and fireflies buzzed around them. The mood proved magical.

Jean-Daniel ran his thumb across her bottom lip. "May I kiss you again?"

After she nodded, he guided her head down until her mouth touched his. An undeniable spark burned between them. Slipping his tongue forward, he wove it around hers. She felt his entire body rise up. When he shifted to a sitting position, he drew her against him and his wild heartbeat matched hers. Dissolving into a giddy puddle, Ella felt a stirring between her legs. *Will he try to do more than kiss me tonight?*

Suddenly, she was scared. Jean-Daniel entwined his fingers with hers, but she retracted her hand.

"Tell me," he urged, "why are you so shy?"

"I'm shy around men."

"Why?"

"I was in a situation once," her gut clenched at the memory, "where I didn't feel safe."

He lowered his timbre. If a voice could sound like satin, his did. "You're safe with me, Ella."

She gulped.

Gently, he snaked a hand around her waist and drew her close. With his other hand, he fingered the strands of hair that escaped her cap. "May I?"

She nodded and he tugged off the cap. Her hair tumbled down in one swoop. She tucked a large piece behind her ear.

"My God." Jean-Daniel gasped. "It's beautiful. Like the color of sunshine in the morning."

Her eyes widened. *That's what he said to me in my dream!* She couldn't help but tremble. Would they act out her erotic dream right now?

His admiring gaze slid over her. She remembered the feel of his mouth on hers and she wanted it again. Could he give her the life she'd always dreamed of? More than that, she wanted to be the beautiful girl *he* loved.

Perhaps they could defy the odds and be together under the most unusual circumstances.

Throwing inhibition to the wind, Ella reacted when Jean-Daniel drew her into a flaming kiss. As he clamped his mouth over hers, all of her emotions, hopes, and dreams spilled forth. The tight way he grasped her told her that he desired to be with her. Maybe, just maybe, it meant he'd never treat her as inferior or discard her.

In fact—though it might be unfair to him—she was placing the gambit of having any faith in men in his hands.

Jean-Daniel devoured her with more kisses . . . each hotter and richer than the one before. As he held her face in both hands, he trailed his tongue over her bottom lip, scorching her skin with it, tasting her flavor and readying her lust. Slowly, carefully, he inserted his tongue past her lips. Like hot caramel, it melted with hers.

Giving her a small tug at the waist, he eased her onto the ground. Once he placed his weight on one hip, he slipped a hand under her head. The other hand roamed her body, deftly tracing her skin from her collarbone to her cleavage. Her low neckline gave him a peek at the rise of her breasts. The sight made him grunt.

"You're my perfect woman," he whispered.

Jean-Daniel kissed her neck and proceeded to untie her *fichu*. Before she could protest, he slipped the neckerchief off and stared at the Egyptian amulet.

"This is beautiful," he said. "Where did you get it?"

"It was a gift from someone special."

"Someone . . . special? Should I be jealous?"

"Not at all."

"Good."

Ella held her breath as Jean-Daniel's tongue traveled the expanse of her neck, and then lower, to her chest. Tugging at her dress, he kissed her shoulder before he exposed a breast. As he pulled her peach-colored nipple into his mouth, she saw heavenly angels. Like an expert, he nipped and laved at it—and even used his teeth.

Squirming against the scalding fire that burned between her legs, Ella closed her eyes. The darkness heightened the feel of Jean-Daniel at her breasts and she gasped as he sucked her nipple into a taut peak. His manly scent surrounded her. Swearing she'd never known such bliss before, she pulled his head closer to her bare breast.

The hard ridge of his shaft pressed against her thigh. Although it was long and stiff and frightened her slightly, it offered her evidence of his attraction. How many times had she thought herself unattractive and unworthy? Not now. She trusted Jean-Daniel. He seemed to desire her, too.

"As you can see, I want you." He gave her a dashing grin. It lifted the mood, but Ella's pleasure still pounded in her ears.

He rolled his weight over her halfway. As he dragged up her skirts, the sound of rough muslin filled the air. Unabashedly, Jean-Daniel ran his fingers higher. She bucked her hips a little while he splayed hot kisses along her neck.

"I want to pleasure you, Ella. Has anyone done that before?"

She blinked up at the haze of twilight, too tense to answer him. This is always where she stiffened.

"Hmm," he purred as he located her fleece and slid his fingers along her folds. They were damp, ready for him. But then Ella froze some more.

"I'm sorry," she managed to whisper.

He seemed surprised but then he kissed her cheek. "It's all right, my lovely."

"You've turned me into a puddle of want. Then I clammed up. You're probably angry."

"I'm not angry at all." He removed his hand. She studied the sincerity in his handsome face. "It's my fault. I should have gone slower."

"It's not you. It's just . . . memories."

"Some bastard really hurt you, didn't he?"

She nodded. "He stole my innocence away." A tear slipped from the corner of her eye.

"With me, you don't have to be afraid." Jean-Daniel wiped the tear away before it drizzled into her ear. "You're so beautiful that I want to be intimate with you, but we can certainly wait."

But we don't have much time . . .

There was a crunching of grass. Ella's heart thrummed. A shadow fell over them.

"Ella!"

Ella recognized the woman. She was Adelaide, risen from the grave.

CHAPTER 19

Jean-Daniel helped Ella cover up. Then he assisted her to her feet. "Madame Fouquet! What are you doing here?"

"I came to fetch my servant. At the château, someone suggested she was outside." She tried to grab Ella by the arm, but Jean-Daniel pulled her away just in time.

"You want Mademoiselle Ella to return to you now?" he asked in alarm.

"Yes. It's a good thing I arrived when I did. How could you shame yourself like this?"

Ella's head reeled. The ground shifted and nausea stuttered up her throat. *This can't be happening!*

Like a raging storm pouring on a merry parade, Adelaide had showed up to ruin the moment. It's what she'd always managed to do before she died.

Confused, Ella tried to sort things out. Was this woman the reincarnation of Adelaide? Or rather, had Adelaide been reincarnated in the future from this time period?

If Ella expressed her questions to an ordinary person, they'd insist she'd see a physician. But she had just traveled three hundred years through a painting. She wasn't exactly fazed by the idea of reincarnation.

Like a rattling bag of bones, Hervé arrived by horseback. He dismounted as hastily as he could. "What is going on here, Monsieur? Is Madame Fouquet creating trouble?"

"Yes," Jean-Daniel answered firmly.

The noblewoman pointed a finger at Ella. "This girl is my servant. Her name is Ella and she's on loan to the château, but I need her back."

"She's staying," said Jean-Daniel firmly.

"Monsieur." Hervé's face flushed. "This is hardly the time or the place to discuss such matters."

If Ella had been a cat, her claws would have come out. As it was, she stood helplessly by.

Jean-Daniel placed Ella behind him. "Ella is a person, Madame. For God's sake, show some compassion."

Madame Fouquet raised her chin. "I mean no disrespect, Monsieur. It's just that my husband passed away recently. I've been left with no money so I've had to rent out my servants. Now I'm suffering from having no help at home."

Hervé raised an eyebrow. "As I recall, you have two daughters— and a stepdaughter."

"Espoir and Charité are weak and fragile." Madame Fouquet sniffled. "In fact, they're very sick. And my stepdaughter is no longer with us."

Espoir and Charité. *Hope and Charity?* Now Ella was the one who felt sick. It was her worst nightmare to be under their thumbs. Or to be at Adelaide's beck and call.

Her nerves teemed, but she tried to calm herself. *At least Espoir and Charité aren't my stepsisters in this century.*

"Ella," Madame Fouquet commanded, "come with me at once. There is much to do at home."

"If you have a servant's contract with Ella," Jean-Daniel addressed the cruel woman with authority, "that contract is under my jurisdiction."

"Sir, we must draw up a formal demand to see Madame Fouquet's documentation concerning Mademoiselle Ella," Hervé reminded him. "Then something can be done about her position."

"We'll speak more about this, Madame," Jean-Daniel promised dourly.

Shock and frustration flushed through Ella as the disagreeable woman gripped her arm. *Why can't I get away from her?*

Jean-Daniel fastened his hands on his hips. "Ella, I hope to see you at the ball."

"Vile, disgusting girl!" Madame Fouquet snarled as she dragged Ella to the Fouquet house. "I've always said you were. Your actions today prove it."

I love Jean-Daniel. Ella wanted to say as much, but since this woman was a version of Adelaide, Ella knew she wouldn't have room in her heart for sympathy. What's more, what did Adelaide know of love?

Ella turned and saw Château de Maincy disappear in the distance. Her heart plummeted. She'd just been pulled out of what could have been the best moment of her life. Perhaps she hadn't been ready to make love to Jean-Daniel, but being in his arms had certainly reaffirmed her faith in intimacy.

His patience and gentleness were all-important. Eventually, he could help Ella overcome her fear of giving herself to somebody physically. She knew it. Considering his tenderness, she might even become an experienced, avid lover.

Madame Fouquet yanked Ella toward a stately house perched over a stream. Smoke blew from a chimney stack at its rooftop and chickens roamed a wide yard that bordered a flower-laden field. It seemed a quaint, nonthreatening place, but if a form of Adelaide and her two daughters lived here, Ella knew better.

Still holding Ella's arm, Madame Fouquet trudged up a small knoll. The sour-faced woman was going on and on about how Ella had embarrassed her.

"I didn't mean to," Ella murmured under her breath.

"What was that?" Madame's eyes narrowed. "You know I hate it when you mumble."

I know.

"I sent you to Château de Maincy as a representative!" the woman said as she shoved her through the front door. "And what do I find? You lying on the ground like some courtesan!"

No one was supposed to see. Trepidatiously, Ella stepped into the parlor. She held onto a chair back to steady herself.

"Charles would have been appalled at how you've represented this household." Madame Fouquet placed a hand over her heart.

Charles, was it? Poor fellow. Had he actually loved his wife the way Ella's father had loved Adelaide? Pain—both sentimental and raw—tore at Ella. Her father wouldn't have been appalled at her liaison with Jean-Daniel. He'd have wanted her to find true love.

Suddenly, she yearned for the copy of *Wuthering Heights* and the glass slippers her father had given her.

Gad! She'd left the slippers and the Egyptian bracelet behind at the château!

She needed those. Perhaps tonight she'd slip back to the château and retrieve them from under her bed.

Espoir and Charité came bounding down the stairs. The hair on Ella's arms stood on end. Rustling with crinoline and hanging on to their poorly starched skirts, the sisters tried to shove each other out of the way. One sported a broken dress strap while the other had food stuck in her teeth. Ella hadn't missed the girls at all. In fact, the sight of Hope and Charity struck her with dread.

Not Hope and Charity. *Espoir* and *Charité.*

"We've been so helpless without you, Ella!" the girls crowed simultaneously.

Ella's hands curled into fists. Body trembling, she hankered to tell the girls and their mother to go to hell. Yet a blockage in her throat materialized. It was the same debilitating lump that'd been ever-present in 2015.

Espoir wagged her finger. "My laundry pile is sky-high and my mending basket is overflowing!"

"My hair," Charité lamented. "I can't do a thing with it!"

"Girls!" Madame Fouquet said sharply. "There are house chores Ella must complete first."

"Why did you let her go to the château in the first place, Mother?" Espoir drew her over-plucked brows together.

"Madame Manard was paying handsomely for extra help. Considering the way you girls spend money, we need income."

The cruel woman of the house came closer to Ella, her hazel eyes full of disdain. "The bequest money is gone. That means we have to work twice as hard to keep this house in order."

You mean I have to work twice as hard.

"Speaking of handsomely—" Charité clasped her chubby hands together. "The vicomte . . ."

"You mean 'speaking of handsome . . .' You're so dense, Charité!"

"Shut up, Espoir. You're no smarter than me."

"I am smarter. Plus, I'm more charming. In fact, I plan to charm the vicomte at the ball with my graceful dancing."

"Graceful dancing? Don't you mean plow him down with your big feet?"

"And what do you plan to do? Knock him over with your foul breath?"

A sense of déjà vu weaved its way around Ella. Tears sprang to her eyes as it tightened its grip.

This is so bad! She leaned against the wall as the girls piled laundry in her arms. *God in heaven. Where was Jean-Daniel? Why doesn't he ride in on his stallion and whisk me away from here?*

She bit her lip. Her situation seemed bleak, but she needed to deal with it herself.

"Ella," Madame Fouquet commanded, "snap out of your trance! It's late but we haven't eaten. You must prepare supper. Unfortunately," malevolence darkened her face "you don't get any. Unless you want to share the hog's slop as you sleep with them for a week."

"What?" Ella asked sharply.

"You didn't think embarrassing me would go unpunished, did you?"

Jean-Daniel reclined in a chair. The sitting room inside his apartments felt lonely without Ella. In fact, every room in the château seemed hollow without her. She'd only been here a few days, but she had been an undeniable bright spot.

Actually, she was much more than that to him. With Ella around, Jean-Daniel had no desire to ride into town and drink with friends. Nor did he feel like staying up all night at the château, carousing and indulging in God knows what. Gone also was the urge he always had to sleep until noon.

She inspired him. Not only was she interesting and beautiful, she was honest and hardworking. Qualities he admired.

Damn it. He crossed his arms. Ella was all he could think about.

It was a new reality for Jean-Daniel. For once he became focused on a goal. Come hell or high water, he was determined to have her in his life.

Maybe this betrothal focused ball isn't such a bad idea. If Ella shows up, that is.

A plan began to form in his head.

"Good Lord!" Hervé entered the room. The elderly man threw his hands in the air, his joints cracking. "That Fouquet woman is too maddening!"

"She's horrible." Jean-Daniel squeezed a tennis ball he held in his hand. Rémy panted at his feet, ready to fetch it. "Sorry, boy. I don't feel like playing tonight."

Rémy sank to the ground and placed his head over his paws.

"Later, I promise. That's a good boy." Jean-Daniel smiled.

Hervé watched him. "Too bad you couldn't charm Madame Fouquet with those dimples of yours, Monsieur."

"They don't work on everyone." Jean-Daniel frowned. His knuckles turned white as he gripped the ball.

"You felt sorry for that servant girl," Hervé said. "What is her name?"

"Ella."

"Yes. Ella."

"I feel more than that for her," Jean-Daniel said. "She and I have developed feelings for each other."

"Feelings?" Aghast, Hervé shuffled to the door and locked it. His voice dropped to a whisper as he returned. "Feelings for a servant girl? You can't mean it, Monsieur!"

"I do. She's special, Hervé."

"There are rules against such a union!"

"Christ. Must there be a rule at every turn?"

"Rules and laws are set for a reason, sir. It's called government."

Jean-Daniel slammed the ball to the ground and caught in on the bounce. "Well, I find most notions of government lacking. Why can't a man be with the woman he loves without a rule getting in the way?"

"A common man can. But you're a vicomte."

Jean-Daniel rolled his eyes. *I'd rather be a scientist studying plants. Or a physician who cares for animals. Then I could live in a small country house with Ella.*

It sounded like bliss.

"There will be other eligible women at the ball," Hervé reminded him.

"Women like Madame Fouquet's unattractive daughters?" Alarm surged through him.

Hervé leaned on the desk. "Madame Fouquet's daughters have replied to your mother's invitation, yes."

"Good God!"

Hervé gave a solemn nod.

Jean-Daniel pushed himself out of the chair and paced the room.

"Monsieur, you must forget about Ella," Hervé said. "She is not the kind of girl a vicomte marries."

Jean-Daniel threw the rubber ball against the wall with a loud slam. *We'll see about that.*

That night, Ella was grateful for the full moon. As she crept toward the château under its bright light, she wiped the perspiration from her brow.

Stealing out of the Fouquet household had fueled her nerves. "Thank goodness Madame took her headache medicine," she whispered as she waded through the field of lavender. It would help her sleep soundly.

As far as Espoir and Charité were concerned, the wrinkle-preventing "beauty" ribbons they'd tied under their chins and over their ears would muffle most sound.

Once Ella reached the château, she planned to tiptoe through the back door, climb the rear stairs, and snatch her belongings from the room she shared with Claudia. She'd be back at the Fouquet home in an hour.

That was her strategy, but as she neared the stately palace, she noticed guards atop the turret's ledges. It seemed Jean-Daniel had taken Colbert's advice to protect himself. Should she pretend she hadn't been snatched back by Madame Fouquet? No, she couldn't just waltz into the château. The last thing she wanted was to alert the vengeful woman.

She must come up with a different plan of attack. Perhaps she could use the secret passageway Claudia had told her about—the one inside the well.

Praying that no one saw her, Ella brushed aside a tree branch and located the structure. In the summer breeze, the well's water bucket swung gently over its circular opening.

She grasped the edge of the shaft and looked down. The moonlight disappeared into a pit of blackness. As she tried to put her fear aside, she grasped the rope with two hands and clambered over the sill. Once she situated herself in a rock-climbing pose, she sucked in a breath. With her feet braced against one side of the interior wall, she leaned her back on the opposing one. Carefully, she used the bucket's rope to inch her way down the dark well.

About ten feet into the shaft, she started to second-guess her decision. She still couldn't see the bottom. And was it really possible to enter the house this way? What if the door to the tunnel had been locked—or sealed off since Claudia had used it?

Palms perspiring, she looked up. Unfortunately, it would be much harder to climb out at this point than to continue down.

She inched her way lower, wishing she had her cell phone's flashlight to aid her vision. *People in the eighteenth century don't know what they're missing.*

Ella told herself not to be scared. She refused to let someone get hold of the glass slippers her father had made just for her, so she continued on.

Her left foot dangled as she braced her right one against the stone wall. Much to her dismay, gravity pulled her clog off. The shoe plunged into the darkness and landed in the water with a splash.

Pulse stuttering, Ella placed her bare foot on the slippery wall. She slid down. When she reached the well's bottom, she stuck both legs inside the cool water and stood. The water level came up to her armpits. Letting go of the rope, she managed to grab hold of the wooden clog that floated there.

Overcome with relief, she tried to find the secret door Claudia had spoken of. With wet hands, she pressed on the stones that touched the water. Then it dawned on her. The entry to the secret passageway had to be above the water level. If a door were located at the very bottom of the well, water would rush into the passageway every time the panel was opened.

Lifting her arms out of the water, she began to grope for a lever. Or a handle. But only the smoothness of the stones greeted her. Her arms ached as she searched in the pitch black. She was about to give up, when her fingers caught a groove. Tucking the clog beneath her arm, she pulled back on the groove and a panel sprung open.

"Thank God," she whispered.

Now, she needed to get inside. Unfortunately, pulling herself out of the water proved difficult. Her drenched dress weighed her down.

Teeth chattering, she heaved herself through the opening in the stones and crawled a few feet. To her relief, the tunnel widened and she was able to stand. After wringing some of the moisture out of her dress, she walked a little farther up a long ramp. Once she slipped the clog on, she climbed a set of stone steps and heard voices.

Colbert and Jean-Daniel were engaged in a discussion beyond the wall. Where did Claudia say the passageway led? The drawing room.

Ella pressed her ear to the cold wall. A gap in it let her clearly hear what was being said.

"I think you've had enough brandy, Colbert."

"There is still some left in the decanter."

"You're being a shit." Jean-Daniel paused. "At least *I've* had enough wine." He set his glass on something solid with a loud *thud*.

"I've come to tell you that a rebellion is brewing," Colbert said darkly.

"A rebellion?" Jean-Daniel asked grimly. "I find that hard to believe. Louis is too popular."

"The rebellion is local. Citizens of Maincy are becoming incensed that I might govern them in your absence." Colbert slurred his words.

"How did they find out, Col? What's more, why can't you agree with my views instead of fighting me at every turn?"

There was a sharp silence. Then the sound of Colbert guzzling more alcohol penetrated the wall. "It's foolish and unfair of Louis to spend so much money on this war in Spain. Why can't you agree with that?"

"Louis must think it necessary. Besides, he has ultimate say," Jean-Daniel pointed out.

"Ah, yes. That infernal notion of absolute monarchy."

"It's proven itself to be a good approach. So much so that I think it will stay in place for a long while."

Ella thought back to her history lessons. Absolute monarchy was a view strong enough to stay in place until the French Revolution. Because it created a centralized state governed by the capital, which seemed to work, it came to be held in high regard.

Jean-Daniel had impressive instincts.

Ella leaned closer to the door. She could hear one of the men roam the room restlessly.

"Remember those Protestants Louis ran out of France? And those citizens who want this war to end?" Colbert said. "I'd be careful if I were you."

"I've posted the guards you hired everywhere," replied Jean-Daniel darkly. Then he added, "Are you sure you aren't the one behind this uprising, Colbert? It strikes me as something you would do."

There was a troubling moment of silence. "All I'm saying is watch your back, Jean-Daniel."

"Thanks for the warning, brother."

"What are twins for?"

The drawing room door opened and shut. Ella pressed her ear tighter to the stone wall. Although the room beyond it offered no sound, she stood frozen for a while—to give Colbert and Jean-Daniel time to venture back to their apartments.

Ella needed to gain access to the drawing room. After she squeezed more water out of her dress, she searched for a latch. In the distance, the longcase clock chimed eleven o'clock. She hoped the house's inhabitants would be asleep by now.

It took Ella a long time to find a groove in the stones. When she did, she yanked on it impatiently. The wall slid slightly to the side and she entered the drawing room on silent footsteps. Thankfully, a moonbeam angled into the room and illuminated the way. Ella hurried to the door the Girard brothers had exited through.

Once inside the hallway, she discovered it was empty. Filled with relief, she made her way up the rear staircase, being careful not to make any noise. When she reached the third floor landing, she hurried down the corridor.

As she was about to enter the room she shared with Claudia, someone grasped her arm.

CHAPTER 20

Colbert spun Ella around. "I heard footsteps on the rear stairwell."

She looked into his hungry eyes. Fright churned inside her. "I was just—"

"Heading away from my bedchamber door?" he interrupted. "As I recall, we have some unfinished business between us."

Ella was tempted to scream, but decided against it. If she woke the household, Madame Fouquet would learn she'd snuck out.

"You're no longer on loan here," Colbert said.

Being on loan humiliated Ella, but Colbert managed to humiliate her more.

"Speak up, girl." Nostrils flaring, he resembled a cunning tiger.

"I didn't have a chance to retrieve my things."

"Why didn't you plan to come back in the morning?"

What was this? Twenty questions?

"Madame Fouquet wouldn't allow it. She's a merciless woman."

"Poor Ella," he said as place his rough hand on her cheek. "Treated as if she's the lowest rung on society's ladder."

She flashed him a dark look. "You're no better, Monsieur."

He bent his head back in hysterical laugher. "The kitten has claws! I like that!"

She tried to wriggle free, but he tightened his grip on her arm. It made the previous bruise he'd given her throb.

"I can be nice and gentle, like my brother." Hot liquor fumes poured out of Colbert's mouth. Ella turned her head away. "It seems that's the kind of man you prefer."

"I prefer no nobleman. I'm a servant," she spat.

"Don't worry. Our liaison will be secretive, Ella. And I'm good at keeping secrets." He pulled her toward him, her wet dress darkening his jacket.

"Why are you all wet?" he asked as she squirmed against his solid chest. "It's no matter. I like the way your bosom stands at attention when it's damp."

"You're despicable!"

Like an archangel swooping down, Jean-Daniel appeared. He yanked Colbert off of Ella. And when he landed a ferocious punch across his twin's face, Colbert lost his balance and fell to the ground.

"Stay away from her, Colbert!"

"Christ, Jean-Daniel. We were getting along so well."

"You cannot treat women like pieces of meat," Jean-Daniel said hotly.

Doors began to open. Seconds apart, Claudia and Madame Manard stepped out of their chambers.

"Are you all right?" Claudia asked Ella.

Infuriated, Ella shook her head. "I came to get my things."

Claudia moved back to allow Ella in. Without looking at Colbert, Ella entered and made straight for the bed. Once she'd retrieved the glass slippers and the bracelet, she reached for a piece of burlap to wrap them in.

Thank God no one discovered them.

Bundling the items in her arms, she exited the room.

Wearing a concerned expression, Jean-Daniel led her away. Ella glanced back at the housekeeper and Claudia. Claudia and Madame Manard's mouths hung wide open as Colbert stormed off.

"Where are we going?" she asked Jean-Daniel.

"To my apartments."

Ella almost suggested she go back to the Fouquet home, but she wasn't that desperate.

"Colbert seems to be in rare form tonight," Jean-Daniel went on. "I don't want him anywhere near you."

"What makes him think he can treat a woman that way?"

He glowered. "Colbert has a problem with entitlement. If he can't have my title, he settles for bullying everyone else."

"Well, it's wrong," Ella said softly. Colbert's motivation didn't erase the trauma he'd caused her. Nor did it excuse his barbaric actions. Suppressing tears, she could still feel the baron's tight grip and smell his drunken breath.

Jean-Daniel ushered her into his apartments. Rémy was curled up in a chair in front of drawn curtains. Once Jean-Daniel closed and locked the door, he set her package on a nearby credenza and embraced her gently. "You're trembling," he whispered.

"Your brother scares me."

"I'll never forgive him for what he did." He took in a breath. "But you're safe now."

Ella leaned her head into the silken fabric of Jean-Daniel's shirt. As he hugged her, his strong arms fended off some of her disquieting thoughts.

"How did you come to be in the hallway?" she asked.

"When I have trouble sleeping, I like to roam the house. It helps me think."

"Thank goodness you showed up when you did."

"I'll never let anyone hurt you, Ella." She raised her head as her tears began to flow. He wiped them. "You mean a great deal to me."

"I didn't want to go with Madame Fouquet," she choked out.

"I didn't want you to go, either. We have so much to learn about each other." As he took a wide stance, he stroked her hair. "You've been gone mere hours and I already missed you."

"I missed you, too."

Smiling gently, he took both of her hands and squeezed them. "You're still shaking."

She nodded and hiccupped a little.

"Come with me." He guided her into his bedchamber.

She eyed the bed with doubt.

"Don't worry," he said. "I promise I won't take advantage of you. I just want you next to me so I can protect you. Is that all right?"

Ella dipped her chin in response.

Jean-Daniel handed her a nightshirt. Once Ella entered the dressing room, she peeled off her wet dress and slipped on the dry garment. She returned to the bed where Jean-Daniel joined her. She lay flat on her back while he rolled to face her. "Try to sleep. I'll watch over you."

She folded her hands over her stomach. Her sobs had finally decreased to whimpers. In an attempt to relax, she shut her eyes.

In the awkward silence, she opened one eye. Jean-Daniel was gazing at her. Reaching out, he languidly traced a wave of her hair. "I'm here, Ella. Drift off to sleep now."

"Would you talk to me?" she said. "I like the sound of your voice."

"What should I talk about?"

"Plants. Or animals."

He rested his head on the pillow. "There are almost thirty breeds of hounds. Afghan, Basset, Bluetick, Beagle . . ."

Lulled by his low voice, she fell asleep.

When she awoke, it was still dark. Perhaps five o'clock in the morning. Jean-Daniel had one leg laid over both of hers. At the sight of his arm nestled protectively around her waist, she smiled.

He'd slept beside her all night! She snuggled against him, content and cozy. *There is nothing more wonderful than waking up next to him.*

Ella studied his peaceful face. His black eye hadn't quite healed and his chin showed signs of stubble, but he was still incredibly handsome. Chiseled and defined, his cheekbones gave him a sophisticated look, while his shaggy hair made him appealingly boyish.

Ella wanted nothing more than to spend eternity with him. *What if I'm pulled forward in time a moment from now?* The thought pierced her with panic. Being yanked away from Jean-Daniel was a possibility she was beginning to dread. Perhaps she should enjoy every second with him.

Slowly, she ran her fingertips along his angular jawline. He grunted something inaudible in his sleep. Because he hadn't awakened fully, she lifted her head and kissed him tenderly on the lips.

"Ella—" he murmured.

Was he dreaming of her as she'd often dreamt about him?

Tremulously, she lifted his arm from her chest and wove her fingers through his. She wanted him to know how she felt about him. Without words. Without tears.

Better yet, she'd *show* him how much she cared.

Tamping down her insecurities and fears of intimacy, she placed his hand across the open expanse of her chest. Her breasts tingled as Jean-Daniel stroked them. Smiling in his sleep, he moaned and caressed her skin. And when she pressed another kiss to his parted mouth, he peeled his eyes open.

"God," he said in a groggy voice. "I want you."

"We don't have much time together," she said softly. "I can't explain why, but it's the reason I want you to make love to me."

He seemed fully awake now because he smiled brilliantly. "I'd be honored to."

After he yanked his shirt off, he drew her into a passionate kiss. Heat radiated from his body. And when he slipped his tongue into her mouth, Ella tasted fiery remnants of wine. Her senses spun. Jean-Daniel's tongue intertwined with hers and she heaved forward in what was a bold move for her. Time wasn't on their side at the moment and they were past chaste kisses. Ella pressed her breasts to his chest to show that she was willing to give herself to him completely. In return, she felt ridges of every kind harden against her: his pectoral muscles, the dense ripple of his stomach and his long shaft. Aroused, his penis rose and strained against the fabric of his breeches. She could feel it through her nightclothes.

"Some would say you're just a servant girl—unassuming and shy. But I'm overwhelmed by you," he said.

Fire coiled around Ella's spine at the admission. Then a stirring sparked between her legs. *Can this really be happening?* She longed to make Jean-Daniel understand how much she'd given up for him. How much she *would* give up for him.

They melted together and their red-hot desire escalated. After he kissed her deeply, he lifted her arm over her head. Then he glided his fingers down its length, caressing her skin at every inch through the fabric of her nightshirt. When his touch reached her breast, he cupped its underside and parted his perfect lips.

"You make me want to be a better man—and vicomte, Ella. No woman has ever done that."

His words cut through the strain of her encounter with Colbert. For the first time in a long while, she meant something to someone. Someone who had positive things to say about her.

Jean-Daniel slanted his mouth over hers and sampled her lips again. His tongue brushed across her mouth in slow, sultry flicks. Her body rose. While he cradled her head, he planted his hot mouth along the column of her neck. And when he tilted her head to the side, he traced his tongue against the juncture of her nape and shoulders.

"That feels so good," she rasped.

He nodded, the satiny layers of his hair falling across her collarbone. "Let me kiss that adorable little birthmark. Then I'll taste your breasts." Slipping her sleeve from her shoulder, he tugged the material down until her right nipple was exposed.

"Beautiful," he murmured. He lifted the weight of her bosom in his hand and then outlined the circumference of her bud with his tongue. Her pulse raced like a wild mare. He looked so handsome, hair damp with enthusiasm and muscles swelled from working magic at her breast. She loved the sight of him.

"Look at that," he said, pulling back to admire her peaked nipple. "Magnificent."

When he held her gaze, Ella's breath came in fast bursts. "I'm ready for you to touch me, Jean-Daniel."

"Are you sure?" He raised a brow.

"Yes."

"Completely sure?"

Trying not to appear shy, she said firmly, "Yes." She knew Jean-Daniel had gone down in history as a womanizer, so why was he being so gentlemanly? Perhaps his chivalry made him popular with women, but Ella preferred to think he was being gentlemanly in her honor.

Desire glistening in his eyes, he bunched up the hem of her dress. Sliding his hand up her thigh, he whispered, "Don't be afraid, my sweet. I'll be tender."

She put her lips to his bent neck and clung to him. His fingers found her center. As Ella held her breath, he stroked her curls. His hand on her mound felt like heated velvet and for once, she liked it.

Using his fingertips, Jean-Daniel fondled the pleats around her core.

"You're moist." His lips quirked in a sideways grin. "Christ. You're just as aroused as I am."

Anticipating the feel of him inside her, she wet her lips.

"Let your knees fall away," he instructed gently.

Until then, Ella hadn't realized she'd drawn up her legs in a rigid pose. It took every ounce of trust she had to let them separate and fall to the mattress.

"Yes. Just like that."

"Will you teach me what to do?"

He flashed a dazzling smile. "This part is all me, so all you have to do is relax. But I'll show you how to make love in a moment."

Unhurriedly, he caressed her fleece. She wriggled and moaned against the feather-soft sensation—and had no desire to snap her knees shut. As he reclined on one elbow, he stiffened two fingers of his free hand and swept them down her slit. In an earth-shifting moment, he penetrated her folds and explored her womanhood.

While he teased and provoked her, he watched her face. Then his mouth was on hers again. In a harmonious rhythm, Jean-Daniel increased the heat of the kiss while he increased the intensity of his fondling. And when he began using his thumb against her bead—

There! Ella's pleasure built to a deafening crescendo. The room hummed with her pants and moans until there was a burst of wetness between her legs. She cried out before she glanced at Jean-Daniel. Grinning, he didn't withdraw his hand until her climax stopped.

"Now you're ready for me."

Ella wasn't a virgin—though losing her chastity hadn't been her choice.

Fortunately, making love to Jean-Daniel tonight would be strictly voluntary. The best part was: he knew her history.

Assisting her to a sitting position, he peeled the nightshirt over her head. And once he tossed the garment to the floor, he eyed her throbbing breasts.

"By God, you're aching with lust. That excites me." Smiling, he captured one of her nipples with his mouth while she sat up. As he lapped and flicked at it with his tongue, it turned dark pink.

She began to grow self-conscious about the state of her body. Hands nicked and calloused, shin bandaged, and ankle bruised. She worried she was rough and not pretty until Jean-Daniel murmured, "Incredible. Your skin is so . . . sun-kissed."

Tan, Ella corrected him silently. The word didn't exist in 1703, but suddenly she preferred "sun-kissed."

He laid her back down and rolled toward her on one hip. Slowly, his gaze roved to her pelvis and groomed mound. He sucked in a breath. "Holy Mother and Country! Your nest is exquisite."

Ella smiled at the euphemism.

Jean-Daniel traced her tattoo. "What's this?"

"It's a fleur-de-lis."

"Drawn with some kind of body paint?"

Since it would be too difficult to explain the idea of a tattoo, she nodded.

"Charming." He paused. "Now it's your turn to feel me."

Ella hesitated. She looked down at the contour of his cock. It protruded with a host of veins and a pair of bulging testicles. She *was* curious . . .

"Stroke it." He reached for her hand. "Like this."

Fingers quivering, she let Jean-Daniel guide her hand to his crotch. As she caressed his sex the way he instructed, signs of pleasure washed over his face. But then he frowned.

"This won't do," he said gruffly.

Standing, he stripped his breeches off and revealed a thick, lengthy penis. Nested in golden-brown curls, it stood erect and pumped with masculine desire. Once he lay atop the sheets again, he retrieved her hand and urged her to ready him more.

"Hmm," he hummed at her up and down motions. "You're beautiful *and* talented."

Lord. This man was everything: kind, smart, funny, handsome, and sincere. How had she gotten so lucky?

Ella knew she loved him. But it was important that he say the words first. Would he?

Jean-Daniel scrambled to position himself between her legs. While he leaned forward on locked elbows, his slim torso and eager shaft brushed against her center. A new wave of yearning flooded her. Firmly, he fisted his cock and opened her core with it.

Giddy with anticipation, she snaked her arms around his sturdy neck. He bent over and kissed her deeply. Hotly. Easing his shaft inside her, he moaned.

Astonishing! Unbelievable! Fulfilling! Every affirmation in the dictionary sprang to Ella's mind. But it was only when Jean-Daniel looked her straight in the eye and said, "I love you," did she know she'd died and gone straight to heaven.

CHAPTER 21

Romeo and Juliet were a perfect example of it. Antony and Cleopatra were lucky enough to experience it. As were princes and princesses in fairy tales. Love at first sight . . . that overwhelming sensation. A mad desire to affirm what one felt so soon after meeting one's true love.

Both Jean-Daniel and Ella were overcome by that feeling right now.

In a passionate frenzy, Jean-Daniel didn't just make love to Ella, he devoured her. Thrusting into her like a fiery cannonball, he fisted her hair and then grabbed her buttocks. Like a wall of protection, he bundled her around the waist as if he never wanted to let go.

Abandoning all resistance allowed Ella to enjoy the most fantastic moment of her life.

"Christ," he said breathlessly, "your body is so sweet and supple."

As he worked hard for his climax, he exhibited an army of flexing muscles and rippling tendons. And when he raised himself on locked elbows again, he pumped until his facial expression changed. "I can't hold out!"

Ella's center vibrated. Like a charge of electricity, they peaked together. Jean-Daniel's warm quicksilver spilled inside her and he came in repeated spurts.

Gasping, he heaved his body over Ella's. His ragged breathing rang in her ear and she realized she'd never been more satiated. Or happy.

He shifted away. Lying on his stomach, he reached over and stroked her cheek. "That was incredible."

Ella placed a hand over her hammering heart. *Best day ever.*

He kissed her full on the mouth.

"The sun is rising," she whispered as he broke contact. "I should go."

Disappointment shadowed his face. "Must you?"

"If Madame discovers I'm gone, she'll punish me."

Scowling, Jean-Daniel hung half his body over the side of the bed and retrieved the nightshirt. "That vulgar woman better not hurt you—"

To Ella, it seemed more than unfair. She'd journeyed through time to be by Jean-Daniel's side. Now a version of Adelaide was preventing her from being happy even here.

Could this be the last happy moment she shared with Jean-Daniel? Visions of the television episode *Ghost Catchers* flashed before her. Him lying face down in the bloody lake on the night of the ball. Floating motionless . . .

She shook away the vision. He couldn't die! She was here to help him. But how to redirect his fate?

Her mind wandered in all directions. If Jean-Daniel lived, she was desperate to know how it would impact the next three hundred years. Ella had considered it numerous times, but she couldn't answer that question. To her knowledge, no one had ever altered the past.

She dressed and he followed suit.

A sheepish expression crossed Jean-Daniel's face. "A moment ago, when I said I loved you, I know it sounded crazy."

Not any crazier than me traveling through time to be here. "Skeptics would argue that we've known each other too briefly, but I love you, too."

Joy replaced his sheepish expression.

"About the ball—" they said simultaneously. Chuckling, they each urged the other to go first. Those words overlapped as well.

Jean-Daniel said, "I'll wait for you to speak."

Ella's tone turned solemn. "Don't ask me how I've come to this conclusion, but I know you're in great danger."

"You've heard rumors of political unrest, too?"

"Something like that."

He laced his fingers through hers.

Ella went on. "Something terrible is going to happen at the ball."

"Yes. I might have to dance with one of the Fouquet women!" He gave a great big laugh.

"Please be serious," she implored.

He caught his breath. "Why are you so worried?"

"You wouldn't believe me if I told you. But we need to have a plan."

"A plan?" he asked. "That's funny. I was thinking the same thing."

"Make it a masquerade ball, Jean-Daniel."

"Why?"

"It might come in handy for you to be disguised."

"Disguised—for what?"

"Just don't go outside. Don't go to the lake."

"But that's where I thought we could meet. Once we're outside, we could disappear together."

"Disappear?"

Concern creased his forehead. "We can't be together, Ella—unless I give up my noble status. After we run away, we can live a simple life somewhere in the country."

Ella's spirits sang. Jean-Daniel intended to be with her. Elated, she let the realization sink in.

"I was going to become a courtier to the king, but you are more important."

Was he actually willing to give everything up for her? What if he did and she suddenly returned to her own time period? She didn't think she could bear going back to the future without him.

Deciding to take things one step at a time, she repeated, "You mustn't go to the lake."

"Aye, aye, Captain," he teased her.

"I'm serious, Jean-Daniel. I've seen what happens there."

He cocked a brow. "How?"

"Like I said, it's too complicated to explain."

"I wish you would tell me."

"I can't."

He sighed. "Very well. I trust you. I'll stay away from the damned lake. And I promise to come up with another plan of escape."

He clasped her hand—and she was grateful for its comforting feel. Still, other issues brooded over them like a storm cloud. "If you leave this place," she said, "will Colbert be in charge even though he doesn't care for the king's philosophy?"

"Have you been listening at doors?"

She blushed.

"Colbert is far from being a supporter of the king, yet he won't have a choice but to follow Louis's commands."

"Won't it be hard for you to leave the people you've been governing?" she asked.

"It will be the hardest thing I've ever done."

"In that case," Ella said, "are you certain you want to give up your title . . . your life here at the château for me?"

"I'm sure."

Jean-Daniel walked her to the door and offered her a final kiss. "A footman will spread the word about making the gala a masquerade ball," he said. "Then I'll have Madame Manard deliver an exquisite costume to you."

She cupped his cheek tenderly. "I'll recognize you behind any mask."

He took her hand and planted a kiss across her knuckles. "And when I spot you at the ball, my beautiful Ella, you'll look like a princess."

Her cheeks warmed.

"That night, you must meet me at the longcase clock at midnight. I will tell you what I've worked out then."

Nodding, Ella turned to retrieve her package. To her horror, the burlap bundle holding the glass slippers and the Egyptian bracelet weren't there.

"My belongings are gone!" she cried.

"Jesus." Jean-Daniel ground his teeth. "Someone must have stolen in while we were sleeping."

"Or while we were making love."

He raised an eyebrow. "I hope we weren't observed."

"I thought you locked the door," she said urgently.

"Several people have a key."

Ella bit her lip.

"Don't worry," he said. "I'll tear this château apart looking for your things. What, exactly are you missing?"

"A pair of shoes my father made for me. Plus, a bracelet that matches my amulet."

"I promise to find them and deliver them with your costume."

"I *have* to have the items," Ella said. She presumed that one of the items or perhaps a combination of them had allowed her to time travel.

He nodded.

After Ella changed, they left Jean-Daniel's apartments. Thankfully, they managed to make it outside without being seen. Jean-Daniel informed his guards that Ella was his guest and then escorted her as far as the well. Once they parted, she ran to the Fouquet house quickly. Mere seconds after she entered, Espoir called for her.

"Ella! My morning tea!"

In a sort of exhausted daze, Ella prepared a tray. It nearly slipped out of her grasp as she brought it upstairs. *Gad*. Which room was Espoir's?

She wasn't about to go around opening doors at the risk of waking Madame Fouquet.

"Ella!" Espoir's screech came from a room on the left.

Relieved, Ella entered. "Good morning, Espoir."

"What's so good about it? I've been eating too much and I can't fit into my dress for the ball."

Snuggled in bed, the girl pushed herself to a sitting position.

"I have some good news." Ella set the tray down. "Word has it that the vicomte prefers the ball to be a masquerade. Soon he'll inform every attendee."

Espoir climbed out of bed. She moved unnervingly close. "Then I'll have to buy another dress! How is that good news?"

"Perhaps you can create some sort of costume instead of purchasing something new."

"I hardly sew."

Ella made for the door.

"And where did you hear all this?" Espoir stopped her. Her eyes narrowed. "Did the vicomte whisper in your ear as you lay beneath him like a whore?"

Ella's mouth went dry. The debilitating lump in her throat returned. Hope was even worse in this century. Why couldn't she tell the vile girl to shut up?

Because it'd been ingrained in Ella's nature to be subservient, that's why. It wasn't possible for a person to change her ways overnight.

"Mother told Charité and me how she found you. You were another notch in the vicomte's pleasure belt yesterday. That's what I think."

"Another notch?" Ella nearly choked on the words. In her present day—when she'd gazed upon Jean-Daniel's portrait—she had sensed that he liked to have a good time. But here in the eighteenth century she didn't want to hear about his roguish escapades.

Espoir put her hands on her hips. "The vicomte enjoys a different woman every week."

Ella felt sick.

"And I hear he has an eye for fair-haired women."

"You know nothing of what went on at the château," Ella spat back. *Wow. Maybe I'm growing a spine after all.*

"Mother wouldn't lie about finding you spread-legged under a tree." Espoir dropped her sleep mask on the floor. "How clumsy of me. Now—pick that up."

It was hardly a battle of wills. Ella relented and retrieved the item . . . although she took her sweet time doing it.

Jean-Daniel didn't bother knocking at his brother's door. Marching in, he scooped a tasseled pillow off a sofa and threw it at Colbert, who lay in bed. "Wake up, you bastard!"

Colbert grunted. Facedown, he dangled one leg over the side of the mattress. As slow as a sloth, he rolled over, holding his head. "Christ, Jean-Daniel! This is an ungodly hour!"

"Did you steal into my apartments last night and take Ella's belongings?"

"You're accusing me of thievery?"

"Just answer the question."

"No, I didn't steal in. I came back here and continued drinking."

"After what you pulled, you should have retreated like a dog with its tail between its legs." Jean-Daniel began to tear the bedchamber apart looking for Ella's items.

"Thanks for adding to my humiliation." Colbert watched Jean-Daniel with disinterest. Then he let his head fall on the pillow. "If I say I didn't take them, I didn't take them."

"Did you actually say 'humiliation'?" Jean-Daniel thundered. He kicked a chair over.

Colbert pried himself out of bed. Body hulking, he slung a bed-sheet around his waist as if it were a towel. "Yes, humiliation. Rejection can damn well lead to it. But I forgot. No one has ever rejected *you*, brother."

"Forget our history of competition, Colbert. I don't want you manhandling Ella again."

"Why? Have you developed *feelings* for her?"

Jean-Daniel's eyes narrowed. "Who told you that?"

"Hervé. Give the fossil some rum and he'll spill national secrets."

"Shit, Colbert. I love her!"

The words exploded in the air like fireworks. Colbert's face went white. Unsteadily, he came to stand before Jean-Daniel. "You *love* her?"

"I do."

"That's something new for you."

Jean-Daniel raked his hand through his hair. "I can't describe how I feel. I thought it was impossible to fall in love at first sight, but now I know I can."

"For Christ's sake—" Colbert put his fists on his hips "—Ella is a servant. What could you want with her?"

"You don't see something in her?"

Colbert's face reddened. "I . . ."

Jean-Daniel waited for his answer, but Colbert spun away.

"Stammering and flushed, are you?" Jean-Daniel raised a brow. "If I didn't know better, I'd say Ella has melted your icy heart."

"What are you talking about?" Colbert filed around the room. "I've never said more than two words to her."

"You didn't have to. It's her essence that captures people."

Colbert came to a halt. "There's no doubt she's beautiful. But her best quality is her ability to refrain from swooning at your feet like most women do."

Memories of making love to Ella rose in Jean-Daniel's mind. She hadn't swooned. Rather, she'd offered herself to him with aplomb. Their passion had been mutual and *that* was something new to him, too. His lips quirked.

"I hoped to have a chance with her," Colbert went on.

Jean-Daniel snapped to attention. "I'm sorry to disappoint you, brother."

"Disappointment is nothing new to me, Jean-Daniel!"

"I'm leaving. Take care of that hangover."

Just before Jean-Daniel exited the room, he ran headlong into his mother. She put a hand to her heart. "What's all the fuss in here? Listening to you boys argue is putting the servants in a dither."

Madame de Maincy laced her hand around Jean-Daniel's elbow and steered him back into Colbert's suite. Before Jean-Daniel shut the door, he caught an astonished look from a hall boy.

"Heavens, Colbert!" Madame de Maincy said. "Put some clothes on."

"You've seen me in my birthday suit more than once, Mother." Flopping into a chair, he shot her a grimace.

"When you were nine months old, son." She averted her eyes.

Leaning against the wall, Jean-Daniel crossed his arms impatiently. "I need to summon a footman."

His mother looked confused. "Whatever for?"

"I'm changing the ball to a masquerade."

"A masquerade?" She blinked. "How will you spot a wife behind a sea of masks?"

"It will make the hunt more interesting."

"But the invitations have already been sent out," she protested. "With beautiful calligraphy, I might add—"

"I don't care," he interrupted. "If you want me to have this damned fête, it's going to be a masquerade."

Misery flooded his mother's face. "We'll notify everyone. But I've already had a dress made. *Now* what will I wear?"

As Jean-Daniel's thoughts flew to Ella's assertion that he'd soon be in great danger, what his mother wore was the least of his worries.

She removed her spectacles. "Is there a reason you want to make the ball a masquerade?"

"Yes. I cannot go into details, but we need to heighten protection during it."

"Done." Colbert said.

Madame de Maincy hesitated. "I've made no secret that I have mixed feelings about you going to Versailles and leaving Colbert in charge." She slid Colbert a critical look.

"It's a little more complicated than that, Mother." Colbert craned his neck over the back of the chair.

"What do you mean?"

"Forget Jean-Daniel's political aspirations and forget the ball. Another matter warrants your immediate attention."

"Such as?"

"Jean-Daniel has something to tell you."

"Shut up, Colbert." Jean-Daniel flashed a look that could kill.

"Tell me?" The vicomtesse smoothed her dress and took a seat. "Very well. I'm listening."

"I have no idea what Colbert means."

"I'll help you along, brother. There is no need for a matchmaking ball because Jean-Daniel has already fallen in love."

Madame de Maincy lit up. "That's wonderful!"

"With a servant girl," Colbert added darkly.

Shock made her hands tremble. "A *servant girl*?"

Jean-Daniel strode over quickly. "I know it sounds unsavory, Mother, but I assure you this girl is special."

"I don't care how special she is! She's beneath you." Madame de Maincy's chest heaved with anxiety. "The whole point of this ball is to find you a *suitable* wife."

"If you do, maybe you'll grow up," Colbert sneered.

"I am grown up."

Madame de Maincy tsked. "There is a rule against nobility marrying commoners."

Colbert folded his hands and looked up at the ceiling. "The worst part is this girl isn't just a commoner. She's in service."

"Not helping, Colbert." Jean-Daniel gritted his teeth.

"I'm afraid your brother is right," Madame de Maincy said. "You must forget about this girl, whomever she is."

"I don't want to forget about her."

"Jean-Daniel, come sit beside me."

He did.

"Let's go back in time a bit." Madame de Maincy gazed wistfully into space. "You were an adorable baby."

Colbert groaned.

His mother told him to shush. "You were lovable and strong-willed and rambunctious. I couldn't believe the amount of energy you had! Now that you're a man, your charms know no bounds. People gravitate toward you, but some say you're untamable, careless. I, however, have faith in you."

"Faith?" Jean-Daniel frowned.

"Yes. Faith that you'll dedicate yourself to the challenges and duties your father passed on."

"Father died at thirty-five," Jean-Daniel reminded her.

Eyes misting, she hesitated. "Is that why you're so opposed to conformity? So bent on having fun because life is short?"

"Perhaps," he replied thoughtfully.

Madame de Maincy placed her hands primly in her lap. "Well, life isn't always about having fun, Jean-Daniel. Not when you have a title."

"I'm sure Father would have packed in more fun if he could have."

Tears spilled over her cheeks.

Jean-Daniel softened his tone. "I'm sorry, Mother. That was insensitive. You know I miss Father as much as you do."

She patted his hand. "I know."

"Christ," he said in frustration. "This is a bunch of horseshit!"

"Jean-Daniel! Calm yourself," Madame de Maincy said. She watched him slide down in a chair and spread his knees wide. "Let's get back to your father. He was a fine man and we were very much in love."

"Having the kind of marriage you had is my ultimate goal." Jean-Daniel leaned over and took her hand. "Did Father fall in love with you at first sight?"

She blushed. "I don't know."

"I do. When Father found out he was sick, we took a walk one day. He told me that he was overwhelmed when he saw you. He spoke of being hit by the 'thunderbolt'."

"What nonsense is that?"

"He said that if I was lucky enough to fall in love at first sight— as he did with you—I should revel in it."

"Is that what you've been waiting for?"

A smile tugged at the corner of his mouth.

"That may be well and good for you." She withdrew her hand. "But this is too painful for me."

"Father may have spoken about the 'thunderbolt'," Colbert said curtly, "but he also read you fairy tales, Jean-Daniel. I think that explains your sense of frivolity, brother."

"Frivolity?" Jean-Daniel sprang out of his seat. "True love is anything but frivolous, Colbert. But you're too pigheaded to see that."

Their mother stood as well. "Know this, Jean-Daniel. You may be head over heels in love with this servant girl, but the only way you'll be with her is if you give up your title."

Jean-Daniel said nothing.

She gasped. "You wouldn't dare . . ."

CHAPTER 22

Spending five nights with the pigs was tremendously uncomfortable. The last evening had been the worst. Ella hadn't gotten a wink of sleep. Now she smelled of hogs and slop and hay.

Up at the crack of dawn, she emerged from the barn and watched the sun crest over the horizon. Warmed by a tepid breeze, she studied the valley dipping before her. Gone were the power lines visible in her day—power lines she'd seen from the top floors of the château. She hadn't ventured this far away from the château then, so she had no idea if the Fouquet house still existed.

As Ella stood facing east, the sun rose rather quickly and woke a host of birds in a nearby tree. The sound of their merry chirping made her smile ruefully.

At least the birds are happy. She was far from that without Jean-Daniel.

Assuming she was up before everyone else, she filled two pails with water. Then, padding inside the house, she transported them to the third floor. Surely one of the modest rooms tucked away from the others belonged to her.

Yes. A corner bedroom containing a tiny bathtub, a wardrobe screen, and a creaky bed appeared inhabited. Ella set the pails down without spilling a drop of water.

Peeling off her dress, she tossed it in a corner and then filled the tub. Amid the summer heat, she stepped inside. The cool water felt heavenly. How people had survived without air-conditioning boggled her mind!

Then again, she thought as she picked up a sponge, *I'm doing it right now.*

Her stomach rumbled. Every meal she'd prepared for Espoir and Charité they had consumed like wild beasts. With nothing left over for her last night, Ella had been too tired to make more food. She went to bed hungry and dirty. Surely most animals didn't do that.

She soaked for at least twenty minutes. Then, like a firebomb, the sound of Espoir's voice exploded in the air.

"Ella! There's someone at the door!"

Would it break Espoir's legs to go downstairs and let the caller in?

Moaning, Ella pushed herself out of the tub and put on a fresh dress. Simple and unattractive, the gray muslin garment rustled as she hurried to the door. A footman wearing a periwig presented a card wrapped with a red ribbon. Ella thanked him and then turned to face Espoir and Charité. The girls let out a yawn—before they eyed the regal invitation, that is.

Eyes as big as saucers, Espoir snatched the card from Ella. In turn, Charité ripped it from Espoir's grasp and tore the ribbon away. She scoured the invitation while Espoir tugged at her shoulder.

"The vicomte is insisting that the ball be a masquerade," Charité said.

"You were right, Ella," Espoir murmured darkly. "I, for one, have a problem with the change. If we're wearing masks, how will the vicomte see our beauty?"

Charité tossed her hair over her shoulder. "It'll shine through, don't worry."

Ella rolled her eyes.

"Oooh, a masquerade. How mysterious!" Charité added.

"It's going to be so much fun!"

The girls turned to Ella.

"Too bad *you* can't come." Tauntingly, Charité waved the invitation in front of her face.

Ella grabbed it and read it. "It says every unmarried maiden in the province is welcome."

"Madame le vicomtesse isn't inviting *servants*."

"I'm going no matter what," Ella said firmly.

There was another knock at the door. Ella opened it to a smiling Madame Manard. "Good morning!"

"Good morning, Ella." The woman held a gorgeous dress across her arms. "May I come in?"

"Who are you?" Espoir asked snidely.

"I'm the housekeeper at Château de Maincy. Monsieur le vicomte specifically wanted me to deliver this to Ella."

Madame Manard looked so much like Mimi that Ella was tempted to hug her. She greeted the kindly housekeeper and showed her in. Madame Manard bustled across the parlor's threshold and laid the ball gown on the divan.

"Is it really for me?" Ella sucked in a breath.

"Yes."

"Thank you for delivering it. It's stunning."

"It's very beautiful, I agree." The housekeeper wagged her finger. "But it's on loan."

On loan. Ella winced at the words.

Madame Manard swept past Espoir and Charité and took Ella's hands. "The vicomte had me pick it up and tuck it away when Madame de Maincy changed her attire for the ball. She's dressing as a peacock now." The housekeeper giggled.

"So this is what Madame de Maincy was going to wear originally?" Ella asked.

"Yes."

Ella moved closer. She ran her fingertips over the silken material. Sparkling with a wall of crystals and shimmering with yards of gold trim, the sapphire ball gown possessed a square neckline, puffed sleeves, and a dramatic over train.

"You'll need hoops and petticoats for this one." Madame Manard's eyes glimmered. "Then you'll look like a princess."

Ella smiled. To dance in Jean-Daniel's arms . . .

"I've also brought this." Madame Manard withdrew a bejeweled half-mask from her cloak. Attached to a short pole adorned with ribbons, the gold mask emanated daintiness and elegance. "Madame used it during an earlier masquerade."

"Thank you so much. But won't the vicomtesse recognize that I'm wearing her dress?"

"It's the latest fashion from Paris. Another guest may also be wearing something similar."

"Thank you," Ella said again.

"It's nothing, my dear. Now, the clock is ticking. I must get back to the château."

Ella escorted her to the door.

"Be careful with the vicomtesse's things," the gray-haired housekeeper said. "I expect them back."

"I'll take very good care of them, I promise."

As soon as the door closed behind Madame Manard, Madame Fouquet stepped forward. "Espoir and Charité. What do you think of Ella's new dress?"

"It's beautiful." Espoir pouted. "But it's outrageous that it's meant for a servant!"

"I agree." Charité crossed her arms and looked every inch the spoiled daughter.

"There's no denying the gown's splendor." Madame Fouquet's eyes formed slits. "You are very lucky, Ella. It seems the vicomte has taken a liking to you."

Ella backed away. "It isn't my doing."

Madame Fouquet clenched her fists. "It seems you've been giving the vicomte a great many ideas lately. Rumor has it he's losing interest in his noble title."

How did gossip spread so fast? Did the château have ears?

"What?" Charité shrieked. "Interest in *her*? Look at her calloused hands. That can't be!"

"The ultimate question is," Madame Fouquet said, her timbre dropping to a harsh whisper, "will Monsieur le vicomte give up everything for a servant girl?"

"He wouldn't!" cried Espoir.

Madame Fouquet turned and looked at her daughters. "Don't worry. It's a good sign that the ball is still taking place. But I have my work cut out for me. I must make sure the vicomte dances with you, Espoir and Charité."

"Yes, Mother. Please do!"

"I must also make sure this servant girl is nowhere to be found."

Ella wanted to scream as Madame Fouquet and the selfish girls left the room. How dare the woman try to prevent her from attending the ball! Jean-Daniel cared about her and she had every right to be there.

Furthermore, if Ella disguised herself as elegant nobility, no one would know she was the servant girl Jean-Daniel preferred to spend his time with.

Ella scooped the dress off the divan and scampered upstairs. She intended to lock the garment in her wardrobe and protect it with her life.

Jean-Daniel meandered into the gardens. The evening was clear. Its air fragrant. A slew of gardeners had been pruning and grooming the gardens for a week now. The grounds looked spectacular. And just in time. The ball would take place tomorrow night.

Jean-Daniel had a lot of thinking to do. Rémy panted beside him as he walked.

"It's infernally hot this evening, isn't it, boy?"

Rémy's tongue hung loose. He seemed thirsty, but he kept in perfect step with his master, nonetheless.

Jean-Daniel circled the fountain and plopped down on its edge. He faced the château while Rémy halted in his tracks. "The house looks lovely at night. Everyone has worked so hard to polish it to a high shine."

Rémy took a look and then dipped his head slightly.

"Did you know that my father built this house for me? Of course you do, boy. You know everything."

The canine's eyes glazed at the compliment.

"Now I'm about to abandon his legacy."

Rémy seemed sad, so Jean-Daniel scratched the dog's head. "You're right. It's very confusing. Father put the romantic notion of a thunderbolt in my head, but in the same breath, he advised me about my duty to the people of Maincy."

Rémy planted himself on his haunches.

"I fear for what Colbert would do if he were given free rein."

The hound whimpered.

"What is a vicomte in love to do?" Jean-Daniel smiled ruefully.

Rémy listened intently. He was a very good listener.

Jean-Daniel crossed his ankle over one knee. "You sure have it easy. Don't you, boy?"

Rémy pinned his ears back.

"Then again, you don't know what you're missing. Ella is as soft as a rose and as intriguing as a good mystery. And she desperately wants to be with me."

He glanced down at Rémy. The dog seemed to ask, "Do *you* want to be with *her?*"

Jean-Daniel exhaled. "I want to be with her more than anything."

His gaze returned to the house. Its windows were lit with the impending excitement of tomorrow night's ball. "But don't worry, Rémy. Ella and I will take you with us when we leave."

Jean-Daniel rose and gave the house a forlorn look over his shoulder. "However, I will miss this place tremendously."

CHAPTER 23

By sunset the next day, Ella was exhausted. Madame Fouquet had managed to keep her busy the entire afternoon with endless chores. She'd dusted the whole house, scrubbed the floors, changed the beds, and washed and styled Espoir and Charité's hair. She'd even cleaned the chimney flue. A face full of ashes had gotten a rise out of the girls.

"*Cinder* Ella!" They'd taunted her cruelly.

Well, Ella had a few choice nicknames for them, but she was too ladylike to spew them. Wiping the last of the grime from her cheeks, she climbed the stairs. It was six o'clock. Just enough time to bathe, arrange her hair, and change into the borrowed gown before the carriage arrived.

Heart pounding, she entered her tiny bedroom and unlocked the wardrobe. *Thank goodness!* The dress was still there.

Ella set a pail of water down, took a quick bath, and then stepped into the dress. It smelled of sweet perfume. It also held an unfamiliar aura—one of opulence and reverential attention. The kind a servant gives a noblewoman.

She smiled. For once in her life, she was going to live like a princess.

Once she was ready, she stared at her appearance in a cracked mirror. She hardly recognized herself! Back in the twenty-first century, she rarely wore dresses and she never applied this much makeup, but somehow, for this sole night, it suited her.

If only I could don Dad's glass slippers. They'd complete the ensemble. Her heart sank a little at the loss.

Grasping the half-mask, she hurried downstairs. The carriage transporting the Fouquet women to the ball was to arrive any minute.

Espoir and Charité stood at the bottom of the stairs. Espoir gasped when she saw Ella. "My costume looks like horse dung compared to Ella's, Mother. It isn't fair!"

Madame Fouquet stepped forward, her pewter gown rustling. "Ella does look lovely."

A compliment? Ella didn't trust Madame as far as she could throw her. What did the malevolent woman have up her sleeve?

"Mother!" Charité tugged on her arm. "You're not *really* going to let Ella go to the ball, are you?"

Madame Fouquet arched a brow. "The invitation said every unmarried maiden." She paused and shot a conniving glare. If looks could kill, Ella would have been dead that minute.

"Still," Madame came closer, "I find something wholly unfair about this situation."

Charité and Espoir's eyes grew beady as they waited for their mother to continue.

"You girls are jealous of Ella's dress, are you not?"

"It's gorgeous," Espoir huffed.

"It puts ours to shame and there's no justice in that!" Charité stomped her foot like a petulant child.

Madame stood practically nose-to-nose with Ella. At the close distance, Ella studied the woman's deep wrinkles, hawk-like nose, and downturned mouth.

"What *really* isn't fair," Madame said darkly, "is being left in the lurch by your deceased father, Ella."

"My *father*?" Ella could hardly get the word out. "I don't understand."

"Don't play dumb. The money Charles left us is gone."

In a heart-thudding moment, Ella remembered that her father's middle name was "Charles." Obviously, it's what Madame Fouquet had called him. "But you told the vicomte that your stepdaughter was dead!" she protested.

"I'm surprised you didn't say anything contradictory," Madame said. "Then again, I've ingrained it in your brain not to."

"I'm your stepdaughter and you told people I passed away?" Ella said. "How could you!"

"Shut up, you insolent girl. If I hadn't allowed you to stay here after Charles died, you'd be on the street."

"Allowed me? I'm part of the family!"

"It doesn't matter. Now what's important, " Madame indicated the borrowed dress, "is that you have something nicer than my girls. Do *you* think that's fair?"

Ella's nerves rattled. "Wearing the dress is the vicomte's idea. Not mine."

"To be fair," Madame de Maincy suggested, "perhaps the eldest girl should wear it."

"That's me!" Espoir jumped up and down.

"No!" Ella cried.

Before Ella could back away farther, Espoir snatched at the gown. A sash ripped off.

"Then again." Madame Fouquet shrugged. "There are three of you. Maybe what's best is to take this beautiful ball gown out of the equation altogether."

Ella's stomach roiled.

Like vultures on a carcass, Espoir and Charité attacked the dress and tore it to shreds. Trim went flying, crinoline floated in the air, and material sliced in half like crackling lightning. In the aftermath of the frenzy, remnants of the dress lay pitifully on the rug.

There was a knock on the door. "Madame Fouquet. The carriage is here."

"You have nothing to wear now, Ella." Madame Fouquet grimaced. "But you couldn't have gone anyway." She reached for a bag of lentil beans that sat on the entryway table. A release of the drawstring sent hundreds of beans spilling on the floor. "I was going to instruct you to pick up every last one."

"You had this planned?" Ella shouted.

Her stepmother laughed. It echoed like a dark sound in a demon's cave. "You may be worthless, *Cinder* Ella, but at least you catch on quick."

Madame Fouquet and her daughters bounced out the door. Devastated, Ella rushed upstairs. Sobs wracked her body as she threw herself on her bed. If she couldn't be a guest at the ball, how could she possibly save Jean-Daniel from his tragic fate?

She cried for a long while. Finally, she pushed herself off the bed and went to the window. Her soul plummeted to a low point and moroseness flooded over her. The moon hung closely over the gleaming turrets of the château. *If I am a Fouquet, how could my stepmother treat me like that?*

Wait. *I'm a Fouquet.* The fact erupted an epiphany inside her. It meant she wasn't the lowest rung on society's ladder. Instead, she was a girl worthy of marrying Jean-Daniel.

She *had* to find a way to get to that ball.

Jean-Daniel eyed his clean-shaven face in the mirror. It had taken him a while to dress and now the collar of his new jacket was too damn stiff and his three layers of clothing were making him sweat.

"And I just took a bath," he muttered.

"Stand still, Monsieur," Hervé insisted. "Maybe you won't perspire so much."

"Wouldn't you, old friend, if the shoe were on the other foot?"

The advisor laughed. He gazed at Jean-Daniel over his spectacles. "To be young again and surrounded by eager ladies would be a dream come true."

"I'd officially give anything to avoid tonight's ball. Riding through the woods, sleeves rolled up, hair blowing in the wind sounds much grander—"

"Greetings, brother." Colbert stepped into the dressing room.

Jean-Daniel scowled. "Colbert. What the hell are you doing wearing the same jacket as me?"

"Mother had two made."

"She hasn't dressed us alike in fifteen years."

Colbert shrugged. "This is our costume, brother. We're *twins.*" He said the word as if he wanted to expel some kind of revolting cough medicine. He circled the room. "What do you think of my appearance? Dapper, eh?"

With his hair slicked back and his face smoothly shaven, Colbert almost looked respectable. Almost.

"If you two had your masks on, I wouldn't be able to tell you apart," Hervé said.

"Fantastic," Jean-Daniel remarked sarcastically. He lifted one arm as Hervé slipped a regal sash over it and then secured a cutlass to his belt. "Why are you here, Colbert? To torment me?"

"To wish you a good ball." Colbert glared. "If there is such a thing."

"You're here to stir up trouble."

"Why don't you ever give me the benefit of the doubt?" Colbert searched for some liquor. "No brandy?"

"Yes," Jean-Daniel growled. "On the bureau. Lucky for you, a new chambermaid brought me brandy instead of wine tonight."

"Splendid." Colbert poured himself a glass.

Jean-Daniel's cheeks grew hot. "I have no inclination to argue tonight. I just want to get this ball over with."

Colbert splashed on some of Jean-Daniel's cologne. "Here's my advice. If you see a pretty girl, you can chat her up without Ella knowing. I doubt she's coming. It would be above her station."

"You're disgusting, Colbert."

"Come now. You can't deny you've had your share of satisfying women."

Jean-Daniel clenched his fists. "That's in the past."

"Do you really think you can be loyal to one female? You've had difficulty dedicating yourself to *any* one thing, Jean-Daniel."

"You're resentful, Colbert. Resentful that I'm the heir. And as the heir, I'm growing a sense of responsibility."

"Responsibility? Do you call abandoning your people 'responsible'?"

"Mother wants me to marry. I'm being responsible in that regard."

"At what cost?"

"Get out!" Jean-Daniel raged. Stepping off the clothing podium, he picked up a bottle of champagne and flung it as his brother. Colbert ducked. The bottle smashed against the wall, sending frothy bubbles and streams of liquid down the wallpaper.

"Careful now." Colbert cocked a brow. "We don't want all these eligible ladies thinking you've lost your charm."

Music from the château reached Ella on a warm breeze. Spurred by an idea, she shut the window and spun around. "If only I can find proof that I'm a Fouquet, Jean-Daniel and his mother will know I have aristocratic blood in my veins."

Her pulse sped at the possibility.

Dad always wrote me notes. Maybe he wrote me a note or a letter in this century, too.

Ella raced downstairs and entered Madame Fouquet's suite. Yanking open drawers and tossing papers from an armoire, Ella searched for what seemed like hours. In the end, she found nothing. No documentation. No letters. Soon she came to the conclusion that people weren't given birth certificates in this century.

Is there no record of me being Charles Fouquet's daughter?

Despondent, Ella left the room. She trudged downstairs, past the mess of the beans Madame had left, and went outside. The music lilted louder in the garden. Closing her eyes, she pictured the ball in progress. The room was filled with swirling, sparkling costumes, accomplished musicians, gourmet food, and handsome men.

But the only handsome man she cared about was Jean-Daniel.

She plopped into a garden chair. Glancing down, she spotted a fat pumpkin nestled in a patch. Running her fingertips across it she said, "What will Jean-Daniel think if I don't show up?"

Enormous sobs shook her body. Ella sank to the ground and hung her head.

Suddenly, a shadow fell over the pumpkin. Ella looked up. Madame Manard stood over her, her face awash with sympathy.

"Goodness child! The vicomte was right. Something *was* wrong when you didn't arrive with the Fouquet women."

Ella fingered her frayed dress. "Tell Madame de Maincy I'm sorry."

"Did those horrible Fouquet girls do that?

Ella nodded.

Madame Manard's cheeks turned crimson. "I'll explain to the vicomtesse." Obviously riled, she extended a hand from her billowing cape and helped Ella stand. "We can't have you go to the ball looking like that."

"I don't have anything else to wear."

"My daughter, the one whose self-worth was crushed by Madame Fouquet, says I have an uncanny ability to sense the future."

"Your daughter was abused by Madame Fouquet?"

"She spent time here as a servant."

Ella pushed a dry lump down her throat. "And she said you can sense the future?"

Madame Manard patted her arm. "I *foresaw* this happening."

Wiping her tears, Ella said nothing.

The housekeeper looked embarrassed. "Sounds batty, eh?"

"Oh, no. I've heard and seen crazier things."

"You have?"

"Much crazier."

"In that case, you'll understand why I made another dress. It's a costume really."

"You made—"

As if the heavens had opened up to shower Ella with renewed hope, Madame Manard pulled a shimmering white dress from the folds of her cape. The stunning dress boasted a fitted bodice, yards of crystal trim, flowing sleeves, and a glimmering trumpet skirt. Completing the costume was a set of transparent wings edged in feathers.

"You'll be an angel tonight," the kindly housekeeper said.

"It's beautiful!" Ella gasped. "Thank you so much!"

"Its color means you can still use the half mask I gave you. Plus, I have shoes."

Like a magician producing something out of a top hat, Madame Manard pulled a bag from her cape—Ella's burlap bag that'd gone missing.

Ella's heart galloped. "Where did you find it?"

"In the baron's chambers. That devil. The bag was stuffed in the back of his wardrobe."

He must have been the one who took it from Jean-Daniel's room.

Madame Manard put her hands on her hips. "I always clean Baron Girard's suites personally. He should have known I don't miss a thing."

"You're wonderful!" Ella hugged the woman, as she'd been longing to do since she set eyes on her. There was no doubt in Ella's mind that Madame Manard was Mimi . . . her guardian angel.

Laughing, the housekeeper opened the bag and extracted the glass slippers. They glittered in the bright moonlight like polished diamonds. "These are gorgeous. Thank goodness I didn't break them."

Ella and Jean-Daniel had agreed to meet at the longcase clock at midnight. Could she still make it?

"Hurry, my dear. Let's get you dressed!"

Madame Manard helped Ella into the angel costume. It looked breathtaking on her—even better than Madame de Maincy's sapphire gown. Although the dress showcased her creamy bosom and the curve of her waist, it hid the amulet by way of a lace trim.

Despite the way the costume hugged her curves, Ella wasn't self-conscious for once. The wings and a halo added the finishing touches and when Madame Manard swept a layer of sparkling powder across her cheeks, she felt like a bona fide princess.

After watching Ella slip her feet into the glass slippers, the house-keeper proclaimed her ready. "Take the carriage that brought me here. I shall walk."

"No—"

"We don't want my presence to alert the Girard family. Besides, I want you to arrive in style . . . with all the mystery and grandeur a no-blewoman would command."

Ella picked up her skirts, grasped the half-mask, and climbed aboard the white and gold carriage.

"The vicomte looks very handsome tonight." Madame Manard blushed. "In case you don't recognize him behind his mask, he's out-fitted in a silver-gilt jacket lined with red silk."

Ella smiled.

"Dance and have fun, my dear!" Madame Manard waved to her as the coach sped forward.

"I'll never forget your kindness!" She poked her head out the window.

The carriage raced over twisting dirt roads and cobbled streets. As Ella jostled about, she peeked inside her handbag, to make certain the Egyptian bracelet was still placed inside. She wondered if com-bined with the amulet the bracelet was the catalyst that had allowed her to leap into Jean-Daniel's painting and travel back in time.

Swallowing, Ella patted the handbag. She intended to guard the piece of jewelry very closely.

CHAPTER 24

The beautiful coach reached the château's portico. Before Ella knew it, she was in line behind two other carriages. While she waited for her coach to pull up, she wondered if she was one of the last guests to arrive.

She also wondered how the night would go. What if Madame de Maincy spotted her as the servant girl who'd served her tea? And what would happen if Colbert—or Madame Fouquet—exposed her true identity?

She'd suffer mortification and humiliation, no doubt. But that was nothing new. Worse would be Ella's failure to be with Jean-Daniel. Or her inability to save him.

After she accepted a footman's help in alighting, Ella entered the château. She noticed that the house had never appeared so magnificent. Candles flickered, chandeliers glittered, ropes of roses and bellflowers adorned the staircases, and the marble floors shone like glass. While she hid behind her mask, Ella touched her neck. It was damp with perspiration and she was glad she'd worn her hair piled in a high chignon.

As she strode past the foyer, she noticed a group of chirruping girls at the edge of the drawing room. Looking past them and into the room, she smiled. Jean-Daniel's newly-commissioned portrait hung in plain sight.

"He's so handsome!" swooned one girl.

"I'd give anything for one kiss," said another.

"Rosemary! Get those naughty notions out of your head."

"You're thinking the same thing, Marie. Admit it."

"Have you seen the vicomte tonight?"

"Not yet."

Ella left the giggling girls and made her way to the ballroom. Blending in with a group that had arrived in front of her, she studied costumed guests from the edge of the room. Geese, dolphins, fairies, swans, Snow Queens, and sea horses stood fanning themselves. Few couples were dancing. After all, this was a matchmaking ball. Women made up a majority of the guests ... women who were waiting to catch Jean-Daniel's eye.

The crowded ballroom—larger than two basketball courts—whirred with excitement. Ella searched for Jean-Daniel but didn't see him. Then she snatched a glance at the longcase clock. Its face read eleven thirty-nine.

After she entered the room, she brushed past a butterfly and accepted a glass of champagne from a footman. The music soared. As she drank the champagne quickly, the melody and the libation wove threads of intoxication through her. Suddenly, a strong hand clasped her elbow and steered her to a corner of the room.

Tall and powerfully built, the masked man wore a silver-gilt jacket edged with red silk. He was the man from her vision.

She cried, "Is it you?"

The man nodded.

"Jean-Daniel?"

He smiled.

Perhaps his silence is part of the charade he's planned.

Jean-Daniel's mask, which was settled on his nose and fastened behind his head with a black ribbon, disguised his handsome face. The idea of a masquerade rained excitement on Ella. She knew all too well what charismatic features lay beneath, but it was great fun pretending she didn't.

Grinning, Jean-Daniel swooped her onto the dance floor. Her mind whirled in time with the music. Thankfully, he'd swept her into a classic waltz and Ella knew the steps. When Jean-Daniel grasped her around the waist and pulled her to his hard chest, she gave a little cry.

Jean-Daniel seemed different tonight. Frisky. Possibly charged with the danger she had predicted.

Ella gripped the pole of her mask tightly. "Who is the vicomte dancing with?" she heard a guest whisper.

"Certainly not that filthy servant girl we've been hearing about."

"The vicomte certainly changes his mind quickly!" someone else said.

Although she was getting dizzy, Ella caught sight of Madame Fouquet, Espoir, and Charité through the crowd. Charité's giraffe headpiece sagged, Madame Fouquet gripped her Harlequin mask, and Espoir's sparkling bunny ears sat slightly askew. The girls and their mother removed their masks for a moment. Ella held her breath. Thankfully, their faces housed unadulterated jealousy—but no recognition.

Jean-Daniel drew Ella closer. She smelled his cologne mixed with the fragrance of milled soap. Ecstasy flooded her every sense because it was pure joy being in his arms. She also loved being the envy of every unmarried woman in the room—for once in her life.

Jean-Daniel nuzzled her neck. Then the ridge of his erection surged against her silken dress. He seemed especially sensual tonight and due to the champagne she had chugged, she responded.

Boldly, she put her mouth to his ear and whispered something suggestive. He stopped dancing in a sudden halt and led her out of the ballroom. Ella felt all eyes on them, but soon they were alone behind the locked door of the library. She lowered her mask. In an instant, his hot lips were on hers. Darting his tongue into mouth, it jumbled with hers and stoked her desire. Sighing heavily, she enjoyed the taste of brandy and cheroots on his tongue. In fact, they made her breathless. When he dropped his touch from her nape to her protruding décolletage, he fondled the mounds that spilled over the top of her dress and grunted.

"Take off your mask," she whispered.

Slowly, he shook his head. This was so unlike Jean-Daniel, but a part of her liked it.

He kissed Ella deeply again. Her blood heated to the degree of a crackling fire. After he skated his hand from her breast to her stomach, it descended to her core. Once he hiked up her skirt, he flattened his palm against her mound then curled his fingers into her moist folds. Ella sucked in a breath. Music and chatter droned around them, which made their liaison more exciting.

Jean-Daniel pleasured her with two fingers. She moaned against his lips. As sounds of his nimble handiwork filled the air, Jean-

Daniel lowered his head to kiss the rise of her breasts. Letting her mask drop to the floor, she wrapped her hand around his head. The movement knocked *his* mask off. Jean-Daniel snapped upright.

But it wasn't Jean-Daniel at all. It was Colbert!

Ella stepped back, shoving her dress down. "How dare you!"

"Some women say I'm a better lover than my brother."

"I doubt it," she spat.

"Oh, I see." Colbert drew his brows together. "You enjoyed my brother taking advantage of you in his bedchamber."

"You saw?"

His mouth quirked.

"He didn't take advantage of me."

"That means you're less than a respectable girl."

"You stole my things from the vicomte's room. Why?"

"You were so intent to get them back. I wanted to see what they were."

"No," Ella fumed, "you were going to use them to blackmail me. To persuade me to do what you want."

Colbert secured his mask over his face. "I want you, Ella. You're smart and beautiful. And I can see why Jean-Daniel fell in love with you."

She jerked her head away.

Gritting his teeth, he clamped his hand over her wrist. "Perhaps you don't know much about twins, but *we share everything*."

A tremendous crash sounded and Jean-Daniel barreled through the latched door. "You'll have to do more than lock yourself in the library to stop me, Colbert!"

Severed ropes hung from Jean-Daniel's wrists. As he yanked them off, he shot Ella a concerned look. "Are you hurt?"

Relieved, she shook her head.

"Get away from her, Colbert." Jean-Daniel stalked forward.

"Mind your own business, brother."

"Did you really think tying me up and throwing me in the attic would keep me from Ella?"

"I hoped to God it would," Colbert ground out.

Jean-Daniel drew his sword. Colbert did the same. While Ella leapt out of the way, the points of their tapered steel blades met and the duel was on. Jean-Daniel seemed to have the upper hand. Sword clanging against Colbert's, he inched his twin backward . . . into a

Beauvais tapestry. Colbert seemed to get his second wind. Growling, he maneuvered his cutlass with expert speed.

"Remember, Jean-Daniel, I've had more fencing lessons than you," he boomed.

"But I practice more."

Jean-Daniel ducked and swerved out of the way. He leapt atop a tulipwood desk, followed by his brother. Jean-Daniel shuffled forward, sword swinging. Colbert toppled backwards off the desk, but managed to scramble to his feet just as Jean-Daniel jumped down.

Their duel took them underneath an enormous pair of deer antlers. Jean-Daniel's sword swept across Colbert's arm, drawing blood.

"You'll pay for that," Colbert yelled.

As quickly as they moved and without them speaking, Ella couldn't tell them apart. The brothers were the exact same height, rivaled one another in muscularity, and with their hair slicked back and their masks on, they looked like genuine twins.

Blades clanking, the Girard men spilled into the hall. Colbert scratched Jean-Daniel's neck with the tip of his sword. Jean-Daniel did the same to Colbert. Blood trickled on their jackets, sending the guests into a dither. Guests gasped. Servants flew out of the way. And as the fight moved into the ballroom, more people scattered. Colbert landed against the food table and got a heavy dose of frosting as a three-tiered cake slid down his shoulder. Jean-Daniel lunged for him. They tousled on the ground, smothered in foie gras, more frosting, and red punch. Both men lost their swords, but then retrieved them before they sprang to their feet.

"Colbert and Jean-Daniel. Stop it this instant!" blazed Madame de Maincy. "You're acting like animals!"

The brothers paid no mind. Ella trailed behind them, rooting for Jean-Daniel. She wasn't a violent person, but right now, at this moment, she wanted him to rip his twin's head off.

The men dueled toward the longcase clock. The clock began to chime midnight and Ella's blood froze. Everything decelerated into slow motion. With an exaggerated swing, Jean-Daniel sliced at the clock's topmost ledge. The force halted the timepiece in mid-dong.

With a ragged breath, Jean-Daniel said, "That's enough."

The brothers ceased fighting and looked at each other. Ella was about to run to Jean-Daniel, but someone tore her mask away from her face. Horrified, she wheeled around and stared into Madame Fouquet's grim expression.

"It *is* you," Madame Fouquet hissed. The cruel woman yanked a ruffled cap off a parlor maid standing next to her and set it on Ella's head. "You see? This girl's an imposter! She's my servant. Not a member of the gentry!"

Sharp gasps pinged around the room. Jean-Daniel stared on in sympathy. Even Colbert dropped his expression of derision. As hot tears stung Ella's eyes, she could barely see through the veil they created. "I'm your stepdaughter!" she said.

"A likely story," Madame Fouquet bit out.

Madame de Maincy gasped along with everyone else. "Madame Fouquet. You claimed your stepdaughter succumbed to consumption in Paris."

"She did. This girl is lying. Her greediness led to this charade."

"What do you mean?" asked Madame de Maincy.

"All Ella has ever wanted to do is live the life of a princess."

"One moment." The vicomtesse moved closer. She braided her elegant fingers together. "Jean-Daniel. Is this the girl you've fallen in love with?"

"Yes," he said breathlessly.

The noblewoman turned to Ella. "What proof do you have, child? Proof that you are Charles Fouquet's daughter?"

Bile traveled up Ella's throat. She tore the servant's cap off and stuffed in into her handbag. "I have none."

Jean-Daniel looked at her imploringly. "Why did you tell me your name was Ella Benoit?"

My life is over.

Refusing to be gawked at another minute, she fled. Scooping up a bottle of champagne, she hastened through the open French doors and raced into the night. Someone ran after her, but she didn't turn around to see who it was.

"Ella!" a man's voice reached her along a sharp breeze.

Down the outside staircase she ran, her heels tapping over the stones. One of the glass slippers slipped off. With no time to retrieve it, she streamed into the gardens. She felt desperate to disappear, get drunk, and lick her wounds.

Footsteps pounded behind her. Her heart ached with a sorrow

she'd never known. Her fairy tale night had been ruined. She'd known humiliation and effacement before, but this was different. Now people considered her a liar.

"Ella! Stop!" The voice belonged to Jean-Daniel. He caught up with her at the edge of the lake and halted her in her tracks.

She didn't turn to face him. "Go, Jean-Daniel. Dance with other women. Meet your future bride."

"I don't want to meet other women. I want you."

Carefully, gently, he slipped the angel wings from her back. Then with infinite patience, he slowly placed his hands on her shoulders. She closed her eyes and released a maelstrom of sobs.

When he gathered her toward him, he wrapped his arms around her middle. "I'm going to have Madame Fouquet drawn and quartered in the morning."

Jean-Daniel's torso felt strong against her back. "She's right," Ella said. "I was playing dress up tonight. You have no idea how far I've come to be with you, but maybe it was a mistake. We come from two different worlds."

"You're talking nonsense, Ella," he whispered in her ear. "I plan to be with you despite what happened tonight."

He let her release more sobs.

Hervé emerged from the château and shuffled halfway down the staircase. His voice reached them. "Monsieur!"

"What is it, Hervé?"

"A group of men are trying to infiltrate the château. You must flee!"

"Christ! Where are the guards?"

"Gone! Somebody released them."

"Must Colbert betray me at every turn?" Jean-Daniel tightened his grip around Ella's waist. "Hervé! Instruct my male servants to apprehend the intruders!"

From over her shoulder, Ella could smell the fumes of brandy rolling forth.

"You must hide and I must make sure my mother is safe," Jean-Daniel said quickly. "But I want to know: are you really of aristocratic blood?"

Before she could open her mouth to answer, he added, "It's no matter. I'm going to marry you anyway. Meet in me ten minutes by the well."

"Thank you," she murmured as he pressed his cheek to hers.

"For what?"

"For being so wonderful."

"You can thank me later."

The words chilled Ella's blood. It's what her high school boyfriend had said. It's also what Colbert had said before he pawed her like a mindless animal. *Was this man Colbert?* Ella's hands trembled around the champagne bottle. The smell of brandy. Jean-Daniel drank wine. It could be Colbert. Surely he could imitate his brother's voice.

When he curled his lips around her ear, she panicked. Whirling around, Ella swung the champagne bottle in the air. Colbert had his neck bent forward. The champagne bottle came crashing down on the back of his skull. Under the impact, he lurched forward and fell face down in the lake. Blood poured from his wound. Slowly, the water carried him away from the bank.

Ghost Chasers had reenacted the scene perfectly.

Wait. This was Jean-Daniel's fate. Had Ella been wrong? Had she clobbered the wrong twin?

Sloshing into the water, she lifted the floating figure's mask away. With quivering hands, she rolled him over and lifted his head out of the water.

It *was* Jean-Daniel. The universe came crashing down upon her.

"*I'm* his murderer!" she gasped. It's why his ghost had been so insistent on summoning her back in time. He wanted her to reverse her deed. *She* had killed him and he'd been counting on her to change his fate.

She'd failed on all accounts.

A mournful cry escaped her throat. *He can't die!* Clutching him to her chest, Ella cried, "I love you more than life itself."

Voices filtered from the ballroom, replaced by the sound of violent scuffling. At least twenty men emerged into the tepid night, but she paid them little mind. She needed to save Jean-Daniel. Bunching her skirt in one hand, she tried to stop the flow of blood with it. It did no good. The water around Jean-Daniel undulated and he began to sink.

Although he was heavy and limp, she managed to plant a tender kiss on his lips.

"Don't die," she whispered desperately.

He stopped breathing.

As if the ground had been yanked out from under her, Ella felt dizzy. Crazed with despondency. She was tempted to pick up the cracked champagne bottle and—

Her handbag swung on her wrist as she contemplated killing herself. What was there to live for? Nothing in this century. Nothing really in the present day, either. She had ended up alone.

Then a thought struck her. In her handbag sat the Egyptian bracelet. Her mind raced. Could their magical powers reverse what she'd done? Could the amulet and the bracelet together send *both* of them into the future?

With nothing to lose, she withdrew the item. Body shaking, she studied the bracelet. Its design was masculine. Should she put the band on Jean-Daniel's wrist?

She did. For the second time that night, time seemed to slow. A shooting star streaked across the sky. Hastily, she made a wish. Wind picked up. Edged with forceful sparks of the unreal, it blazed across the lake toward the house. Rigid, Ella watched Jean-Daniel. He gave no movement and her lungs constricted. At least ten men moved in her direction, pitchforks and shovels in hand.

"Come on!" Rattling the bracelet, Ella pleaded with Jean-Daniel in a sharp whisper. "We need to time travel now!"

Two of the men came closer. Luckily, they hadn't seen her yet. She shook Jean-Daniel again. He lay immobile in her arms.

"Please." She put her mouth to his. "I love you."

Ella wasn't giving up. If they weren't going to leave this century together, at least she wanted him to be alive in 1703. Pressing her lips to his, she kissed him with all the passion, emotion, and potency she could muster. Miraculously, Jean-Daniel squeezed her hand.

"I love you, too," he whispered back.

"Jean-Daniel!" She hugged him, never wanting to let go.

"What are we doing in the lake?" He opened his eyes and cocked a brow. "I thought you said to stay away from it."

Laughing, she sputtered through her tears, "Come on. We need to hide."

"We haven't danced together yet," he quipped.

"Be quiet," she said gravely. "The men your brother summoned are nearby."

Groaning, Jean-Daniel held his head. Using a lifeguard move she'd seen in the movies, Ella dragged him ashore. She helped him from the water, sagging under his weight. As they hunched over, they managed to hide themselves behind a wall of willows. The intruders scattered around the lake, eyes blazing.

"You can't hide from us, Vicomte!" one called out.

"Bastards," Jean-Daniel muttered.

"The well," Ella whispered. "Do you think you can climb down it in your condition?"

"I'm damned willing to try."

After moving through bushes as quietly as they could, they reached the darkened structure. It looked even more intimidating than it had when Ella braved its stone walls. She helped Jean-Daniel swing his legs over the edge. Then she secured the pail's rope around his waist.

"I'll lower you down as long as you can hold some of your own weight," she whispered.

"My head is leaking like a sieve," he admitted. "What the hell happened to me?"

"It was me. I thought you were your brother."

Jean-Daniel's mouth quirked. "Then all is forgiven."

He slumped over and Ella started to question her plan.

"Vicomte!" came a different, more threatening voice.

"I'll start lowering you down," she said in a hushed tone. "Try to stay alert until you reach Hervé."

He looked at the bracelet around his wrist. "What's this?"

"I'll tell you later. But don't take it off."

The pulley creaked as she threaded the rope through it. She cringed.

"Aren't you coming?" Jean-Daniel whispered.

She shook her head forlornly. "As I told your mother inside the ballroom, I have no proof that I come from respectable lineage."

"And I told *you* it doesn't matter."

"Jean-Daniel. Being with me means you have to give up so much. You need time to decide if this is really what you want."

Sitting on the edge of the well, he threaded an arm around Ella's waist and drew her close. "I know it is."

In spite of his food-layered shirt, blood-spattered face, and mussed hair, he looked incredibly handsome.

"I haven't felt love and acceptance since I was eight years old," she said. "That's why your love means the world to me. But people are depending on you. I can't ask you to give that up for me."

The intruders' footsteps came closer.

Jean-Daniel gathered her into a scorching kiss and leaned back. "Will you be safe from these buffoons?'

"They aren't after me. Besides, I know a shortcut home." *One I discovered during my run into town.*

"Don't disappear on me, Ella Benoit Fouquet. I'll find a way to be with you."

She watched him vanish into the blackness of the well. As she raced to the Fouquet château she fingered the Egyptian amulet. *I'll try not to disappear.* Although the amulet and the bracelet hadn't pulled her and Jean-Daniel forward in time, she wondered if they could still be hurled out of this century unexpectedly.

CHAPTER 25

Lungs stinging, Ella reached the Fouquet château. She had run all the way, leaving a slew of unanswered questions behind.

Had Jean-Daniel escaped the intruders?

Had what she said made sense to him?

If so, would he abandon their love affair? After all, who was she to barge into this century and ask him to give up all his noble rights?

As she crept up to the front door, she frowned. If she hadn't appeared in 1703, he wouldn't have been hit on the head and needed saving.

The Fouquet house lay in darkness. She crept in. Apparently, Madame Fouquet and her two beastly daughters hadn't returned from the ball yet. Making her way to her room, she heard the rolling wheels of a coach.

They're back. Ella's nerves jump-started.

With nothing to say to the woman who'd single-handedly ruined her life, she hurried upstairs. And when the female terrors swept through the front door, she refused to answer their demands for tea or even open her door.

Jean-Daniel had been awake all night. After lowering himself into that dank well, he'd stolen into the bowels of the château. Hurrying as fast as he could, he'd gathered his mother, Rémy, and Hervé in the music room to guard them in the hushed darkness. He wasn't going to be fool enough to take on twenty men by himself. Thankfully, his servants apprehended the intruders before they were found there.

Colbert was nowhere to be found. Jean-Daniel discovered that the coward had taken his things and disappeared. The action spoke volumes. When Jean-Daniel stared at his twin's empty wardrobe in the morning light, anger rolled over him like a tidal wave.

"I've been too soft until now," he told Hervé after the château had emptied out and his head had been bandaged. "I've been too distracted by what pleasures and interests *me*. No longer."

"What's brought about this change, Monsieur?" Hervé asked.

"Ella was right. I have a duty to my people. Louis can do what he thinks fit for the nation. I'm going to do what's best for the citizens of Maincy."

"You're staying, sir?" The advisor smiled hopefully.

"Yes."

"Wise decision."

Jean-Daniel hadn't seen the old geezer this happy in years.

His head throbbing painfully, Jean-Daniel patted Hervé on the shoulder. "Now, I just have to ensure that I can remain a vicomte *and* have Ella's love. Any suggestions?"

The advisor shook his head forlornly.

Jean-Daniel looked down at Rémy. The dog kept a pleasant enough expression, but didn't appear to have any ideas.

"Not as easy as it sounds, eh?"

As the men stood in the main hall of Château de Maincy, sunshine filtered through a group of windows. Cut crystals on the chandeliers streamed colored hexagons in a brilliant rainbow against the wall.

"Astonishing," Jean-Daniel murmured. "I wish I could be illuminated like that."

As stiff as a piece of wood, Hervé paced the long hall. Stopping, he asked in a thin voice, "Shall I check on the vicomtesse, sir?"

"Please." Jean-Daniel bent to pet Rémy. When Hervé reappeared, Jean-Daniel asked how his mother was.

"She's asleep." Hervé paused. "She was terrified last night. Apparently, one of the intruders threatened her."

"Fiends!" Jean-Daniel's face flamed. "Colbert may not have arranged that, but I definitely think he intended I be the target of the attack. It would break my mother's heart to know the level of his deceitfulness."

"I agree, sir."

"I don't know where Colbert is now, but promise me my mother will never know about his scheme."

"Of course." Hervé cleared his throat self-consciously. "I'm very proud of you, sir. Your staying in Maincy will make people believe in you even more."

Jean-Daniel smiled broadly. "Thank you, old friend." Grateful for the man who had been a father figure to him after his own father died, Jean-Daniel squeezed the advisor's arm affectionately.

"Sir," Hervé continued. "I didn't want to say anything last evening in front of Madame. But now that she's resting—"

"Yes?"

Hervé withdrew the dainty glass slipper from his jacket. "I found this on the outside staircase."

"It must be Ella's!" Jean-Daniel took it from him and turned it over in his hands. "She was the only lady wearing glass slippers."

The elderly man nodded.

"Hervé, you've given me an idea!"

"I have?" He blinked behind his spectacles.

"You're always speaking of unbreakable laws and rules, correct?"

"Yes."

"On that note, I have a plan."

Espoir and Charité lay sprawled across the sofa. They'd been too exhausted to go upstairs and change out of their costumes. Now their limp headdresses tilted under their chins and their dresses bunched up in crinkled messes.

Espoir opened one eye. "For the love of France, Ella. Draw the blinds!"

Charité shook her head. Scratching her behind, she groaned. "Impudent girl won't come out of her room. Mother really humiliated her last night."

"Poor Ella," Espoir replied. Then the girls twittered obnoxiously.

Charité looked out the window. A cloud of dust streamed along the country driveway. The girls heard the rumble of horse hooves.

"It's a coach and four," Charité cried. "A *regal* coach and four. I think it's the vicomte!"

"I look a mess!" wailed Espoir.

"*Maman*!" the girls shouted simultaneously.

Madame Fouquet came downstairs, back erect. "I saw the coach from the upstairs window. Try and calm yourselves."

"But it may be the vicomte!

Like a pair of rabbits, Espoir and Charité bounded to the window. The tails attached to their costumes drooped behind them while they pressed their noses to the glass.

"It *is* him!" Charité cried.

With startling composure and to-die-for sex appeal, Jean-Daniel emerged from the coach. Muscles rippling, hair flapping in the breeze, and a smile dashed across his face, he embodied the very notion of a prince coming to the rescue. Dressed in an aquamarine jacket buckled at the waist and ecru pants tucked into shining brown jackboots, he strode determinedly to the door. Hervé was right behind him.

As he moved, Jean-Daniel peeled the bandage off his head.

Espoir held her heart. Charité desperately tried to order herself.

Pinning her shoulders back, Madame Fouquet let the men in. "Messieurs. How nice to see you."

Jean-Daniel dropped his smile.

Hervé held a plush gold pillow in his hands. Atop it sat Ella's single slipper. "The purpose of the ball you attended last evening was for the vicomte to find a wife," he announced. "By noble proclamation, Jean-Daniel Girard, vicomte de Maincy, will marry the girl who left this slipper behind."

Madame Fouquet offered a cultivated smile. "Monsieur. Won't you sit—"

"Proceed with the fitting, Hervé." Stern-faced, Jean-Daniel cut her short.

Both Espoir and Charité ripped one of their shoes off at lightning speed. Hobbling forward, they pushed and shoved to get to Hervé first. Meanwhile, Jean-Daniel rolled his eyes.

"I'm the eldest," said Espoir. "It's only fair I try it on before you, sister."

"Mother!" whined Charité.

Madame Fouquet shot them a disapproving look. "I'm sure the vicomte will give both of you a fair turn, my dears."

Jean-Daniel frowned at her sweet smile.

Sitting on a small tufted ottoman, Espoir raised her large foot in the air. Bones cracking, Hervé removed the dainty glass slipper from the pillow and tried it on her foot.

"You can push harder," she said, her smile disappearing.

"I'm afraid it doesn't fit, Mademoiselle."

"Bunions," she said, her cheeks rosy. "You see, our coach broke down last night. We had to walk home."

"Yes," Charité fibbed. "That explains the hole in my stocking, too." Jean-Daniel grimaced.

Charité sat down next. Wincing, Hervé stepped forward. He attempted to put the tiny slipper on, but he couldn't get it past the bridge of her pudgy foot.

"It fit last night," she said, going pale. "I swear."

"I don't think so," Jean-Daniel said. "The shoe belongs to another lady of the house. Ella Fouquet."

"At the ball, we established that she is not of gentry status." Madame Fouquet's face darkened.

"No, you *lied* about her birthright at the ball last night," Jean-Daniel fumed.

She clasped her hands together until her knuckles cracked. "Whatever do you mean, Monsieur?"

He took a wide stance. "I haven't made it a secret that I think serfdom should be a thing of the past. But before I suggest its abolition to the king, I stand before you as your lord. Your landowner. If you don't tell the truth about Ella being your stepdaughter, I shall, by law, strip you of your house and property. You'll be forced to live in the seediest, the dirtiest, the foulest section of Paris."

She took a step back. Face as white as a sheet, she reached for the staircase banister.

Hervé unrolled a document and was ready with pen and inkwell.

"Sign it." Jean-Daniel gritted his teeth. "Sign this unbreakable acknowledgment that Ella Fouquet is the daughter of the deceased man of the manor, Charles Fouquet."

Madame Fouquet glanced at Espoir and Charité Their faces were as pale as hers. "We don't want to lose our home, Mother."

Madame Fouquet penned the document with a shaking hand. Afterward, she sunk on the staircase's bottom step and hung her head.

"Hervé?" Jean-Daniel gave a nod to the second level of the house.

"I will fetch Mademoiselle Ella right away."

"There's no need," came Ella's voice. "I heard the entire thing."

Beaming, she hurried downstairs and grasped Jean-Daniel's hands.

"I'm ready to try the slipper on, Hervé," she said without tearing her gaze away from Jean-Daniel.

"It would be my pleasure, Mademoiselle." As easily as silk glides over satin, Hervé slipped the glass shoe on her foot.

"A perfect fit." Jean-Daniel helped her to her feet. "For a perfect wife. Ella, I don't care *what* your last name is. Now we can marry and live in the château." He nuzzled her cheek. "I love you."

"Ella, you can't marry him!" shrieked Espoir.

Ella turned to face her stepsisters and her stepmother. "I could say a lot of vicious things right now, but I'm better than that. With the vicomte, I'm going to live as I've always dreamed of. But you—you must face what karma has in store for you."

"Karma?" screeched Charité. "Who's Karma?"

Jean-Daniel took one look at Charité's twisted expression and let out a booming laugh. Bending his head, he claimed Ella's mouth with the most passionate kiss she'd ever known. Through decades and centuries, through time and space, they'd found one another. And the last thing Ella thought before he swept her out the door was that her father would be happy. Like Heathcliff and Catherine in *Wuthering Heights,* she'd finally found a love that extended beyond the grave.

CHAPTER 26

Three months later

A lazy sun settled over the harbor that bordered Cairo. Unfortunately, the last week of Ella and Jean-Daniel's honeymoon was upon them.

"It's damned hot here." Jean-Daniel slipped off his shirt and padded to his wife. Inside the spacious bedroom of the cottage they'd been staying in, Ella sat at the vanity. She tingled with joy as Jean-Daniel placed his hands on her slim shoulders.

"Still"—he frowned—"I'm dreading our return to France."

"Aren't you a new sort of vicomte now?" She teased as she met his gaze in the mirror. "Serious about business and all that. Eager to get back to your people."

A barge sounded its bell on the Nile before he spoke again. "Yes, I'm serious about my title. It isn't that. I just like having you all to myself here."

"It *is* nice."

Jean-Daniel undid a few of Ella's hairpins. When her locks tumbled down, he purred. Gliding his lips across her shoulder fueled her lust. One touch from him could do that.

"I know we're supposed to cruise the Nile tomorrow," he said as he pressed more kisses along the curve of her neck, "but I have a better idea. We should stay in bed all day."

"How about we stay in bed this evening, too?"

"Done, Madame le vicomtesse."

Their wedding had been the grandest spectacle in Maincy history. Mountains of flowers had lined the altar, guests garbed in their finest regalia had cheered them on, and Ella's spectacular wedding gown had her floating down the aisle. Even Rémy looked very distinguished as the ring bearer.

What had been missing from the affair were champagne bottles, Colbert, and the horrid Fouquet women.

Since the elaborate ceremony, Jean-Daniel and Ella had stopped talking about the women. Of course, they'd learned that Madame Fouquet lost her house due to poor investments. Penniless and forced to fend for themselves, she, Espoir, and Charité left Maincy on a shameful note.

Since their wedding ceremony, what Ella and Jean-Daniel *hadn't* stopped doing was making love. Besides Jean-Daniel eating Ella's cooking, it was their favorite thing to do.

Ella swiveled around on the seat. Jean-Daniel pitched to his knees.

"Have I told you that a new hobby of mine has replaced my interest in animals and plants?" he asked.

"What is that?" She smiled.

"Your beautiful body."

She blushed. Gingerly, he slipped her transparent dressing gown from her shoulders. Before he lowered her chemise he said, "Time to hide your eyes, Rémy." Obeying, the dog inched his head under the bed skirt and settled down for a nap.

With hunger in his stare, Jean-Daniel tugged at Ella's straps. Her nipples, exposed, erect, and eager, begged for his attention. As he licked the firm buds, he murmured, "I'll never grow tired of these."

Ella ran her hands through his caramel-colored hair. His strands had gotten lighter during their time in Egypt. No, she corrected herself. *More sun-kissed.*

With a pleasurable squeak, she gave her breasts a wanton thrust forward. As she coiled her fingers around his golden-brown waves, Jean-Daniel emitted loud sounds of pleasure. Here in Cairo, the cottages were packed closely together, but he didn't care. He told Ella as they'd made love last night that if he could shout his affections for her from the rooftops, he would.

Drawing away, he sat back and studied the rest of her body. "I love your tiny waist and the curve of your hips." Then he traced her tattoo with his finger. "I don't know how you keep applying that body paint, but don't stop."

Ella grinned. She still hadn't told him the entire story. That the artwork was permanently inked on her hip. That his ghost had urged her to travel three hundred years back in time so they could be together. That she'd seen him floating in a pool of blood on a twenty-first century television show just before that.

She shuddered at the memory.

Fortunately, all had turned out well. Now Ella's constant fear that she'd be sucked away from him through a wormhole was gone. If she hadn't been driven to the future by now, she probably wouldn't be.

Jean-Daniel's kissed her hotly. Then he stood and extended his hand. "Come with me, my sweet."

While he stood before her, Ella eyed the bulge in his breeches. She'd never pleasured him yet. Something made her want to try today. "Wait," she said.

He raised a brow. She nearly reverted back to her shy self, but then she reached for his laces. After unthreading them rather clumsily, she pushed his pants to his knees and released his throbbing cock. Engorged with bluish veins and shining with his excitement, it curved upward at the level of her mouth.

"The Giza pyramid has nothing on me, eh?" he joked.

There is truth in jest, Ella thought. His staff was incredible, like something out of a fantasy. Moistening her lips, she took him in her mouth.

"God in heaven." Jean-Daniel threw his head back.

Ella's movements were awkward at first—as she tried to figure out if she should use her teeth or her tongue. But he didn't seem to mind. Eventually, she fell into a rhythm. Gauging by Jean-Daniel's moans, she knew she was doing something right.

She stole a look at him. His mouth twisted into an expression she'd never seen before. Part grin, part ecstasy, it made her smile. He looked down at her. Breathing heavily, he smoothed her hair out of the way. And after he tilted his pelvis forward, he urged, "Don't stop."

As if his erection had a mind of its own, it bobbed in Ella's mouth. She grasped the base of his penis and slid her mouth up and down it.

A month ago, she would have sworn she'd never perform this act of intimacy on any man. With Jean-Daniel, she actually enjoyed it.

"Fist me tighter," he rasped.

She did. His cock hardened even more.

"Now use your tongue."

As she flicked over the crown of his staff, Ella felt his entire body grow rigid. Pressure built inside Jean-Daniel's sex, prompting his moans to grow louder.

"Now!" He popped himself out of her mouth and shot his cream into the palm of his hand. He hadn't wanted to get her face wet, and she silently thanked him.

He pulled her to her feet. Then, craning his neck forward, he kissed her deeply.

"Hold that thought." He gave a disarming smile as he disappeared to wash his hands. When he returned, he spread her enthusiastically across the bed.

"Now it's your turn to feel good," he said.

Brushing her skin with his fingertips, Jean-Daniel patiently caressed every inch of her limbs and torso. "I know I repeat myself a great deal, but you are the most beautiful woman I've ever seen."

Crystal blue eyes lit with desire, he dipped a finger between her legs. "You're moist." He grinned. "I'm glad pleasuring me made *you* excited."

Nodding, she snaked her arms around his neck. He reclined on one elbow and she glanced at his abdomen. Cut with ridged muscles, it rose and fell in shallow breaths and his biceps bulged as he stroked her.

"I want to see you rumble with delight." Flattening his hand, he spread her thighs apart. Then he skimmed his fingers along her moist folds. With the right pressure, he located and pulsated her bead. A few moments later, she came on a blinding wave.

To Ella's surprise, Jean-Daniel kept his fingertip against her swollen pearl. "I'm going to make you see heaven again." Lifting himself to his knees, he grasped his cock. Then, rocking forward, he slipped his sex into her core.

Holding himself up on one stiff arm, he thrust in and out of her like a bucking horse. Pressing on her clitoris all the while, he sought her lips. Sweat glistened off his body as he murmured wayward things against them.

When he raised his head to look at her, he smiled so broadly his dimples showed. That did it. Ella climaxed as forcefully as a hurricane. As her shuddering shoulders showcased her excitement, Jean-Daniel bent forward and locked her in a kiss. She came and came, as if there was no tomorrow.

Once her shudders subsided, Jean-Daniel lay on his back and drew her against his chest. Absentmindedly, she traced the Egyptian amulet around her neck. She hadn't taken it off since she had arrived in this century.

Jean-Daniel glanced down at it. "Are you ever going to tell me about that necklace and this bracelet?" He held his wrist up and rattled the band.

"All I can tell is that they're very powerful objects."

"I agreed to take you all the way to Egypt because of these blessed things and that's all I get?" He let out a huge laugh and snuggled his head against hers.

The glow of an orange sunset streamed into the window. Ella sat up and looked him straight in the eye. "Tomorrow will you do what you promised?"

"Bury your amulet and my bracelet in the Valley of the Kings? Yes, anything for you."

Ella smiled.

"Now can we take off these heavy objects?"

"I suppose."

She removed the amulet while Jean-Daniel slipped off the bracelet. He set both items on a nearby table.

Content beyond belief, she snuggled against him again. Her method for setting things up for what needed to happen in the future was almost complete. She'd tucked her servant cap into a trunk in the attic of Château de Maincy before coming to Egypt. Her father would find it after he purchased the estate. And the British archaeologist Pénélope Toulouse spoke of would unearth the enchanted amulet and its matching bracelet years from now.

If Ella didn't hide everything at this juncture, she would never get to this point. To this amazing honeymoon.

It was all very complicated, but there it was.

As Ella rested her head on Jean-Daniel's chest, he reached for her hand. She loved him more than the sun, the stars, and the moon. Luckily, her attempt to shift the hand of fate had paid off and her wedding to Jean-Daniel had sealed the love they'd managed to save.

It was a perfect time in Ella's life and she never wanted it to end.

Suddenly, her hand tingled. Then, she lost all feeling in it. "Jean-Daniel! Look at my fingers!"

She held her hand up. His palm was clasped around it, but her fingers grew transparent.

"What the hell?" Jean-Daniel yelled.

Seconds later, Ella's hand, wrist, and arm faded from sight.

"No!" Ella cried. "We shouldn't have taken the jewelry off!"

Reverberation shook the bed. Reality waved in and out of focus before her eyes and in a cruel reversal of events, she was snatched away from Jean-Daniel. Through a spiraling tunnel she flew backward, facing him but moving rapidly away. The sight of his devastated face vanished.

Ella fell into the château's drawing room with a *thud*. Her head hurt and her body ached, but more than that, her heart had been ripped away—left with Jean-Daniel back in 1703.

Crying hysterically, she eyed the quiet drawing room. *This can't be happening! It just can't!* Would she ever see him again?

How could she? It was three hundred and eleven years later and she didn't have the necklace to transport her backward in time again.

Pulling herself to her feet, she pounded on Jean-Daniel's portrait, crying all the while. She attempted to put her hand through the painting, but it was no use.

How would she survive without Jean-Daniel? He was everything to her. She'd given up her entire life for him and now she had nothing. Her happiest moment had turned into the most scarring. What had she done to deserve it?

She slid down the wall to the floor. Wondering how many days she'd been gone since she was sucked into the portrait, she quickly decided it didn't matter. She was alone, without her soul mate—and now the world closed in on her.

Under the gloomy haze of a rainstorm, Ella listened to the pelting at the window and cried herself to sleep.

Ella had no idea how long she lay there. Her soul yearned for Jean-Daniel and she had no desire to leave the portrait. A torrential downpour continued to pound the rooftop, counteracting the silence in the drawing room. For all Ella knew, it had been raining for days.

That's how long she'd probably been lying there in a fetal position, in a depressed and devastated trance with no inclination to eat or drink.

Outside, car tires squeaked to a halt—although Ella barely registered the sound. Had Hope and Charity returned to torment her? Did the girls intend to take over the estate after Ella got sucked into Jean-Daniel's painting?

Thankfully, there were no signs of them. The girls were either alerting the press about what they'd witnessed or they'd gone back to America.

There was a knock at the door. Eyes bloodshot and stinging, Ella curled into a tighter ball on the floor.

Knock. Knock. Knock.

"Is anybody home?" A man's muffled voice reached her.

"Go away!" Hoarse from crying, Ella squeaked out the words.

"I hate to bother you," came the same voice, "but I'm looking for my dog."

Ella sat straight up. The voice belonged to Jean-Daniel! *My God!* How could that be?

Nearly tripping over the blanket she'd pulled off the sofa, she hurried to the door and opened it.

"It's raining fiercely, and my pet—" Jean-Daniel, dressed in a white physician's jacket and dark trousers, stopped in mid-sentence.

She stared into his handsome face. Time froze. Tears pricked her eyes and she shivered. Should she rush into his arms? Or was she hallucinating—dreaming up something that was too good to be true?

He smiled, his aquamarine eyes glowing a bright blue amid the gray haze. Wearing the same expression of infatuation he had worn the day they first met in the hunting park, Jean-Daniel took a step closer. Ella read the embroidered writing on his lab coat. *Dr. Jean-Daniel Duquesne, D.M.V.*

Docteur en Médecine Vétérinaire. He was a veterinarian!

Speechless, she stood in the doorway. Jean-Daniel stood out of the rain underneath the portico, dimples showing.

"Mademoiselle, my name is Jean-Daniel Duquesne and I just bought a neighboring house. I let my hound out a little while ago and I think the lightning scared him. He ran into the woodland that joins our properties. Have you seen him?"

She wiped her tears away. "No, I'm sorry."

"Are you all right?"

"I am now."

He grinned. "What is your name?"

She laughed with joy. "Ella Benoit."

"A pretty name for a very pretty girl."

A dog that looked just like Rémy bounded out of the hedges. He galloped over to Jean-Daniel. Sitting on his haunches, the canine panted and shook the rainwater from his coat.

"There you are!" Jean-Daniel knelt to scratch the dog behind the ears.

"What's his name?" Ella asked.

"Rémy."

More elation poured over her.

He stood. "You are very lovely, Mademoiselle Benoit. If you don't mind my saying so."

"Thank you." She blushed.

He brushed a wet lock of hair off his forehead and asked, "Have we met before?"

"We have," Ella said.

"When?"

She sucked in a breath. "Once upon a time."

AUTHOR'S NOTE

Growing up, my two favorite love stories were Shakespeare's *Romeo and Juliet* and Charles Perrault's *Cinderella*. In fact, they still are. Perhaps it's because the stories have more in common than people give them credit for. Mistaken identities. Passionate couples facing devastating roadblocks. And love at first sight.

One story ends well while the other one doesn't, but is there anything more romantic than sacrificing everything for the person you love? That's the question I was struck with when I first saw the film, *Somewhere in Time*. Back in 1980, it honestly changed my life. *"Beyond fantasy. Beyond obsession. Beyond time itself, he will find her . . ."* I can still remember what the tag line on the film's poster read. I became inspired to write a love story filled with just as much fantasy and emotion. More than that, I was determined to write a story that brings joy to others—and opens people up to the possibility of love being magical.

So, I hope you enjoyed this "Somewhere in Time in reverse" story. In *Cinderella and the Ghost,* my heroine becomes obsessed with a man in a painting, just like Christopher Reeve falls in love with Jane Seymour's image in the movie.

As I close out my Cursed Princes series, I'd like to extend many thanks to my wonderful readers. It's my sincerest wish that my fairy tale retellings have brought a touch of magic into your lives.

About the author

Although Marina Myles lives under the sunny skies of Arizona, she would reside in a historic manor house in foggy England if she had her way. Her love of books began as soon as she read her first fairy tale and eventually led to a degree in English Literature. Now, with her loyal Maltese close by, she relishes the hours she gets to escape into worlds filled with fiery—but not easily attained—love affairs. She's busy being a wife, a mother, and a member of Romance Writers of America, but she is never too busy to hear from her amazing readers. Visit her at www.marinamyles.com

Don't miss any of the Cursed Princes series!

Beauty and the Wolf

A UNION OF CURSES

Isabella Farrington's marriage was hasty. For all her new husband's riches, Lord Draven Winthrop is whispered about, avoided, and feared. Yet Isabella is drawn to Draven's dark good looks, his strength, the charm he can turn on as easily as she can blink. The impoverished daughter of an Egyptologist, she knows there are rumors about her, too, and the amulet she wears. Nothing more than superstitious babble . . .

But when Isabella returns to Draven's remote coastal manor, she senses there is something more at work in the grim gardens of Thorncliff Towers than superstition. Draven is passionate and seductive, but he has a brutal, uncontrolled side, and a history of secrets. To live in peace she must discover the reasons behind a gypsy curse and a mother's scorn. Especially when she learns Draven believes his sweet young bride is doomed to a fate even darker than his own . . .

"Dynamic and sensual; paranormal readers will gobble up this sexy read."
—Donna Grant, *New York Times* bestselling author of *Midnight's Warrior*

"*Beauty and the Wolf* is a deliciously dark retelling of the classic tale that will make you fall in love all over again."
—Erin Quinn, author of *The Five Deaths of Roxanne Love*

THE CURSED PRINCES

HUNGER AND DESIRE
CAN TWINE INTO
MADNESS...

Beauty and the WOLF

MARINA MYLES

Snow White and the Vampire

FOG AND FASCINATION

Alba Spencer thought her past in Romania and the dark magic that haunted it was behind her forever. She is one of the first female barristers now, safe in London. But London has its dark side, too. A man called the Ripper stalks the midnight streets. There are rumors that her hated stepmother has found her again, suggestions that the nightmares of her childhood are returning. And with them appears the cursed Gypsy boy she once loved, grown into a man more seductive and more terrifying than she ever could have dreamed . . .

Dimitri Grigorescu has become a surgeon, a gentleman—and a vampire. The lusts that drive his body are scarcely under control, and even he does not truly know what he is capable of. To fight evil and confusion, Alba must rely on her wits—and a desire that overwhelms her doubts . . .

"A story to remember. LOVED EVERY THRILLING MOMENT OF IT!"
—Addict of Romance Blogspot

"Definitely a series worth watching!"
—Bodice Rippers, Femme Fatales, and Fantasy

THE CURSED PRINCES

WHICH IS STRONGER:
FATE OR DESIRE?

Snow White
and the
VAMPIRE

MARINA MYLES

A Warlock's Dance

A Cursed Princes Novella

ENCORE, PLEASE

Giselle Swenov is a radiant opera star whose beauty is second only to her voice. That is, until a jealous enchantress strips away her talent and looks, transforms her into a mute and haggard old woman, and forces her to leave the man of her dreams at the altar on their wedding day. Now there's only one person able to reverse the spell: Giselle's warlock ex-fiancé, Lucian Ivanu.

But three years have passed, and the ever-dashing Lucian seems to have moved on—he's inherited a vast fortune, forsaken his scandalous powers, and is even set to marry again. Will he recognize his former flame when she shows up at his engagement party and begs for help? Can she recover the powerful magic ring needed to break the curse before it's too late? Giselle's plight has a darker twist as she discovers just how far the enchantress's grasp reaches . . .

". . . a sweet, sweet read. Like a fairy tale for grown-ups!"
—BookBeauty's Reviews

A CURSED PRINCES NOVELLA

A WARLOCK'S *Dance*

MARINA MYLES

Sleeping Beauty and the Demon

SLEIGHT OF HAND

Dragomir Starkov poses as an illusionist, a showman performing tricks, his Romanian accent and dark good looks all just a part of the drama. That's how Rose Carlisle first sees him. She's a respectable girl—she wouldn't accept witchy birthday gifts from a demon. But the hustle and bustle of 1912 New York City offers plenty of ways to slip around the strict old rules of propriety. A good thing, too, because once Rose meets Drago, she no longer cares about being respectable.

But the only illusion in Drago's act is that his magic is smoke and mirrors. Every word of power he speaks is as real as Rose before him, in thrall to his lust and adoration. Drago knows about Rose's curse, that she will die on her next birthday. But the shadowy threat that stalks her hasn't won her yet. If she can trust him, perhaps he can save her too . . .

"An intriguing twist on a classic fairy tale."
—Jennifer Estep, *New York Times* bestselling author

THE CURSED PRINCES

Seduction can save her...

Sleeping Beauty
and the
DEMON

MARINA MYLES

Christmas at Thorncliff Towers

A Cursed Princes Novella

THE WEREWOLF'S SERVANT

Thorncliff Towers is done up for Christmas, secure against wind and wolves. But Karina Petri is shut out, too, and the gypsy witch wants what's inside. She envies the gifts, the feast, the pretty clothes, of course. But her true desire is for the love of Constantin Stoica. Her smolderingly handsome childhood friend agreed to serve Lord Draven after his brother was caught stealing last year. Constantin suspects Karina was involved—and it would take more magic than she possesses to make him forgive . . .

Constantin has always been drawn to Karina's dark curls, flashing eyes, and reckless ways. But trusting her has proven dangerous before, and this night holds more to fear than most. The wrong decisions could cost him his job, his safety—even his life. But letting Karina go could cost him his heart . . .

A CURSED PRINCES NOVELLA

Dark power and
sweet desire
collide...

Christmas
AT THORNCLIFF
TOWERS

MARINA MYLES